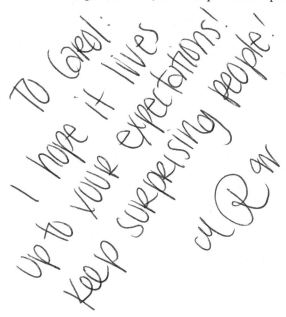

To Carol,
I hope it lives
up to your expectations!
Keep surprising people!
JRS

I dedicate this, my first novel, to my beloved husband with A.M.E. You always keep me on my toes with your constantly loving, sometimes brutal honesty, and I adore you for it. You challenge me, cheer me, and make me feel like a goddess every day.

Chapter One

It seemed she had been waiting hours for the taxi to come and fetch her, but in reality, it couldn't have been more than twenty minutes. The funeral had been bleak and somewhat sentimentally false, as most funerals are apt to be. As people filed from the church, Hattie noted those whose handkerchiefs were truly damp, and she chuckled to herself as she witnessed others make a show of dry, meaningless sobs. Though she continuously scanned the crowd, she didn't recognize a single individual.

However, one rather buxom young woman in a hat far too flamboyant for such an austere occasion did catch her eye. The affected sniffles issuing from her were more than distracting to the boyish, rather foolish-looking young man standing in the corner. He stepped somewhat awkwardly toward the young lady, offering a few muttered words of consolation. But as Hattie leaned forward to catch a better view of what would next ensue, her eyes became unfocused, and she could no longer distinguish the couple clearly. She wondered if it was one of her headaches coming on again, and she leaned back against her seat to relieve the dizziness.

"Your taxi, madam," a firm, respectful voice spoke behind her.

Hattie jumped.

"Oh, yes – yes, thank you," she responded, nervously gathering up her gloves and satchel.

"Allow me to relieve you of this, madam," said the tall, moderately slender man in chauffeur's uniform, as he took her satchel in his hand.

"Oh! Thank you...?" she trailed off expectantly, willing him to tell her his name.

"Bertram, madam – John Bertram. You may remember me – I was in your service a number of years ago, employed as your chauffeur."

She puzzled it out in her mind.

"Oh, Bertram – yes. What a funny coincidence!"

A vague recollection of an elderly, stooped man with spectacles came to mind, but this man was young and strong – with spectacles, yes, but bearing only a small resemblance to the man she had in mind.

The ride was long, but Hattie was content to sit in the open car and watch the fields and trees as they drove along. Nature gave the impression of growing greener and more fresh with each mile, and she seemed to breathe the good, crisp spring air into her very soul. She felt younger, more at ease in the knowledge that she was going home. Bertram must have sensed her introspective mood and left her alone, avoiding the meaningless small talk she dreaded in any situation.

Suddenly, a dark cloud overshadowed the horizon ahead. The landscape began to turn dull shades of gray and brown, and Hattie's heart sank within her at the thought of arriving drenched and shivering in the open automobile.

Bertram seemed to perceive her worry and disappointment: "Don't worry, madam, we shall arrive in a few minutes, before the rain comes."

Hattie smiled to herself, relieved in his comforting words, and the wrinkle that had furrowed her already care-lined face dissipated.

They soon turned down a gated, wood-lined drive, and the eagerness to arrive that had rested in her heart was shocked abruptly into an overwhelming sense of fearfulness and tremor, as the realization came upon her that she'd no idea where they were. At whose house was she arriving? Although her surroundings looked slightly familiar, she could not recall her destination. Had she promised to stay with a friend? If so, which?

Desperation gripped her mind; her breathing became labored. Was she, prim, stately Hattie Vavaseur, going mad at last? She realized she was up in age, but her memory had never failed her so blatantly before. As they rounded the front drive of the large, white house, her eyes widened.

It looked empty – run down, as though no one had possessed it for years. A sweeping wind rushed through the trees and up the drive, causing the unfastened shutters to beat a doleful rapport on the side of the house as though announcing her arrival. It was cold.

Hattie drew her black shawl more tightly around her shoulders and shivered. Bertram's hair was ruffled only slightly as the wind passed. He turned to her, his eyes bright and oddly mischievous. A smile seemed to twitch at the corners of his thin mouth. He almost spoke, stopped himself, then climbed out of the car instead. As he opened the door for her, his eyes were downcast in an attitude of respectful obsequiousness. Hattie had caught the momentary look, however, and longed to ask him if this was some sort of absurd joke. But the lingering fear at the back of her mind stirred up her natural stubbornness, and she abruptly stepped down from the car, grasping his proffered arm. Head up, shoulders squarely set, she walked toward the gloomy edifice that sat like a giant, open-mouthed beast before her.

The bushes on either side of the doorstep were large and overgrown, like two unkempt, messy children whose arms reached toward each other menacingly. The door seemed swathed in moss, which was quite in keeping with the wild, scraggly look of the grounds. As Hattie neared it, however, she realized it had actually at one time been painted green, but the white coats of paint covering it were peeling away from years of neglect, which afforded its feral look. She wondered vaguely why anyone would want to cover up such a lovely shade of green.

Bertram was at her elbow, her luggage in his powerfully large hands. He shifted his weight slightly, balancing on the edge of the step as he rang the bell. Fear struck at Hattie's heart once again, and she dared a furtive glance up at him. He was smiling widely, though staring directly at the door as if he were deciphering a very amusing joke from the peelings of paint.

"Bertram..." Hattie began.

"Yes, madam?" the smile was wiped from his face as

though she'd slapped him.

"I...oh!"

Her body stiffened as she was interrupted by the door creaking open.

A light emanating from the hall within cast the figure before her into complete shadow. She could not distinguish his face in the least, although his tall, prominent figure seemed oddly familiar.

"Ms. Vavaseur," he stated matter of factly, and the man moved aside with a slight bow, allowing her to pass.

Though she did so with much internal trepidation, it was not visible externally, save for a slight nervous habit she possessed of rubbing her thumb along the fingertips of her left hand – an unconscious, soothing reaction to stress. She cast a rather desperate look over her shoulder at Bertram, who had quite suddenly advanced to a symbol of familiarity in these strange circumstances. He winked unabashedly and touched his cap.

Feeling somewhat shocked and affronted at this blatantly inappropriate behavior, Hattie offered a cold, "Thank you, Bertram," and stiffly stalked farther into the hall as the butler took the bags and closed the door in the chauffeur's smirking face.

Hattie was frustrated by this impudent behavior from a chauffeur and was not inclined to encourage the butler into similar effronteries. She therefore refused to look at him, although she very much desired to, in order to assist her in ascertaining her whereabouts.

The butler, apparently sensing her strict formality, lost no time in walking before her with a painfully polite,

"This way, madam, if you please."

Dimly lit gas lamps gave out barely enough light for Hattie to clearly discern the style or cleanliness of the house as the butler led her upstairs, although it was only early evening. Strange shadows flitted across their path as he led her deeper and deeper into the unfamiliar mansion. They walked very slowly and carefully up the large, wide staircase, and he continued through a maze of hallways until at last he paused at a white door that contrasted strangely with the dark paneling which had shadowed their journey throughout the house. He unlocked the door from the outside with an elaborately large, silver key and preceded her into the room. Setting down her bags lightly in all the appropriate places, he left her to herself almost immediately.

The lamp the butler had lit cast but a very feeble light upon the room. It seemed neat and clean enough; relief swept over her. At least in solitude, she could allow her features and her thoughts to relax from their hard, obstinate, self-imposed pretense. Hattie was tired. She was, after all, quite old, and an adventure such as this was proving far too much for her. She straightaway decided on an early retirement to bed.

As Hattie exchanged her dark traveling clothes for her nightdress, she considered the events of the day thoroughly. In all the stress and bustle of the funeral, had she promised an old friend a visit? Could she have forgotten so easily? People from the funeral flashed before her mind...the woman with the over-large, brightly colored hat, the tall, rather gawky young man...

She sat on the large, soft bed, drew the curtains about her, and blew out her lamp. As the shadows of memories passed through her mind, her eyes lazily shut, and she was very soon asleep.

Chapter Two

When Hattie awoke the following day, a deep-settled peace lay in her heart. She took a large, full breath. She hadn't slept this soundly since before the headaches had begun. As her eyelids fluttered open, a slightly reddish light pervaded the thin curtains that hung about her bed.

Imagining it to be the sunrise, Hattie stretched, feeling more flexible than usual and reached out a hand to pull back the drapes.

Shock vibrated through her entire body. She fell back on her pillows, hardly able to bear the sight. The room was undeniably, disgustingly, and uncompromisingly... PINK!

Revulsion echoed through her. Hattie had always possessed a prejudiced repulsion to the color and had consistently refused to have it anywhere in her own house. Even the gardeners had not been allowed to foster any blossoms of the pink variety. She had been careful to avoid the hue completely her entire life, and here she was, absolutely inundated in the beastly shade! She stretched a shaky hand out to the curtains to once again substantiate that her eyes had not been mistaken.

They had not been. Flounces and bows and crinkles in every possible shade of the sickening pigment were flouting themselves unabashedly. There were ruddy curtains floriated with miniature rosettes, rouge ruffles attached to every possible surface – even the furniture was painted with a bright, rosy tint that would make a blushing bride appear pale by comparison.

Closing her eyelids as tightly as possible, Hattie's feet felt their way into her slippers. She peeped just a very little bit in order to make her way across the room to her valise, which she opened to dress. Yes...her nice, brown suit would do marvelously for this occasion to contrast with the girlish, silly shade that surrounded her. Whenever her aunt had made her wear pink when a child, she always had the appalling inclination to giggle uncontrollably; it made her feel downright silly. Somehow, Hattie seemed to always dirty or tear those dresses much more quickly than any of the others...

A knock came at the door the moment she had finished putting her last iron-gray curl in place. There was no mirror in the room, but she was able to manage without it. Hattie always wore her hair up now. In her youth, she had been the owner of lush, dark curls that ran halfway down her back. Her locks were still long and thick, though gray, and she held a particular, secret pride in their opulence.

The knock came, rather insistently, again.

"Come in!" she called, patting her hair reminiscently.

The door creaked slowly open, and the butler stood respectfully in the hallway.

"Breakfast is served, madam," he stated in his low, gravelly voice.

"Why, thank you, Harold," the name slipped out before she'd even thought. "It *is* Harold, isn't it?"

"Yes, madam." He nodded and made to withdraw.

"Just a moment, Harold," Hattie began slowly, "Isn't there another room you could place me in? This one is rather...well..." – a slight cough – "...drafty," she lied, unwilling to admit her true folly.

"This is the best room in the house, madam," he responded. "It has the most beautiful view, and of course, the master *insists* that you reside in this particular room for the duration of your stay."

"Oh," Hattie said timidly, now on very uncertain ground. The mention of the word "master" and the emphasis of the word "insists" momentarily cowed her.

"Will the, um...*master* be at breakfast?"

"No, madam. He will breakfast in his own room, as I am certain you'll remember is his habit."

Harold's eyes flickered momentarily from the floor he'd been studying so assiduously to Hattie's face and back to the floor again.

What was that look? Curiosity? A jab at her stupidity for not recalling her whereabouts? She wondered if it was obvious that she was so completely lost.

"Anything else, madam?" he said, after a slight pause.

"Nothing, Harold. I shall be down to breakfast immediately."

"Very good, madam."

And with a slight bow, he walked noiselessly away.

As Hattie made her way down the broad staircase and to the breakfast room, she was very much aware of her surroundings. The furniture was lush and fairly well kept, though with unmistakable signs of age. Most of the house was done up in a way that just suited her taste, with the exception of a few carpets and knick-knacks. Those that goaded her were of an extremely masculine tenor and seemed ill-suited to the generally simple and even delicate compilation of décor.

She immediately wished to have the running of this household, in order to do away with the ridiculous curios and bring harmony to the mansion. For it *was* a mansion. The rooms were large and open, and she enjoyed wandering through them on her way to the breakfast room. She was surprised that she had discovered this room so easily. It was as though she had a small, internal compass that directed her straight to it. At first, she found this unsettling, but realized it must have subconsciously been the scent of the sumptuous breakfast foods that drew her on to the correct apartment.

Hattie poured out a steaming cup of tea. She had just seated herself, her teeth sinking into a large sausage when the door flew open and a rather elderly, though powerfully built man stormed in through the door, teeming with rage. Hattie's fork clattered to her plate, her shaking hand losing control, and the sausage sailed through the air, striking a candlestick.

"So!" he bellowed, "So! You've come, have you?"

He eyed her between furrowed brows, appraising and distrustful.

"Yes!" she squeaked, swallowing hard. She had no idea who this man was.

"Well, then!" he yelled, "Well! THEN!"

He turned abruptly on his heel and stormed out again.

"Good heavens!" breathed Hattie, her heart beating thrice as quickly as normal; her breath rapid.

"*What on earth was* that?" she thought, as she stared after him.

Hattie was rattled, but she was also hungry, and she speared another sausage.

"*Perhaps if I just have something to eat, I'll be able to think straight and sort this whole mess out.*"

But as she pressed the meat to her lips, the thumb of her left hand began to drift, over and over again, over the tips of her fingers.

Chapter Three

Having breakfasted heartily (nothing ever made a Vavaseur lose their appetite), Hattie arose from the table, more curious than ever about her surroundings. She fancied a walk outside might assist her in clearing her clouded head. The breakfast room possessed wide French doors that opened onto a small terrace on the side of the house. As she passed through them, the fresh country air filled her lungs, and her eyes brightened at the view. Although the grounds were overrun and wild, there was still a sense of majesty in their layout and extent. The hill on which the house was set sloped down onto an expansive, flat run.

A rushing wind whipped over the lengthy grasses, forcing them this way and that, as though driven by the wings of invisible creatures. It made Hattie long to gallop through them astride a horse – she had never ridden sidesaddle, as was considered proper in her youth. She could imagine herself now atop a stately stallion. She would have pushed him hard, up over that fence, and perhaps, if she was feeling dangerous and the horse was a spirited one, farther and farther beyond, into the thick, fern-infested forest, along that delicate-looking path, testing his surefootedness and her own skill at avoiding tree roots and branches. Her heart was pounding when she came to the end of her small fantasy, and she felt a little breathless. What had gotten into her? She hadn't dreamed of riding for decades. She was far too old and weak to do such things now. If she ever had a tumble, it would mean death, or, at the very least, broken bones that would assuredly never heal properly. But it was poignantly pleasant to dream of old days...

So lost was she in her reverie that she jumped when accosted by Harold. Good heavens! If these sorts of surprises continued in the quick succession in which they'd begun, she'd have a stroke before the week was out.

"Does madam desire a walk at this hour?" He seemed to have a window into her mind as he continued, "Or there are some lovely, gentle horses in the stables if madam wishes to go for a ride. There is a young boy by the name of Teddy who would be more than happy to lead madam about the back west garden," he said.

"Riding! At my age!?" Hattie retorted indignantly. She'd almost added, "The idea!" but pulled herself up short, realizing that was a phrase an old, detested aunt had used rather too often.

"I'm very sorry, madam. The master *thought* you might be too weak, but still I ventured to suggest it," replied he, bowing his head deferentially.

"*Did* he?" this last, more to herself than to the butler. "Have a horse saddled immediately, Harold. I shall be riding in the back west garden."

It was the least she could do for so inconsiderate an opinion.

After much quibbling with Harold over "gentle" horses, she was at last seated atop a nice, steady brown mare. Sidesaddle, it's true – she'd yet to win that battle, but as she'd brought no riding habit, or even owned one now, she was forced to concede. Teddy, a pleasantly round, Titian-headed lad led her rather officiously around the garden. There were no gardeners digging virtuously about the estate, as was usual for a place of this magnitude, but the wild, abstract beauty of the grounds still possessed a charm that was difficult to deny. Not a single pink bud desecrated the landscape – a fact that Hattie noted to her infinite satisfaction.

The ride was refreshing, and she somehow didn't mind the senseless prattle of the young boy. His cheeks were so rosy, and his entire aspect was rather too engaging for her to be altogether stiff and formal with him.

Although Hattie didn't say much, Teddy seemed content with the vague, almost inarticulate responses she afforded him. Throughout their ride, his conversation focused respectively on the beauty and gentleness of the horse, his mother's health, the tender and delicious nature of green apples, the accuracy and prowess needed to assault squirrels with catapults, and, that savior of all conversations, the weather.

"Lovely weather, ma'am," said he, in his drawling, country brogue.

A hem of assent.

"Lov'lr than we've 'ad in this h'area for years, it seems to me."

Another hem.

"It will cern'ly brighten h'up the master."

"Indeed?"

"H'oh, yes, ma'am. 'E's been down at the mouth about summat these forty years at least."

This fact interested Hattie very much, and she inquired eagerly, "And why is your master so very angry? What could possibly have happened forty years ago that has continued to have such an ill effect upon his temperament?"

"Beggin' your pardon, ma'am. I've forgot we've been forbidden from talkin' too friendly-like with you."

This abrupt retort rattled Hattie. It brought back to mind the rude behavior of the man she'd met that morning. Strangely, it hurt her, this man's behavior. As a wealthy and respected woman, she was used to being treated with some decorum, so it was natural that she should feel upset, but this man's conduct stung more than was natural. Usually, she'd easily brush off the rudeness of strangers and put it down to ignorance or distemper. But this man had her at a disadvantage. She had no memory as to why she was here and was too proud to ask for help, even from this young, pleasant boy.

Suddenly, her body felt terribly sore. It wasn't merely her joints that pained her – the discomfort was amplified by an inarticulate and unfathomable depth of aching in her heart that inexplicably accompanied Teddy's words.

They had stopped.

Teddy was absentmindedly removing writhing worms from his pocket and unsuccessfully attempting to feed them to the mare, much to the chagrin of that worthy animal. Hattie abruptly demanded that they return to the house, and Teddy shoved the remaining worms back into his pocket, a few struggling out and falling along the path as they continued on. Hattie eyed Teddy's hands warily as he helped her out of the saddle.

Hattie climbed exhaustedly up the stairs and went straight to her room. Stretched out upon her bed and still disturbed by the unprepossessing aspect of the still-too-pink room, she expected to labor in mental and physical agony until suppertime and was exceedingly surprised when she awoke from an unusually peaceful nap. A daytime doze had not been afforded her for many years – it was nearly a decade since her headaches had begun. Usually, any attempt at a respite of that nature resulted in violent wrestlings with severe pain, instead.

Although she smelled horribly of horse, she luxuriated in the odor as she would an expensive perfume. Horses had been her freedom in her youth. Her parents had passed away when she was but a girl, and she lived with the aforementioned aunt, along with an uncle – both rather unpleasant individuals. A brother and sister, they continuously quarreled with Hattie about her financial affairs, education, manners, appearance, and marital prospects. Hattie frequently escaped these painful arguments with a ride through the lush woods near her estate. Aunt Bathilde and Uncle Harvey Ginter were stern, unrelenting individuals who prodded and poked at Hattie's most vulnerable emotions. Always finding fault, they continuously made her feel as though she could never quite measure up to their ideals. Coupling that with an envy for her wealth, which was thankfully independent when she came of age, they made a formidable duo who cut down her original, independent spirit until it hung by a thread.

Hattie's one escape had been her rides on Charlemagne, her favorite horse. It was the only thing they couldn't bully out of her. In thinking back on them, she couldn't quite recall how they died but did remember the liberty she felt when they were no longer in control of every breath, every thought. Perhaps she was heartless to look with such relief upon death, but she remembered staring unabashedly into their faces as they lay, dead and pale, in her parlor. She had ordered the black crepe that covered the windows and doors to be torn down almost as soon as it was put up. When the clocks were stopped out of respect, she followed the servants around the house and wound them up herself as soon as they were out of the room. And when they tried to remove all the mirrors, she refused, relishing the idea that they could be forever trapped, unable to pass to the other side. Such silly superstitions, she always thought. Much more efficient to hold funerals in a church, as the one she'd attended. Less of this country nonsense and more of the modern world after the Great War.

Hattie felt extraordinarily refreshed. She sat up in bed, longing for a large, delectable dish of something savory. Hattie found it curious that she had not been called for luncheon. She rarely lunched herself, but fancied that it was not typical household manners to withhold food from guests, and she hardly believed the staff capable of familiarity with her eating habits. Deciding that she would risk meeting that brute that had so unkindly accosted her at breakfast, Hattie resolved to explore a bit of the house, then ferret out some delicious tidbit to consume.

When younger, Hattie had always felt a reluctance to move about inside a stranger's home, but time had quelled that meekness, and her true independent spirit had manifested itself more and more throughout the years. Besides, any politeness that may have restricted her on this occasion had been subdued by the unutterable rudeness of the unnamed owner.

Hattie began her exploration with a small study that she was certain led to the library. She was correct, and the room's proportions were just as she'd expect in so large a house. It was storied, and there was even a picturesque, winding staircase leading to the upper floor. The wood that encased the room was dark, rich, and smooth; the tapestries were elegant and fine. Her expectations of what the library would contain were meager, however. She anticipated that a man, who was so obviously without manners, to possess nothing but dry sets of encyclopedias and perhaps a few books on history or hunting – whatever unimaginative interest took his fancy. The worthwhile, beautiful books that were so beloved by her, she expected would not be found in the man's library, and if a few had mysteriously wandered in, she was sure she would discover them in some out-of-reach place, dusty and neglected.

As Hattie neared the shelves, however, her fingertips ran over the leather spines of well-known and dearly loved volumes. Not the stiff, identical, gilded tomes she had expected, but worn, ancient editions that smelled of the sea; strong, hardened novels with partially torn pages; volumes of poetry with scribbled inscriptions from persons dead long ago. The exquisiteness of these books surprised and delighted her, even as the worry of her situation lay heavily on her heart.

Just as she picked up a volume that had always brought her comfort, something like a growl erupted behind her. She turned to find the master of the house leaning over her, looking first into her face and then her hands. He was, she was certain, about to unleash another torrential rage upon her, but when his eyes fell upon the volume she clasped so tightly, he merely turned away, went over to his desk, and began writing feverishly. A vessel in his temple throbbed as he did so, and he did not look at her again.

She made her escape.

As Hattie passed quickly through the hall, she noticed Harold coming through the dining room door. She accosted him and commandingly requested that her supper be brought to her room. She would rather face the hideous pink of her boudoir than the temper of that man...that *barbarian* again. Hattie determined that she would stay no longer and that first thing in the morning, she would request that Bertram return her to her own home as soon as possible. She felt so tired, so muddleheaded, which usually meant the onslaught of one of her headaches. As she prostrated herself upon the ruffled, silky, ugly bedclothes, she prepared herself for the pain...but it didn't come. Instead, the deep peacefulness she had felt that morning began once again to dwell in her soul. She reveled in the feeling, losing track of time or thought.

A quiet, mincing parlor maid whom she had not seen before meekly brought in the supper. As Hattie sat down to the meal, she considered the benefits that good, long ride had done her. Her pain had quite gone; she felt refreshed and ate almost as heartily as she'd done as a middle-aged woman.

When the maid returned to fetch the supper tray, the young woman bashfully articulated, "Excuse me, ma'am, but the car will be 'round to pick you up at quarter past nine tomorrow morning."

"To take me home?"

"No, ma'am, to take you to town. It's all been arranged beforehand. I'm sorry, ma'am, but didn't you know?"

Blast the impertinent girl!

"Of course I know! I shall be ready at a quarter past!"

"Yes, ma'am. Thank you, ma'am."

She blushed and curtsied, giggling a little self-consciously as she closed the door behind her.

Sitting down in a flouncy, chintz chair, Hattie determinedly began to read her book, but her mind wandered again and again in curiosity. Soon, the whole house would know that she was suffering from memory loss. She couldn't stand the thought of them all speaking to her like a child or exchanging stories accompanied by muffled laughter in the servant's hall. All this frustration and confusion was too much for her, but there was nothing she could do if she wanted to keep her pride intact. She could, of course, refuse to go on the morrow.

Then again, it would be lovely to get out of this gloomy house, with its silly, pink rooms and tartar of an owner. Perhaps something in town would assist her in remembering why in heaven's name she was here.

Chapter Four

At ten past, Hattie descended the grand staircase in the main hall, smartly dressed in her befurbelowed blue suit, equipped with a short, white fur stole and a white leather handbag. She always felt very confident in this ensemble. It was an empowering yet feminine suit with a fine cut. She'd had a bit of trouble with her hat, given that there were no mirrors in her chamber. It was a very small affair of the same blue, with a little white net around it that formed a largish bow on the side. She wanted to get the bow just right, so she waited for the car to pull around to use the rearview mirror.

Hattie passed the butler who wished her a "Good morning, madam," with an appropriately desultory smile as she stepped out the front door onto the graveled drive.

She allowed Bertram to help Hattie in, and as he walked around the side to the driver's seat, she quickly looked up to the mirror to adjust her hat, but found nothing but an empty space where it ought to have been. Bertram opened the door and slid into the front seat.

"Bertram," Hattie began slowly, "there is no mirror in this car."

"No, madam, there is not."

"Well, whatever happened to it?" she demanded, "I need to put this hat straight."

"I'm very sorry, madam. These young hooligans like having their little jokes."

"You should have it replaced immediately."

"We shall, madam, as soon as the master deems it suitable."

Hattie opened her mouth to retort, but it remained open, and no sound obtruded. Once again in this strange household, she felt rebuffed. She was used to having the run of things and would have very much liked to demand that Bertram rectify the issue immediately. Still, she remembered that this wasn't her home, nor her car, for that matter, and she couldn't give orders quite as imperiously as she was used to. For perhaps the first time in her adult life, Hattie Vavaseur closed her mouth. Shoving her hat upon her head rather more forcibly and less artistically than usual, she settled back into her seat, determined to feel as unpleasant as possible during this little excursion that had been planned for her with no thought of her own pleasure.

The sky was overcast; the air felt dank, but as they drove along, the landscape at least seemed more cheerful and less foreboding. Hurtling along, they passed a sign that read Market Foolsbury. It seemed a sleepy little town, with few people on the streets. As they began to pass the shops, Hattie's eyes were arrested by a large, vibrantly purple sign with gold lettering that read:

Vamelda
Medium of the Occult
Inquire Within

Hattie was surprised to discover that the car not only slowed as they passed this highly colored, elaborate sign but also stopped. Bertram cut the engine and stepped out to open the door for her. She stared at him with incredulity.

"Bertram, what *are* we doing here?" her voice was teeming with supreme disgust.

"Your appointment, madam."

"With an *occultist*? I've never been so...I can't...how *dare* you!" she blustered.

"Please, madam. You shall be late."

"Bertram, I *will not* go into that disgusting place."

"I'm terribly sorry, madam, but it's more than my job is worth not to have you keep your appointment. You *must* go in."

He took her arm and began to forcibly pull her out of the vehicle.

"Unhand me!" she cried melodramatically. She very nearly added, "You villain!" but decided against it.

Instead, she commenced beating Bertram with her purse, but her blows seemed to have as much effect upon him as the raindrops that began to fall on them both. He wrested the handbag from her with one hand as he steered her into the shop with the other. She wriggled and writhed the entire way but continued walking with him, fearing an injury if she ceased keeping his pace.

As she stumbled into the ill-lit shop, Bertram closed the door behind them. At last, he released her from his iron clasp, and her weight carried her into the wall. Slowly regaining her balance, she turned to face the interior of the unfamiliar building, her eyes blinking rapidly to adjust themselves to the darkness. For despite the gloominess of the day outside, the shop was fathoms darker. Lamps were draped with diaphanous scarves of varying colors – scarlet, heliotrope, azure. The tenebrous atmosphere quelled her, and the invective about to erupt from her lips was swallowed back to the depths of rage that lay inside of her.

They waited.

Hattie vaguely wondered whether it was still raining, and what they would be having for dinner. It is at times of great distress that our minds seem to clasp upon paltry normalities. Amidst the essence of the unknown, we are disposed to grasp at the mundane – to invoke the familiar as we steady our spirits upon its seeming solidity. But progression requires unsettlement, and unsettled was the strongest of Hattie's sentiments upon perception of her hostess, who then vibrated into the room.

Vamelda was not a large individual but seemed so due to her height, which was accentuated by Spanish heels. As she traversed the room with some difficulty, Hattie imagined the high-heeled shoes on the woman's narrow, long feet to be a relatively new accessory.

"Oh, I'm absolutely *thrilled* you're here, at last, my darlings!" Vamelda gushed in what must have been a naturally shrill voice, which she was unsuccessfully attempting to make deep and rich. "I've been simply *dying* to meet you...that is...I don't want to seem untoward, but...it's just...you see, your case interests me so particularly, you know, and I want to make certain you're *comfortable* and everything, so don't mind me," she finished incoherently.

Hattie found it difficult *not* to mind this strange lady. Indeed, she found it hard to believe that anyone could avoid being veritably disturbed by her.

Bertram stepped forward at this juncture.

"Ms. Vavaseur, may I present Miss Vamelda Anstruthers."

"Oh, stop that, you naughty boy. He's only being so formal to irritate me. I've known Bertram for eons," Vamelda let out a burst of awkward, grating laughter.

Hattie stiffened.

"I prefer servants to maintain the decorum which is expected of their station," she retorted disdainfully, recalling the recent escapade outside.

Vamelda grinned.

"Well, we'll soon cure you of your snobbishness, darling. Speaking of which, we'd better get started. Come with me."

And turning, she beckoned eerily over her shoulder, one

thinly penciled eyebrow raised. Hattie nearly protested, but as her eyes followed this idiosyncratic woman, the even stranger surroundings piqued her curiosity, and she moved forward, desiring a clearer look at the objects that haunted these rooms.

Tiki figurines lined the walls – their tongues lolling out, making Hattie feel, as she passed, as though they were aching for a taste of human flesh. African tribal masks, eyes shut, made her believe they'd never known sight, but could feel her presence all the same. A giant Egyptian sarcophagus seemed to bear down upon her as it jutted out from a dark corner. The sparse light from between the window curtains glinted against the bright gold of the casket, as though coaxing her to come feel its smooth, macabre shell.

Beads were draped ubiquitously – over the lintels of doors, shadowing bookcases, cornering small nooks. They sparkled in the dim light, combating the hues of the thin cloths that draped the lampshades, creating an illusion of an ethereal world. Hattie couldn't help herself – she almost floated forward, trying to take in all around her.

Passing a bookcase, she observed gilt-edged books about Tibetan Bardo; scrolls of Egyptian funerary texts; scripts in Arabic, Hindi, Korean – even languages she didn't recognize. But everything here seemed to point to one thing: death.

Vamelda had disappeared behind a tinkling string of beads, and as Hattie neared it, Bertram touched her arm, holding her back, then swept away the door covering to allow her to enter.

She was arrested by the bleakness of this room. Hardly any of the atmosphere that had pervaded the rest of the shop existed here. It was still dark, still gloomy, but none of the cryptic and intriguing novelties lined the shelves here.

It was spare, sparse, austere. A single, three-legged, claw-footed table graced the center of the floor, accompanied by three chairs of the same dark cherry wood. Covered in red velvet, they clashed but somehow heightened the sense of terror that began to grip Hattie by the throat.

"You'd think such poor taste would make me more sure of myself," she thought, then shuddered.

It was the strangeness of her environment and companions that made her uneasy. Bertram had heretofore been her mainstay, but his aberrant behavior had quite naturally shaken her confidence in his solidity.

With a brief glance of defiance leveled in his direction, she walked forward and took one of the chairs without invitation. Hattie felt that being forced into such a place allowed her some levity of decorum. Vamelda had crossed the room to a window.

She abruptly swept round to face Hattie, and the room went dark.

An eerie glow lit up Vamelda's near-translucent, blue eyes. They shone terribly in the semi-darkness. The medium drew closer and closer. Hattie grasped desperately for Bertram's hand. It had been on the back of her chair a moment before, but now it was gone. Turning, she was met with emptiness. Bertram had exited the room.

Hattie whipped her head back around. Vamelda was merely two feet before the table now, her arms outstretched, the long, vermillion nails of her hands looking blood-drenched in the half-light. A scream in Hattie's throat clamored to get out – choked her – she could hardly breathe!

"So sorry about that, my dear," Vamelda said, reaching across the table. "The effect is for the other customers, and I neglected to turn it off."

Bending over Hattie, she flicked a hidden switch beneath the table, and immediately, stark white light flooded the room.

Hattie, still nervous, breathed a shaky sigh of stunted relief.

"You see, your case is such a special one – such a *real* one, we can dispense with the fluff...er...the formalities. I'm *not* a quack, you know. It's just that it works so differently than people seem to suppose it should, so I put on a show for them. But you, my dear...YOU!"

Vamelda stared greedily into Hattie's eyes.

The medium seemed less and less coherent as she gushed on, "We'll see what we can do for *you*, my little sweetums."

Hattie straightened up.

She had lost her memory, been compelled to sleep in a PINK room, kidnapped, and forced into an establishment of horror and death, but she absolutely drew the line at being addressed as "sweetums."

"My name is Ms. Vavaseur," she stated firmly. "You will kindly address me as such."

"But darling…"

Hattie's voice rose, "I am most certainly *not* your darling. And you have no right to keep me in this hideous deathtrap of a room. I demand my freedom."

She arose with a royal gesture and strode magnificently toward the door. It was locked.

"Or at least," she continued as she turned from the useless door handle. "I demand an explanation as to why I have been brought here and, apparently, am being held by force."

"Oh, sweetu…"

"*Ms. Vavaseur!*"

"Yes, darling Ms. Vavaseur. You're absolutely free to leave whenever you'd like."

"Then would you kindly explain to me why this door is bolted?"

"Oh, that must be Bertram. He has stringent orders, you know."

"Orders from whom? From you?" Hattie demanded.

"Of course not. I wouldn't dream of ordering Bertram about. He's much too strong and muscular…and rather attractive, don't you think?"

"*From whom?!*" Hattie shrieked in a very unladylike

manner.

Vamelda seemed not to hear her as she gestured toward the hideous furniture.

"Come and sit down, dearie, and we'll have a nice little chat all about it."

Hattie considered. She felt like Eve, confronted with the choice between eternal ignorance or mortal pain. She chose what she hoped was the briefer option and moved to the table.

"That's it, sweetu...Ms. Vavaseur," Vamelda corrected herself after taking in Hattie's stern eye. "Just you rest your old bones down on this chair," she said, letting out another shockingly loud, seemingly erroneous guffaw.

Nevertheless, Hattie took the proffered seat and waited expectantly as Vamelda attempted to sit down. Gathering her long, flowing scarves and robes about her, she was unsuccessfully trying to disentangle them. Hattie wondered why Vamelda would bother trying to make herself neat; her clothes seemed so mismatched and convoluted, no one would ever be able to tell one from another.

While she watched the medium, Hattie's eyes lighted upon a crystal ball that sat in an elaborate silver-and-gold pedestal on the table between them. The ball seemed to breathe the delicate wisps of smoke that swirled around inside it. Hattie shivered and drew her fur more tightly around her shoulders. It was tantalizing, captivating to watch the crystal. It seemed to emanate its own internal brilliance and glowed brighter even than the electric light overhead. Fascinated, she only with extreme difficulty coaxed her eyes away from the orb and rested them on her hostess.

Vamelda's own eyes were sparkling wickedly at her.

"*Gooor*geous, isn't it?" she declared with luxurious satisfaction. "I picked it up in my travels simply *ages* ago, darling, and it's proven my faithful companion and deceptionist for years and years."

The occultist's theatrical intonations were starting to grate on Hattie's nerves.

"Deceptionist?" Hattie inquired.

"Oh, yes, you see, the mystic side of life isn't something that people easily believe in, in these so very *modern* days. You've got to use every trick they've ever heard of, or make something up they've never even *dreamed* of, and put on the most *elaborate* shows, or else they won't believe one bit of it."

Hattie thought of all the invitations to spiritualistic parties she'd turned down and was proud of herself for not being taken in by such absurdities.

"So you're admitting that you're a fraud...that you take good people's money dishonestly. Why are you telling *me*?" Hattie asked, puzzled and affronted.

"I never said that I was dishonest *or* a fraud," Vamelda answered, apparently taken aback.

"Then what was all that rigmarole about using tricks and this crystal, and the lights, and the books, and the beads, and the masks, and the sarcophagus?" asked Hattie, rather winded at the end of her query.

"Well, my dear...it's so difficult to say this...but, you see, I'm afraid you're dead."

Hattie was certain she must have misheard. Her auditory skills had always been quite good, even as she'd aged, but she couldn't possibly have understood Vamelda correctly.

Hattie shook her head and reasoned: "Did you say I'm *red*? Why, of course I am. I'm 63, and I've just been forcibly kidnapped."

"Heavens, no. You look quite ravishing this morning, darling. What I *did* say is that...*you're DEAD.*"

The realization crept upon Hattie slowly. She was remembering now: the headaches, the last illness...

"Oh, I'm dead," Hattie said lamely.

She stared at the woman; all the intricate details of religion and the afterlife came welling up in her mind. The funeral she'd attended only days ago...*her* funeral. She allowed emotion to congeal for an instant, but her stark efficiency asserted itself promptly.

"Well, what are we to do about it?"

"*Do?*" responded the fortune teller. "There's nothing we *can* do, my dear sugarplum. You'll simply have to accept it. There is no reincarnation – no resurrection from the dead. You see, the world of spirits has always been around you, simply on a different *plane*, if you know what I mean, my darling. Now, I know this is a great deal to take in, sugarplum, so we'll take it one, tiny step at a time."

Hattie's mind was exploding with questions, but she couldn't entirely clear the misty spiderweb of her thoughts enough to formulate one into words.

"I'm dead," she said again, passively leaning back in her seat.

Vamelda's eyes studied Hattie's white face.

"What you need, sweetcake, is some brandy."

"No," Hattie declared, shivering at the thought of the giddiness that came upon her whenever she partook of anything but weak sherry. Hattie never did enjoy feeling out of control.

"Some tea will do quite nicely."

Vamelda dramatically shrugged her shoulders, causing half of her wispy shawls to fall to the ground. As she picked them up, she draped them around her neck in progressively untidier layers.

"Tea then, darling dearest."

Vamelda left the room, one of the scarves wrapped negligently around the heel of her left shoe.

Hattie's head began to spin. The palpable bareness of the room was oppressive. Her eyes became clouded. When Vamelda reentered with the tea, Hattie was sprawled across the table in a fainting fit.

The crystal ball had been knocked from its stand and was rolling across the floor, its light extinguished.

Chapter Five

"Ta-ta, darling! I'll see you tomorrow!" Vamelda had shouted from the doorway as the car had driven away. Hattie groaned internally. She was sitting at breakfast with a stiflingly terrible headache. The toast was burnt, the eggs underdone, and Hattie's mood was none the brighter with another trip to the medium ahead of her.

Suffering from the headache, Hattie hardly had time to process the information she'd received the day before. She now morosely dwelt on it. What had happened to all her high ideals of heaven? The situation she found herself in savored much more of Hades than almost anything she could imagine.

Was she, then, in hell, and this outrageous master of the house the devil himself? She couldn't believe it. The man had a temper, yes, but what of the rest of the household? Everyone else seemed reasonably content with their lives.

"Are they called lives, then?" thought Hattie.

Could it be possible that she was doomed to exist in this house, in darkness and torture, always wondering, always wishing? Hattie was disappointed. She'd led what she believed was a good life. Although her bible reading and churchgoing had been respectively minimal and social, she had always striven to be kind. With her vast wealth, she had laid an open palm full of gold to those in need. And gold, quite obviously, had not been enough.

Hattie stretched her mind back to her youth. Yes, she had been defiant and headstrong toward her aunt and uncle, but there was something...something in her past, something to do with...

She lost the train of thought almost before it had begun.

As Hattie wandered out to the garden beneath the terrace, she considered: If she was forced to live in this house, forced to see Vamelda against her will, forced to exist here as an old woman with nothing to look forward to but a continuation of her condition, she might as well give up and stay in bed for the rest of eternity.

But Hattie was not content with the fate that Providence had given her. The marvelous stock of innate courage that had been dormant in her soul for so long began to resurface. She needed a plan – a course of action. Was it possible to alter one's fate after death? Hattie didn't know. She only believed that she could do nothing but try.

Living alone for most of her life, Hattie had developed the habit of mumbling and gesturing to herself. It was an unconscious proclivity, and she would have been supremely distraught if she ever became cognizant of the fact.

Teddy, who was surreptitiously watching from beneath the branches of a Camperdown elm, had seen Hattie's unconsciously dramatic gesticulations and facial contortions as she reasoned with herself. He had stolen a steak-and-kidney pie from the larder and had just beat Harold around the corner before slipping into this secret hiding place. As he gulped down the last bite, upon his face dawned a slow, mischievous smile as he observed Ms. Vavaseur turn abruptly on her heels and disappear into the house with a determined step.

"I 'ave a feelin' the guv'nor's gonna get it," he confided to the leaves.

Hattie's mind was made up. She needed to speak to the master of the house. It was time she found out who he was and whether he knew anything about the reason for her presence here.

As she made her way determinedly through the hall, a slightly sweaty Harold swept to the side of a doorway, allowing her to pass. About to brush past him, she paused and, turning an austere eye upon him, commanded, "Tell me where the master is, Harold."

"He is unfortunately, madam, not to be disturbed at present," the butler responded, meekly and a bit out of breath.

"I will most certainly *disturb* you if you fail to tell me, Harold. His location. *Now.*"

"I regret to inform madam…"

Hattie, ignoring this unsatisfactory response, barged up

the staircase, her adrenaline carrying her up faster than she'd ascended any stairs in decades. She turned to the right, instead of the left, where her own room lay, assuming that such a brute of a man would desire to be as far as possible from his guest.

Giant double oak doors at the end of the hall pointed her toward the master bedroom. Flinging them aside, she charged into the chamber. What she perceived both shocked and stilled her. Huddled at the edge of the bed was the master of the house. The large, powerful man was sobbing violently while holding a luminous object close to his chest. Hattie's own hand fell from the doorknob in surprise, causing the heavy oak to slam forcefully shut. The silver-haired master of the house was so engrossed in this object and in the pain that apparently surrounded it, that he did not notice Hattie's presence until the bang of the door startled him into looking up.

For a moment, more abject human sorrow than Hattie had ever witnessed was displayed before her. He looked as though he was a man driven mad by grief. His eyes were afire as rivulets of hot tears streamed down his careworn face. Her heart fleetingly caught hold of some inherent sympathetic nerve. But as promptly as the feeling had come, it vanished, for the man's face had turned from contorted anguish to distorted rage.

Inhaling convulsively, he roared, "How *dare* you impose yourself on my presence, you meddlesome hag!"

The object in his hands flashed briefly as he tucked it away under a nearby pillow.

Astonished but still indignant, Hattie haughtily lifted

her head up and shook off the heart-wrenching scene that had just unfolded before her.

"I am no hag, sir, but an old woman who has lived a good life. And on this premise, I demand to know why I am here. What is my purpose? Must I pay a fine of perdition or suffer some unbearable consequence for a former, unremembered sin?"

"I haven't the slightest notion what you're talking about, woman!" he barked. "Tell me what you want with me and be done with it!"

Extracting a handkerchief from his breast pocket, he angrily wiped the tears from his face. He made no apology for his former emotion.

"I've *told* you already, *sir*," she coated the appellation in as much sarcasm as she could muster. "It's for *you* to make up your mind to tell *me* about it."

"*You're* the one wanting to purchase this place, aren't you? Why don't you make your decision?"

Then, grumbling under his breath, "Months to decide... what kind of imbecile woman needs *months* to see if she likes a place?"

Hattie was so baffled by this statement that she didn't think to contradict it. The man had turned his back to her, mutely dismissing her from his presence. Hattie walked back through the egress, in yet another rare mood of contrition. This man's sorrow, coupled with such an obvious state of advanced madness, caused her to second-guess herself. She felt that the answers must then lay, not with the master of the house, but with the strange medium she had encountered the day before.

After this unnerving interlude, Hattie was more than happy to climb into the car with Bertram and drive into Market Foolsbury to Vamelda's. Unwilling to speak, Hattie completely ignored Bertram's polite inquiries and attempts at conversation. Her mind was occupied with a mass of questions for the clairvoyant. It also briefly swept through some mild curiosity about the strange object that ostensibly had such power over that miserable man.

As the Daimler pulled up to the occultist's shop, Hattie clamored out on her own, desiring no assistance. She felt defiant, and, energized by her purpose, she wanted no further contact with anyone but Vamelda. In her decisive and somewhat confused state, she did not recognize that only the day before she had harbored feelings of detestation for the lady in question. It probably would not have made a difference if she had realized it. Hattie was so resolute, so sure of her plan of action, that she was determined to plow through any difficulty of personal dislike. Marching straight into the premises, determinately ignoring scarves, sarcophagi, and scrolls, Hattie burst into Vamelda's inner room.

Chapter Six

Hattie was surprised to see the room bathed in darkness, the medium hunched over her crystal. A lumpy little shadow was hovering in the chair opposite. When Hattie closed the door behind her, Vamelda cried out and jumped to her feet. The crystal ball rolled off of the table and smashed into a profusion of pieces on the floor.

A rush of cold wind entered the room from behind Hattie, sending Vamelda's scarves whirling like the tentacles of an underwater creature. Something like a disconsolate moan accompanied the wind. The dismal sound sent chills down Hattie's spine, but she ignored them. The lump squeaked, and a trill of nervous laughter rang through the room. Hattie, too determined in her bullheadedness to care, stalked straight over to the light switch and pressed it on.

"Oh, goodness me!" croaked the lump, which Hattie now observed was a middle-aged woman with large, watery eyes and an indeterminate chin. "Is it a spirit?!"

"Yeeeeaaaas," said Vamelda raspily as she floated over to the wall to return the room to darkness.

Hattie immediately switched the lights on again.

They fought over the buttons twice more before Vamelda said, in an unusually steely voice, "It seems to be a rather *difficult* spirit today."

"Oooooo!" gasped the lumpy woman. "I've never seen one with such a corporeal affinity to light before! In my experience, the spirit world has always enjoyed darkness!"

Vamelda threw Hattie a disgruntled look and returned haughtily to the table.

"Well, my dear, let us continue with our séance. Our spirit is attempting to communicate with us something about light. You should sleep with all of the lights on in your house tonight, or you will be in graaaaave peril!"

"Oh, yes, YES!" replied the lump, seeming unable to communicate in anything but exclamations. "I felt that the spirit was imparting to me the EXACT same message! I shall do so this *very* evening! Thank you, *thank you*, Vamelda!"

"Of course, my deeeeaaar. And perhaps, next time, we shall be able to contact darling Henry once again."

"Oh, YES! How can I ever repay you for your protection this night?"

"I'll send you the bill in the mail tomorrow, my daaahling," rejoined the secretly practical medium.

As the lumpy woman left, Vamelda began to sweep up the crystal shards. Hattie stood over her, becoming slightly more contrite as she observed the disgruntled look on Vamelda's face.

"That crystal ball has been with me for years...YEARS, Hattie. I don't know where on earth I'll find another like it." Then, she relented, "But, of course, I understand, darling, that you must be very upset. Your first encounter with a mortal, you know."

Hattie, her mouth forming a retort, suddenly changed to, "A *what?*"

"A *mortal*, my dear sweetcakes. You know...a live being. You used to be one. Don't you remember?" Then, to herself, "That's very strange. I know there is a history of memory loss associated with death, but at *least* they usually remember *living.* I shall have to look it up."

Vamelda began walking toward the outer room, her eyes set on her books. Hattie followed.

As Vamelda's finger ran along the bookshelves, Hattie, frustrated, practically yelled, "Of *course* I remember being a mortal. I just hadn't thought about what I am *now.* Am I immortal? Am I a spirit? What *am* I?"

"Well, that's completely up to *you*, my sweet," said Vamelda ambiguously.

The medium pulled down a dusty, old volume with silver lettering, written in some unrecognizable language. She opened to a middle page, where Hattie noted an elaborate sketch of an uncloaked grim reaper outstretching his hand to a middle-aged man cowering before him in an armchair. Hattie found the image extremely disturbing, but Vamelda flipped through the pages of increasingly gruesome images without flinching.

"Aha! Here it *IS!*" she cried impressively.

She laid the book down on an intricately carved oak book podium.

"Nope...no...*nooooo*...neeeeooo....naaaao...no...NO!" she said in varying degrees of resonance as she scanned the page. "There is nothing here for *this* degree of forgetfulness...with the exception of...well, that will be coming shortly, now won't it?" she ended hazily.

"But I *do* remember living," said Hattie, shutting the book on Vamelda and narrowly missing her hand as she did so. "Not everything, but..."

"I quite understand, my dear," interrupted Vamelda. "You've relieved me greatly. What we can do is this: We need to make contact with the other side. They are the only way you'll ever be able to sort through this mess. Trust me, Hattie. I've been at this work for *ages*, but I simply cannot do much more on my end of things. My practice is far too busy. Besides, these cases are usually so very straightforward, particularly combined with emotions this powerful, but it's just the *opposite*, you know, from what is usual, and I'll help you all I can, but I am so *limited* by the very act of my profession. One simply *cannot* go *delving* into such personal issues, can one? That is, not in someone else's family that doesn't strictly come to *me*."

By this time, Hattie's mind was awhirl attempting

to keep in sync with Vamelda's both vague and disruptive commentary. Hattie was still calming herself down after seeing all of those alarming paintings and sketches depicting death and dying.

"*Now,*" Vamelda said, rounding on her. "Who?"

"Whom," corrected Hattie absentmindedly.

"Yes, as I said, '*Whom?*'" returned Vamelda.

"Whom what?"

"Whom do you suggest?"

"For what?" replied an exasperated Hattie.

"Why, to contact on the other side, of course," the medium answered.

"Why is this necessary, Vam...Vamelda?" Hattie struggled with annunciating such a ridiculous name. It wasn't difficult for her orally, but morally.

"To do research. There is only so far I can delve into your mortal affairs as a clairvoyant. The general public does not give much credence to my creed."

She snorted with laughter at her own play on words.

"Terribly sorry, my dear, I only..." she began snorting and shaking with mirth again.

Peal after peal rang out as they moved toward the stark room once more. Wiping tears from her eyes, Vamelda calmed herself at last and sat down in one of the chairs, her arm motioning Hattie to do the same.

"Well, what about the woman that was just here? She

seemed foolish enough."

"Oh, *dear* no. The poor woman is having a difficult enough time already. She comes to visit her husband, but she nagged him so during his life that he gets bored of her and leaves at the beginning of the session nearly every time."

"Then why does she stay?"

"Well...*ahem*..." Vamelda cleared her throat, slightly abashed. "The customers don't pay for only a few minutes, now do they? So I rather...stretch it out a bit. The husband doesn't mind. He left her plenty of money, you know, and so long as it makes her happy...he really does love her."

"So *whom* are we meant to contact?" queried Hattie, emphasizing rather grammatically.

"Well, it should be someone in your family. It must be an individual who has a tendency to believe in occultism. Otherwise, all of our efforts will be completely useless. Although I have been known to convince the odd cynic or two. But in this case, we had better get someone very, *very*...sensitive."

"Gullible, you mean," returned Hattie.

"Well, let's not bicker about labels," Vamelda said lightly. "Now, who is it to be?"

Hattie pondered for a moment. There wasn't much she recalled about her living relatives. She remembered her aunt and uncle, of course. There was a halo of haze surrounding the details of anything but her early life. But wait...wasn't there a cousin somewhere? A cousin with a son. The boy used to call her Aunt Hattie. He was a charming little boy…all dark curls and large eyes.

"Gerald Warburton," she stated aloud. "He's my nephew…well, sort of."

"And what can you tell me about him?"

"Well, he has brown hair. He is tall and lanky. "

"No, *no*," responded Vamelda. "I mean, what are things about him that nobody knows, so I can convince him to come *here*?"

Hattie's mind drifted back to her funeral. Her nephew, as she now recognized him, had been the young man who was overly solicitous toward that buxom young woman. She remembered that he had always been a little silly about girls.

"He's rather taken with a certain young woman at present if his actions at my funeral are any indicator," said Hattie savagely.

It was, after all, *her* funeral.

"Ah, young love! Always an excellent subject for predicting the future. Has he any money?"

"Well, he ought to, considering he was my only living relative, and I left no will. If I recall correctly, I was insanely wealthy when I passed away."

"Good," nodded Vamelda.

"Why, you mercenary…" Hattie stood up haughtily.

"Oh, my *DEAR*! You are quite, *quite* mistaken in me. I only meant that young ladies are apt to accept wealthy young men's proposals, so it will be quite easy for me to predict his future nuptials."

"Ah...oh," replied a contrite Hattie.

"Now, you toddle along home, my dearie, and I'll settle everything and try to convince him to come to us. I'll be out of the country for quite some time, so I'll contact Bertram when I'm ready for you."

Chapter Seven

For the next week, Hattie's days passed rather placidly. She would read, sit in the garden, ride in the fields, and above all, eat heartily. In life, she had always enjoyed food. At least, she believed she did. The details of her living existence were incredibly hazy at times. She recalled only her youth and the end of her life when her illness became severe.

There was a block somewhere – something she needed to unearth about her past, but the harder she attempted a thorough look into it, the more she became confused and seemed to lose the little clarity she had gained in her sessions with Vamelda. She had not heard from the medium for nearly three weeks, and she began to wonder whether she would ever see her again. What had started as an annoyance had, in her current loneliness, now turned into an almost craveable necessity.

In order to satiate her desire for entertainment, Hattie picked up book after book from the massive library. She was cautious each time she entered, determined to avoid another disagreeable encounter with the master of the house. She had not for some time seen him and assumed that he kept to his room, as her meals were never shared, and her solitude never interrupted.

Literature had continuously been a delicious indulgence for Hattie. The volumes of philosophy, adventure, and romance had always been great sources of attraction and even endearment for her. Each book was filled with beloved characters, familiar landscapes, and cherished storylines, but all seemed to pale when compared with the current mystery of her own circumstances. Hattie found herself turning, inexplicably, to children's volumes.

Here, she found comfort and distraction in the simplicity of the words and genuine virtue of the stories and people contained in these pages. She was amused at herself in this discovery, for she had always been a quick learner and had neglected and even scorned such publications as a child. Dickens, Goethe, and the Brontë sisters had been amongst her favorite childhood companions, so her current perusal of *Pilgrim's Progress, Gulliver's Travels*, and even the more recent *Grimm's Fairy Tales* formed her vein of study, and she thoroughly immersed herself in the enjoyment of these stories.

Learning and laughing from one such volume in the east garden in the dimming evening light, Hattie was startled from her adventure of "The Devil and the Three Golden Hairs," attempting to decide if the devil or the king more closely resembled the owner of the house, when the very man appeared before her.

"He must be the devil, then!" thought Hattie, only slightly

malicious in the enjoyment of her private jest.

The secret amusement sustained her as the man passed.

Hattie sat perfectly still, not allowing a muscle to quiver, praying that he would not discover her presence. But an ill-placed bunch of pressed wildflowers she had been using as a bookmark fluttered in the slight breeze and carried over to the man's open hand, brushing his fingertips and startling him out of his apparent reverie.

His hand closed upon the small petals, and Hattie gasped for fear that he might crush the delicate things. As he turned at her sharp intake of breath, Hattie noted that his fingers folded gently over the blooms, rather than crumbling them as she had expected.

Hattie cursed herself for her foolish noise. What did it matter if a blossom or two were lost to her? Their eyes met – Hattie's were glowing with the preparation of an argument, but, surprisingly, the man came to her, gently placed the flowers in the palm of her upturned hand, and took a seat beside her.

They sat in silence for some moments before the man faced her and said, in a voice gruff with controlled emotion, "I do not like that you are here."

Hattie began to make an equally rude return, but he held up his palm.

"But the fact remains that you *must* be here. As I am now resigned to the fact, we may as well make what we can of these unfortunate circumstances. You have been allowed freedom in this house, and I have made myself absent on that account. I now find my room too confining and request that we may live here, if not in complete harmony, at least in a fair amount of peace. Is that agreed?"

"Agreed," said Hattie, a little tersely. "But, if you do not..."

He cut her off once again with his upraised hand.

"Let us not argue. I *will not* be bullied by a woman, least of all by one of your age."

Hattie took great offense at this jab at her wrinkles and rheumatism but held her tongue, as she had no desire for him to unleash insults once again.

"I have lived here for decades alone, and I am not used to having company. We shall have to make the best of it. I do not like chattering females, and I especially do *not* like small-minded conversation. If you can conduct yourself in a modest, womanly, and intelligent manner, then we shall be able to tolerate one another admirably. Now, I see you have disarranged several of my books. I wish to have a conversation with you about Nietzsche tomorrow evening, after dinner. Is that agreeable to you?"

Hattie could do no more than give a nod of assent, astounded at this unusual request of intellectual stimulation.

"Very well, I am glad that is settled. Until tomorrow evening, then."

He stood, took a very stiff bow, then vanished back into the house.

That night, Hattie found sleep to be a gossamer web, impossible to catch. She had not looked over Nietzsche in several years, and, aside from his well-known and all-too-traversed quotes about nihilism, she was not certain that she could keep up a conversation with a man so apparently well-read. Clothed in naught but her nightdress, Hattie slipped downstairs to find a copy of *On the Genealogy of Morality*.

After some poking about for the correct volume in the library, the barefooted Hattie began to tiptoe down the hall, her feet cold on the smooth, wooden floor. The rugs had been rolled back for cleaning, so she trod carefully to avoid any creaking in the floorboards.

Looking down at her feet, she was startled to see a sliver of the hallway bathed in light. Glancing up, she perceived that the door to a room she was passing was slightly ajar. She had not given much notice to this particular room before. Peering in blinkingly, she saw the figure of a man in shirtsleeves.

It was Bertram, who began quietly whistling to himself as he polished a mirror in his hand. Hattie's eyes, adjusting to the light, realized that the entire room was filled, from floor to ceiling, with mirrors. Large ones, minuscule ones, mirrors with ornate, gilded frames – even looking glasses framed in pink. They made Hattie shudder when she realized they would have fit perfectly in her bedroom. All of them were bright and clean, down to the one that Bertram was at that moment polishing vigorously.

It was unmistakably the rearview mirror of a car.

Puzzled, Hattie stepped forward for a closer look. The floor squeaked beneath her feet, and Bertram half-turned, the whistle upon his lips silenced. Hattie drew back, embarrassed by her minimal attire, and she rushed up the stairs to the safe confines of her bedchamber. Although breathless and bewildered, she resolved to ask Bertram about this strange room of mirrors when next they met.

Chapter Eight

Humming a little aria, Hattie enjoyed getting ready for the day, despite her ridiculously pink surroundings. She found herself intrigued at the prospect of an intellectual discussion with such a strange character. He obviously had hidden depths...very, *very* hidden, but nonetheless there. Having read long into the night, Hattie felt extraordinarily prepared to bandy ideas with her host.

She went about her day in the usual manner – riding, reading, and wandering the grounds. While she was out, she discovered a small, open summerhouse, quintessentially covered in ivy and climbing roses wherein hung a large, round bed suspended from the ceiling. The wispy, white curtains created a deliciously refreshing atmosphere, and Hattie soon fell asleep whilst the breeze gently rocked her fairy-like bower.

"Aah-hhhhem!" Hattie was startled unpleasantly from sleep by the ridiculously guttural throat clearing of young Teddy.

"You're ter go straight away to Mahrket Follsb'ry to see Vamelder," he stoutly announced, his chest thrust out importantly.

Although groggy from her delicious dreams, Hattie was still strict about proper manners.

"Teddy, how do you address me?"

"By sayin' 'If yer please, Mardarm,' misus," he returned sheepishly.

"That is correct," returned Hattie, smoothing her dress, which seemed to be growing rather large for her.

She should simply have to consume more of that delectable morning sausage. Unconsciously licking her lips, she continued to question young Teddy.

"Now, what is all this fuss about Vamelda?"

"Yer to go un' see 'er straight away. She's got some impre....impra...im-per-a-trive news for yer," he finished, obviously impressed with his clever ability to squeeze the word out.

"Imperative," corrected Hattie.

Teddy's face and chest instantly deflated..

Hattie quickly remedied her unfeeling remark with, "But that was a superb attempt at a very difficult word, Teddy."

The boy's demeanor returned instantly to gloating status.

He had brought the brown, steady mare with him to

make a quicker journey to the house. As they trotted along, a sudden realization came to Hattie. Teddy must be dead, as well. But was he aware of it? She trepidatiously began her pursuit of the truth.

"Teddy, when I first went to see Vamelda, she told me something very...unique. Something shocking that I wasn't expecting. She explained to me that I was in a position that was different and...and...well, *special* from any other I had known. I felt..."

Faltering, Hattie paused, her voice trying its best to sound tender and motherly.

"I was confused and worried when I first heard it and... Teddy...I would like to ask you a question about what Vamelda told me. I...well...I'm not really sure how to put this, but...*what are you sniggering at, young man?*"

The usual sharpness of her voice snapped back into place.

Teddy was doubled-up in laughter, tears streaming from his eyes. He couldn't wipe them away fast enough to see his way through the copse they were traversing, so both horse and leader had stopped.

Affronted, Hattie sat staring at the little roly-poly redhead, her eyes demanding an explanation of this ridiculous behavior.

"I'm sorry, ma'am, but yer so funny when yer tryin' ter be so careful, and of *course* I know all 'long whatcher on about!"

"Oh, *do* you, young man?" she queried skeptically. "What is it, then?"

"Yer want to know if I know I'm *dead*!"

"Ah," she said, taken aback.

She did not expect this humorous acceptance of a situation that would terrify most children.

Teddy finally recovered himself, and he began to lead the horse on again.

"Theodore Alexander Fitzpatrick Scraggins in life. Teddy to me friends."

He touched his cap ceremoniously.

"So when you spoke of your mother's health…"

"I keeps an eye on 'er. Vamelder helps all on us with our loved ones, 'ere and there. She gets caught up in the really *big* cases you know, but she's al'ays got a kind word fer me mum when she needs it. Me mum misses me like mad, yer know."

"I'm very sorry to hear that, Teddy," Hattie spoke in much softer tones than she was used to.

Her heart went out to this poor boy. Hattie's next question seemed rather intrusive, but she couldn't quell her curiosity.

"How did it happen, Teddy?"

"Treacle," the young mite brusquely responded.

"Treacle?" queried Hattie, confused.

"Treacle," said Teddy decisively. "I was eatin' me treacle tart and dropped it into the well and went arter it and fell in. I remember tryin' ter swim, but, as I'm s'little, I didn't know how ter."

"Oh, you poor dear!" Hattie sympathized.

"Coo! What a hey-day that was! They dragged me body up, all blue and puffed up from the water, and me mum was a-wailin' and a-holdin' of me, and all the p'licemen gathered 'round," he continued. "And all me friends at the funeral and that ol'e Annie Whittensprat cried and cried and said she felt bad fer telling the teacher on me fer puttin' those crickets in her desk. Served her right, the tattler!" he reveled.

Hattie was appalled.

"Teddy! You don't mean to tell me you're *glad* you're dead! And that you actually *enjoyed* watching your poor mother mourn at your funeral!"

"No, ma'am. I truly miss me old mater, but it's sure nice to know yer loved, isn't it?" he said, hugging himself, but then had to detangle his body from the reins as a result.

Hattie sighed. She disapproved of young Teddy's light-hearted view of the matter, but it would have been nice to see a *few* more wet handkerchiefs at her own burial.

Chapter Nine

Vamelda was profuse with gushing diminutives when Hattie first entered the medium's establishment.

"Oh, my daaaahling dearest! I *have* missed you so, dearie! It's been simply *ages*, sweetums, and I can't *wait* to catch up on all my little Hattie Patty-Cakes's news! You simply *must* sit down and fill me in. It looks like *you've* been busy!"

"Well, I…" Hattie began to respond as she took a seat upon a plush chair in the anteroom of curiosities.

Vamelda perched, like a bird, upon a table's edge but was up again in an instant.

"Oh, that is *so* fascinating, honeycake, but we mustn't keep *him* waiting!"

For a moment, Hattie thought Vamelda was about to take her to meet her Maker, but the thought of this silly, vacant woman being a keeper of the pearly gates was laughable.

Her curiosity piqued, Hattie strode forward into the inner chamber and nearly collided with the back of a tall, lanky man who was wearing an expensive, but ill-fitting suit. The man moved forward farther into the room as she entered.

Vamelda swept in after Hattie and sat at her table. Hattie observed that a new crystal ball had replaced the one she had broken. This particular orb was much larger and sat in a stand resplendent with what looked like precious gems, but were probably merely cheap imitation glass.

Hattie at once fell under the orb's spell. She was inexplicably drawn to it – even more so than the previous one that had adorned the medium's table of tricks.

"Now, my deeeeaaaah young man, pleeeeaaaase take a seat," she gestured to the guest in her usual, theatrical fashion.

As he neared the table and turned to sit down, Hattie saw his face and gasped.

"Why, it's my nephew, Gerald!"

Just then, the lights went out. The room was shrouded in darkness. All Hattie could see was the glowing crystal ball. It altered from a faint, glistening lavender to a burning, icy blue. Fascinated by the pulsating orb, Hattie walked closer and closer to it, her hand outstretched, her fingers trembling as she felt the heat of it grow more powerful...

"Thaaaa spiraaats are wiiith us!" howled Vamelda.

Hattie reeled backward, utterly disquieted by this unexpected outburst.

"Where?" Hattie exclaimed, realizing too late her mistake. "Oh! I see. I didn't realize…"

"Their presence is stroooong!" the medium continued to wail, drowning Hattie's voice.

"Is it her? Is it my auntie?" squeaked Gerald's weak, tremulous voice.

"Yes, it is me, Gerald. How are you, dear boy?" Hattie responded.

"The spiriiiit is trying to commuuunicate with you!" Vamelda cut in.

"Can't he hear me?" queried Hattie. "I want to speak with my nephew!"

Vamelda opened her heavily painted eyelids and threw Hattie a look that could have killed her if she wasn't already dead. Even in the semi-darkness, Hattie guessed from her look that the occultist was worried about a repetition of the squabble over the light switch.

Hattie folded her hands together, demonstrating her willingness for complacency. Temporarily placated, Vamelda's lids scrunched up tightly once again.

"Yeeeas, yes, it *is* your Auntie Hattie, my deeear boy," she continued in a nauseatingly breathy voice.

"Oh, I knew it! Sweet old Auntie!" breathed the young man.

Hattie drew herself up to her full height. "I have *never* been addressed as 'Auntie' anything in my entire life!"

"Yes, her presence is *very* strong, dearie."

One of Vamelda's suspiciously long eyelashes fluttered open, shooting Hattie another accusatory look.

"What happens now?" questioned both Hattie and her nephew in unison.

"I feel that your auntie was very wealthy," responded Vamelda, whose voice had almost magically turned practical.

"Why, yes, she *was* remarkably wealthy," said Gerald. "As I was her only living relative, her money, as a matter of fact, was left to…"

"Yooouu!" Vamelda screeched, pointing her long forefinger straight between Gerald's eyebrows.

Gerald, obviously taken aback, gasped, "Why, yes! But how could you know…?" He trailed off, puzzled momentarily. "I've got it, by jingo! You're on the level! You're the real thing, aren't you? Now, what's my dearest auntie got to say to me?"

"You're a bit of an idiot, aren't you, nephew?" promptly responded Hattie.

Ignoring her, Vamelda pursued, "She wants you to know that she is pleased with your upcoming nuptials."

"I most certainly am *not*!" Hattie began to say, but Gerald, unable to hear her, interrupted.

"Gee whiz, lady! You really know your onions! I *am* about to slap a handcuff on a choice, little bit of calico. Is that what my auntie wants to beat her gums about? Does she approve? I've been trying to wait it out 'til it was long enough after the funeral for me to propose. It's been six months...do you think it's too soon?"

"Six months?" said Hattie. "Why, he's thicker than I thought. It's only been a few weeks since my funeral!"

"No, she is verrrry, verrry happy for you," Vamelda trilled. "She would certainly support your engagement and recommends that you ask the dear lady in question to wed as soon as possible. There will be no doubt of her accepting you."

"You really think so? I wasn't sure if I should take the chance. Sometimes, I have to get zozzled just to talk to the gal. I thought she might give me the icy mitt! But dear old Auntie Hattie thinks I've got it in the bag, eh? Fancy that!"

"Yeeeeaaas, by all means, my deeeeah boy. Ask the girl to marry you. But once she accepts, there is something you must do before you can go through with the ceremony. Otherwise, yours will be a most unhappy marriage."

"Anything – I'll do simply anything! The game's too good to let *this* Betty get away."

"I could *feeeel* that her name began with a 'B'!" Vamelda cooed.

"Why, it does! It's Beatrice!"

"But you call her by that beloved nickname Bett..."

"Trixie," Gerald broke in.

"Oh, yeeeasss..." Vamelda sounded puzzled.

Hattie thought it was time to rescue her, "It's the patois of the young people these days. A 'Betty' is an attractive young lady, I believe. When I was alive, my maid used to tell me some of the ridiculous vernacular the local shop boy used to say to her."

"Indeeeed! Trixie is *indeeeeed* a pretty 'Betty,'" Vamelda gushed.

She stared hard into the crystal.

"I see her now..." Vamelda trailed off expectantly.

"I *see* her *now*," she repeated and darted an irritated glance in Hattie's direction.

"Oh!" exclaimed Hattie, grasping the clairvoyant's meaning. "She's a voluptuous young woman with light brown hair."

"A voluptuous young woman with light brown hair!" repeated Vamelda.

"You've got it! I know most fellas like their women flat and straight these days, but I like a bird with curves and gams."

Gerald stared into the crystal ball as though willing it to conjure up for him images of his beloved.

"If you'd like your marriage to be a success," broke in Vamelda, her voice textured and full. "The thing you must do is to discover more about your dear departed auntie's early life. There is a great secret you must discover and bring to light before she is able to move oooo-oooooon!"

She trailed up at the end, pointing a long, slender finger into a vague and distant corner of the room. Gerald visibly shuddered in reaction to these dramatics.

"Of course! I'll do whatever it takes to make sure Trixie's happy! Anything else?"

"Yeeeass. Your Auntie Hattie has a few more bits of advice for your personal welfare."

"Lay it on me, baby."

"This could prove to be a veeeerry dangerous mission, dearie. There are evil spirits everywhere, seeking only to disturb the peaceful rest of our dear departed. So I leave with you this wisdom from the beyond! Sprinkle this sacred salt upon your head morning and night...and a pinch of pepper under your arms at least twice per day."

Vamelda pulled two small jade dragons from the inner depths of her crowded attire. They proved to be salt and pepper shakers.

"I have some for you here to begin your quest safely."

Gerald reached out for the precious items, but Vamelda arrested his hand before he was able to take them. She leaned in closer until they were nearly nose to nose. Her voice became even more breathy and deep as she looked intently into his eyes.

"And never, *ever* enter under a door frame without

doing a brief soft-shoe routine."

She allowed Gerald to take the dragons, and he, quelled by her intensity, began immediately to apply her remedy against the forces of evil.

He thanked her, laid a generous amount of money on the table, and, sneezing erratically, commenced an awkward caper out the door.

Raising an eyebrow, Hattie turned from the ridiculous spectacle toward a widely grinning Vamelda.

"None of that nonsense will legitimately assist my nephew in his endeavor, will it?"

Vamelda's face settled back into its usual ethereal expression, and she responded, haughtily, "As a matter of fact, there is some argument in Shinto circles about a practice known as Harai. It is believed that sacred salt such as this purifies the individual and acts as a defense against evil."

"What of the pepper and the...Charleston?" Hattie queried, skeptical.

"*That*, I admit, is for my own enjoyment."

The semblance of a smile began to contort the medium's countenance once again.

Hattie couldn't prevent a secret, little smile from sailing across her lips, as well.

Chapter Ten

When Hattie returned to the house, she went directly to the library. Dinner must have been over for some time – she had stayed too long at Vamelda's.

The room was empty. Feeling slightly disgruntled at the lost opportunity with her host, she turned to exit back to the hallway.

A growl erupted from a darkened corner.

"You're late."

The snarl of a phrase made Hattie's ears tingle with heat. Whipping around, she perceived her host crouching in front of the fireplace, his back toward her. He must have been preparing the fire, for it soon erupted into a blaze. Turning around and placing the matches in his pocket, she could see his eyes take on the glow of the flames.

In the absence of her response, he repeated, "You're late."

Hattie began to speak. He held up his hand – an increasingly annoying habit, Hattie was discovering.

"No excuses. I should have known better than to ask such a *woman* as you to engage in any semblance of intellectual conversation."

He uttered the word "woman" with abject disgust. Hattie, tired from her eventful day and supremely frustrated with this caveman-like attitude toward her sex, was about to parry his remarks with those of anger and hostility. A torrent of words nearly escaped her, but a flicker of light to the left of the man before her caught her eye.

Yet another small orb, seemingly identical to the sphere at Vamelda's, was sitting on the mantelpiece. Placed upon an elaborate silver pedestal, it not only reflected the light of the fire but it also seemed to emit an illumination of its own.

Her lips parted, but instead of the torrent of rage that she expected to release, a calmness overtook her. Somehow, seeing the entrancing, swirling light of the orb gave her an obdurate strength and the presence of mind she needed to brace herself against this man's verbal barrage. Carefully and femininely gathering her skirts, she settled into a chair, prim and erect as a statue.

Hattie began to pour out her theories on metaphysical nihilism and felt eminently prepared, particularly in light of her own situation. Settling on a wide interpretation that did not necessarily include any incidents she'd experienced in the afterlife, she spoke more of the society that must have encompassed them both during life.

His anger suspended, the master of the house eyed Hattie for a long moment in complete silence. Shrugging his shoulders, he sat down opposite her and began to bandy and thrust in full force with his own theories of Nietzsche's intent.

Hattie felt that his theories, though presented with acumen and even sometimes an intriguing hint of wit, were utterly inaccurate morally. He was highly dismissive of ecumenical views and agreed entirely with the ideology of Christianity forming a mere social construct. Although Hattie had never been particularly religious in life, she had always believed in a higher power. On the verge of flinging herself fully into furthering their debate, she instead fell silent.

This afterlife – this place where they both were evidently trapped – wasn't that proof that he was correct?

Where was the peace she should have been feeling? Where were the rest and respite? Where was God?

They had been contending with one another until long after the light in the fireplace became no more than a memory of embers. The darkness of the room had overcome the strength of her arguments at last.

The master of the house lit a candle. Hattie looked up, surprised. Lost in her lingering reflections, she had entirely forgotten his presence. Hattie glanced down at the small pocket watch that was always attached over her heart. It was *very* late, indeed, and high time for her to be in bed. She had enjoyed herself so thoroughly, expostulated so clearly, that she hated to conclude this most satisfactory interaction, despite her brief flight into the dark realm of doubt.

He must have seen the covert glimpse at her timepiece, for he cleared his throat resolutely and, the sternness returning to his gravelly voice, said, "Although your arguments have been just, and, in some cases, even possibly correct, I feel that it is time for us to part ways for the evening."

He stood up and faced the mantelpiece.

"Goodnight," he said.

Hattie, surprised at his abrupt change of manner, but recognizing herself to be exhausted, stood up and gave a curt nod toward his broad back. The orb she had noted earlier now emitted a glow that was stronger than the dying firelight should reasonably have countenanced. She drew closer to it, and, unconsciously, closer to him. Her eyes seemed to burn with the incandescence that emitted from the crystal's very depths.

Just as she was about to reach out to touch it, he turned toward her. Surprised at his unexpectedly close proximity, she took a step back.

"Goodnight," he said again, more sternly even than before.

Hattie fluttered out of the room, head spinning with German philosophy, confusion at this man's erratic behavior, surprise at her own attraction to the mysterious orb, and, more than anything, stunningly ravenous.

Back in her room, sitting on her disgustingly rose-colored duvet, Hattie pondered the overwhelming events of the day. She was about to undress for bed when a knock came at the door.

It was the awkward housemaid with a tray of hot food. Hattie was immensely relieved. Despite her grumbling insides, she was too weary to attempt another furtive excursion downstairs in the middle of the night.

The maid flitted about the room, tidying Hattie's clothes and waiting for the tray to be emptied of its appetizing contents. Devouring the deliciously dripping roast and Yorkshire puddings in much larger bites than were strictly judicious at her age, Hattie engaged in some light conversation.

"How long have you worked here..."

A pause,

"I'm afraid I don't recall your name?" Hattie's voice rose in inquiry between mouthfuls.

"Agatha," she replied, curtsying awkwardly. "I just came to the manor to be of service to you, Miss."

"Well, that's very kind of you," Hattie replied.

Always a bit fussy about her clothes, Hattie was keeping a close eye on how she tucked them away in the large, rose-festooned wardrobe.

"I was wondering," Hattie said, demurely dabbing a bit of dribble from her chin, "Would it be possible to have a mirror installed in my room? It's been most inconvenient for me without one."

Agatha, who had been removing the tray from Hattie's lap, let one handle slip from her fingers and only just caught it in time to save the china. The remnants of Hattie's dinner slid to the floor. Thankfully, Hattie's appetite was such that there was very little left to make clearing up difficult.

As Agatha replaced the dinnerware on the tray and scrubbed the carpet clean with her apron and a little water from the washbasin, Hattie repeated her question. Agatha turned a blotchy beet red – an unfortunate color for her pale skin – and she mumbled something about "the master" that Hattie did not quite catch. Agatha beat a fast retreat into the hall. Hattie was disproportionately frustrated by this girl's clumsiness and her own inability to solve this bizarre puzzle of the missing mirrors.

During the mishap, a paper had fluttered from the tray into Hattie's lap. Catching it up, she was about to call the maid back to return it when she noted the strong, decisive hand it was written in. It read simply:

"Thank you for tonight."

Hattie settled back into her sheets, satisfied with the kind, if brusque, note. With a sigh that filled her lungs with the sleep of more youthful times, she passed into dreamland.

Chapter Eleven

"I *de*mand to know why you've made my de*ar* Ger*ald* prance around in this ridi*cu*lous fashion!" exclaimed Beatrice Bothell – "Trixie" to her friends. "I can't get through a d*oor* without some*bo*dy saying something unpleas*ant*!"

Trixie had an irritating way of placing the wrong emphasis on the wrong syllable in a grossly misguided attempt to sound more refined than, in fact, she was.

"And the smell! Ugh! What am I ev*er* to tell my friends! My *ex*cuse has been a doc*tor's pre*scription for a cold, but Ger*ald* sim*ply* can't have a cold *for*ever!"

She wrapped her fur stole comfortingly around her and shook her head so violently that the gaudy peacock feathers attached to the side of her hat began to unravel from their stitchings.

Vamelda attempted to interrupt, but Trixie rivaled the clairvoyant, not only in fashion, but also in verbosity.

"Hon*estly*," she continued, pulling out an ostentatiously embroidered handkerchief.

She began to emit high, squeaky sobs of an indeterminately realistic nature.

"Hon*estly*," she began again, her already soprano voice progressing to unknown heights the longer she spoke. "I don't know whether or not to call off the wed*ding*. I do love Ger*ald*, but can you ask a wo*man* to live under these *con*ditions? Can *you*?"

One eye, mascara still intact, popped out from behind the hankie and drilled its unrelenting gaze into Vamelda's icy blue ones.

"Can *you*?" she squealed, her tones more aerial than ever.

Hattie and Gerald were seated next to each other near the white walls of Vamelda's spiritual center, breathlessly watching this interaction.

Vamelda had seemed to relent and sympathize with her client's fiancé, but Trixie's gaze prompted her into defensive reaction.

"Yeeeeaaass, my deeeaar!" Vamelda returned with supremely guttural accents that rivaled Trixie's high ones in opposition. "And the spiriiiiits have now advised me that it is absolutely necessary for you to do the saaaaame!"

"Wha*at*?!" squeaked Trixie, aghast that her affecting entreaties had not worked on the seeress.

Just then, another woman entered the room. She resembled Trixie so remarkably in figure and feature that, for a moment, Hattie assumed that Trixie had a twin sister. Her assumption was soon rectified.

"There's my trollop of a girl!" bayed the woman, walking, or rather, marching, up to her.

She bent over and began scrutinizing Trixie from head to toe. "I *knew* she would turn out badly! Just look at that handbag! It's utterly vulgar!"

She turned to Hattie and asked, "Wouldn't you agree?"

Hattie had assumed up to this point that Trixie was too absorbed in feigning sorrow to respond to this woman's effronteries. Hattie now realized that, as she was addressing her, the woman must not be visible to either Hattie's nephew or his fiancé. Nodding insignificantly, Hattie and the woman both turned their attention back to the table where Vamelda and Trixie were spuriously battling.

"Triiiixiiie," breathed Vamelda. "I feeel the presence of a loved one...I feel..." she paused dramatically, and, flipping some hidden switch, she made the lights flicker and turn blue. "Your *mooooother!*"

Trixie's face paled under skin already blanched by far too much powder.

"M...m...my mother?" she gasped, her pitch dropping to a shaky alto.

"I see that she completely ignored my request to be buried with my jewels." Mrs. Bothell turned to Hattie once again. "My dear Henry, Trixie's stepfather...well, we never got around to actual matrimony, but he *did* give me those as a sign of affection, and it was my dying wish that they be laid to rest with my body. Selfish girl!"

Vemelda, overhearing their conversation, turned it to advantage. With a dramatic sweep, she grasped her own neck and began gasping as though unable to breathe.

"Your...your...oh! My fleeeeesh! Something sears the very skin of my throat!"

Alarmed, Trixie unconsciously mirrored the medium, clasping the jewels that festooned her ample bosom. The layered strings of diamonds were entirely too extravagantly ornamental for a simple daytime trip to a soothsayer, but Hattie had a feeling that, uneducated in the wearing of such accouterments, Trixie rarely left them off.

Still scratching and seething as though a firebrand was about her neck, Vamelda howled. "The jewels! The jeweeeeels! They were to have been buried with her!"

Trixie clutched the sparkling collar even closer to her, the cold gems creating a flaming necklace of their own as they pressed deeply into her white skin.

"But how can you know that? Only Mother told me on her deathbed that she..." Trixie broke off, terror overtaking her features like some distorted carnival mask.

"You *must* have them put to rest with her – to make atooooonement!" Vamelda continued, eerily illuminating her face in a resplendently empurpled light with the assistance of some hidden switch.

"I will *not!*" Trixie wailed, rising and stamping her foot, as though the mere memory of her mother transformed her back into a fractious child.

Vamelda commenced once again, "Yeees! You must! You *muuuust*! Or you must at least give it to me, and I will restooooore it to its proper dweeeeelling place!"

"Why, you charlatan!" Trixie's voice was impatient with desperation. "You're merely trying to steal my necklace!"

It was obvious she didn't believe her own words as she twisted the piece of jewelry so tightly against her neck, her breath became labored.

There was a pause, and Hattie glanced at her nephew. Gerald was earnestly observing the interaction taking place before him and tightly clenching a feather that had fallen from his beloved's extravagant headdress. Hattie trepidatiously reached out to steady him by a tender touch, but, unsure of her ability to do so, instead plucked the vibrant feather from his hand and placed it on a convenient shelf nearby. Gerald, a puzzled expression upon his face, watched the feather move about the room, seemingly on its own. However, the distraction must have been a catalyst for encouraging him into action. Faintly clearing his throat, he leaned his lanky, slim body forward, appealingly.

"Look here," he said timidly. "There's no need for calling names and all that. I tell you, she's the real deal, Trixie."

Haughtily, Trixie looked down upon her affianced as though about to tear his body in two, but his imploring, sheep-like face seemed to soften her a bit. She calmed herself and sat down once again.

Vamelda leaped like a hungry tiger at Trixie's temporary mollification: "I have no need for such baubles! It is merely my desiiiire to assist the deeeeeaaaad."

Flickering lights and tinkling crystals assisted in the effect of her words.

"Well, tell me more then," Trixie said, attempting to compose herself. "What else has old Mum got to say to me?"

"Let me see...there is something...something from your childhood!"

"She's got a little scar on her thumb from when she was teasing a dog with a piece of meat," contributed Mrs. Bothell, helpfully.

Repeating the story, Vamelda embellished efficiently, as was her custom.

A few more childhood tales were exchanged between Mrs. Bothell and Vamelda, and Trixie seemed sufficiently convinced.

Stepping back and eyeing her daughter, Mrs. Bothell interjected, "And just look how stout she is," she observed, obviously ignoring her own less-than-slim figure. "I *told* her to lay off the sweets! But she never listens to her poor, dear mother, who is only trying to help her!"

"She is also trying to tell me something...something important about...your *health*!"

"My health? Am I dying? Am I going to be thrown under a tram? Tell me! *Tell* me!"

"She wants you to give up your indulgence of sweet-meats! She feeeeaaars for your...figure!" Vamelda finished histrionically.

"That's mother, alright," grumbled Trixie, sighing dolefully, head bent in full submission at last. "Aside from the neck*lace*, what does she want me to do?"

"She desiiires you to liiisten to me! Take heed to my counsel! Follow the enlightenment of my guidaaaance!" Lights continued to flash as Vamelda manipulated the effects the room had to offer. "You must assist your betrothed in his quest! *And* you must follow all of the very same instructions I have disclosed to hiiiim!"

"I can't! I c*an't!*" wailed Trixie. "What *would* my friends think? What would they *say*?!"

"Then you are destined to become incredibly fat! Your obesity will know no bounds! You are doomed to bursting seams and popping buttons!"

"No! No!" bemoaned the young woman, covering her ears. "I won't hear one bit more!"

"Corpulent! Dumpy! Elephantine! *Paunchy!*" Vamelda swelled.

"Alright, alright! I'll do it!" screeched Trixie.

Launching herself toward Gerald, she violently extracted the small dragon shaker from his coat and thoroughly layered her bare armpits with the spice. With tears overflowing, she then reluctantly unclasped the necklace and laid it upon the clairvoyant's table as though at the feet of a marble goddess. Grabbing her fiancé by the arm, they Charlestoned their way out the door.

"There is that taken care of," Vamelda rose from the table. Gathering up the sparkling layers of diamonds and pressing them against her own breast, she admired their effect in the reflection of the crystal ball. "As long as they are convinced about the superstitions, they will stay on track with the investigation with which I entrusted them. Your nephew has already proven a surprisingly astute detective, despite your tales of his ineptness."

"Perhaps his seeming ignorance is the effect of his education and the society he keeps, rather than a natural stupidity," Hattie rejoined.

Mrs. Bothell stepped over to Vamelda and unceremoniously snatched away the string of precious jewels. Without a word, she stalked out of the room.

"A very rude family, altogether," Vamelda said, dreamily tracing her neckline and staring off into the distance. "I'm surprised your nice nephew set his cap at such a creature. He really is a very nice boy."

"I never knew him well," returned Hattie. "Tell me – what has this detecting work you speak of turned up?"

From within the intricacies of her elaborate robes, Vamelda extracted a bundle of antiquated documents bound together with a ribbon of green silk.

"Here they are. Letters, by the looks of it."

Vamelda unfasted the ribbon and began to read.

"They seem to be a correspondence between you and a childhood friend – Vivienne. She may have been French?"

Hattie neared the medium's table and looked over her shoulder.

"French…" Hattie repeated softly. *"Je pense que je me souviens d'elle."*

Chapter Twelve

26 December 1884
Alverton Manor, Cornwall

My Dearest Vivienne,

Life is not the same since I came away from school. I am so lonely in this enormous house. My aunt and uncle are every day increasingly more unkind – even cruel. If only my parents hadn't left the estate entrusted to them until I turn twenty-one. It seems an age until then, though it's less than a year now. They do still at least allow me my daily rides, but at times, it is not enough to make my captivity any more bearable.

I long for your company, my dearest friend. I miss our late night chats and the bonbons we used to sneak from Headmistress Stufflebeam's desk drawer. Weren't we a rambunctious duo?

In yet another quest to find me a suitable husband, Aunt Bathilde and Uncle Harvey are forcing me to attend what sounds like an extraordinarily tedious Boxing Day dinner with our neighbors. I use neighbors very loosely, of course, for here in the country, we must travel simply miles and miles before we see another human being. Nothing to your dear Paris, where you're gadding about with the most interesting people every night of the week!

There is a duke staying with the Pendulburys, and my guardians are set on my making a good impression. I confess I'm tempted to do something absolutely disgraceful. Perhaps I'll dribble soup down my chin or suck my fingers loudly after each nibble of cheese. Unfortunately, my wealth seems to be such an attraction, that any revolting behavior on my part is overlooked by these fine gentlemen.

Even when I am wholly myself around them, my obvious disdain for their company seems only to encourage them the more. We'll see how this particular upper-crust dandy fares.

Here is my aunt, near to breaking down my door. I must fly!

Yours, etc.,
Hattie

---

19 March 1885
Belgrave Square, London

My darling friend,

I'm thrilled to be in London at last! If it weren't for my aunt and uncle's constant vituperation, I would be less inclined to leave the countryside. At least here, I shall be able to go out more into society. The company we keep motivates Aunt and Uncle to draw a very convenient veil over their true natures, and they are obliged to speak more civilly to me than when it's just the three of us.

You know how I've always longed to attend the opera! I have also made a long list of all the masterpieces I intend to study for hours in endless museums. Aunt Bethilde and Uncle Harvey are so dull, they take no interest in such pleasures, so I'm hoping to escape often.

In fact, there is a group of bright, young things with whom we had dinner last night, and they have promised me sundry adventures. They've invited me for a picnic at Victoria Park tomorrow. Worry not – we shall all be accompanied by a stately chaperone who is someone or other's great-aunt.

I can't think that I shall be able to write to you so very often, as I'll be occupied experiencing all the sights and sounds of this magnificent city. Rest assured that when we return to the country, I shall pour every memory into missives addressed directly to you!

I'm so delighted to hear that you are still enjoying Paris so much. You were born for such places. I, on the other hand, have been so sheltered that I find myself lost in all of the busy streets and pressing crowds. However, I am quite determined to become a refined, cosmopolitan lady, and so I shall devote myself wholeheartedly to my adventure tomorrow.

Yours ever,
H. V.

Postscript:
I meant to post this letter yesterday, but I'm overjoyed to find that I left the envelope unsealed and on my desk. It's very late, and Uncle Harvey will have my neck if he finds that I've lit a candle at this hour, but I simply *must* tell you that I've met the most divine man I've ever laid eyes upon. I won't put a jinx on myself by writing his name here – I'm terrified of even saying it aloud.

It was a very windy day, and the picnic was all but a disaster! Foodstuffs went flying about, and glasses of hot coffee were tipped out onto the dresses of a few very refined ladies (some of whom comported themselves not at all as refined ladies in the aftermath). I would have laughed myself sick if I'd only known my companions better. As it was, I was loath to hurt anyone's feelings, and, indeed, I'm glad I did not, for my own hat flew right off of my head and directly into the lake.

Luckily – if luck had anything to do with it – a group of young men from the Royal Military Academy was rowing upon the water. One brave man dove straight into the depths without hesitation and swam all the way to the edge of the bank to deliver it back to me.

As you might imagine, I couldn't very well ignore him after that heroic feat! The poor man was simply drenched from head to foot, and I couldn't think of anything to do but to offer him my shawl for warmth. He took it with the most daring smile, and I directly ordered that he be given everything that was left of the hot coffee.

We must have looked a sight: me, without a hat and my

hair flying about wildly, and this strange man, wrapped in my bright, yellow shawl – the one embroidered with flowers and birds…

I *can* tell you, however, that I have never beheld such a manly figure before in all my days!

Goodnight, dearest!
H.V.

---

3 April 1885
Belgrave Square, London

Vivienne –

My mysterious gentleman and I have just met in Regent's Park. He was on a military drill and broke ranks to come and greet me. I'm sure he will pay for it later, but it was quite the compliment to me – a well-deserved compliment, I thought, especially as I was wearing the very daring blue velvet hat that you sent me.

It was so delightful to see him once again. I did not believe that it would be possible for us to cross paths – we are from such very different worlds. Although he did not say much, his eyes were as adoring as one could wish.

He would never be good enough for my aunt and uncle, so perhaps I should not indulge in such fantasies, as it would undoubtedly incur their wrath. It can't hurt to dream a bit about him, though, can it?

Yours ever,
– Hattie

8 July 1885
Belgrave Square, London

Vivienne!

Prepare yourself to feel an excess of pea-green envy, for I am currently wearing a piece of jewelry that has yet to grace your delicate fingers! It's true – my own love has proposed!

Shall I tell you how it all came to pass?

I was longing to see him, but he has strictly been denied entrance to the house. So your clever, little Hattie devised a most devious plot to ensure my aunt and uncle would be out of the way.

Under the guise of generosity, I wrote out a check for a large sum to each of them. Uncle Harvey has been looking a little pale about the ears, so I knew he was craving a return to one of those loathsome opium dens. And Aunt Bathilde has been begging for money to feed her disgusting bridge habit. She gambles simply the most exorbitant sums, and she always loses. Of course I do not approve of either of these appalling habits, but I longed to see my love and so threw over my morals – just for an afternoon!

After my successful ploy, I retired to our little back garden to await his arrival. I was posed romantically, albeit prosaically, under an overgrown tree when he came. I had just plucked a lush rose from a bush and pricked my fingers in the process. Kneeling before me as the knights of old, he took my fingers in his and wrapped them in a handkerchief. Then, with that deep line that wrinkles above his right brow (which means he is about to be desperately serious), he very sweetly and gently asked me to be his wife.

I couldn't help myself – I dropped the rose directly and took his face between my hands. I kissed him before I said yes – brazen and forward, I know, but I couldn't contain another moment without feeling that we were one. He laughed at my haste, picked up my rose, and, placing it in my hair, folded me into his arms and said in the tenderest voice, "You are mine now."

I am not certain, to this moment, if I ever gave him a verbal answer to his exquisite question, but my heart and soul cry out together, "Yes, yes, YES!"

Your divinely blissful,
– *Hattie*

---

17 August 1885
Alverton Manor, Cornwall

My darling friend,

Yes, I write to you from the countryside once again. My beloved and I were embracing tenderly in a darkened corner of the British Museum when my aunt and uncle happened upon us at a most interesting moment. I have been escaping more and more often, growing careless as I used various excuses to meet my betrothed, and they had grown suspicious and followed me. My true one has wanted for so very long to let the engagement be known to them, but I, who understand their evil natures, begged him to wait until I come of age, when my fortune and independence are completely my own at last.

Needless to say, they are utterly furious at the match and have forbidden our union. They have other, more prestigious men in mind for me still. I have sworn on my life that I will not marry any one of them! Each they've introduced me to has been absolutely vile.

Truly, I believe they could forgive a man who murdered several of his past wives and intended the same black fate for me, so long as they could bury me with a title placed anteriorly on my headstone.

Yours in agony,
H.V.

---

7 November 1885
Alverton Manor, Cornwall

My darling friend,

My heart must be breaking in two, for I cannot hold my pen steady. I've attempted to write to you many times. My darling betrothed (for I am *still* determined to marry him, despite my aunt and uncle's displeasure) has been sent to Burma with his regiment. He has high hopes that the assignment will be brief, and then he's decided to leave the army and make his way to America to seek his fortune. I've told him time and again that I have enough money for the both of us, but he won't hear reason. He's determined to make his mark on the world somehow.

I am so happy to hear about your young man. He seems a delightful match, and I sincerely wish you all the best in your union. Of course, you *would* happily and easily fall in love with a wealthy Marquis who is a poet to boot!

Leave it to me to find a poor but honest young man with nothing to show but a good heart and his passion for me. I want to hear every detail of your trousseau! I expect your next letter to be a bulging envelope stuffed full of long lists and elegant details. I am overjoyed for you, my dearest friend, and please don't let my troubles be a burden to your well-deserved happiness.

I apologize for my brevity, but I cannot stop weeping at the thought of my own love so far away from me. I feel a headache coming on and must rest.

Yours, etc.
Hattie

---

23 December 1885
Alverton Manor, Cornwall

Happy Christmas, my dearest Vivienne!

I'm so glad you loved your wedding gift, and my heart thrills for you and your Marquis. Imagine – a Christmas wedding! I only wish I could be there. My aunt and uncle are quite determined not to let me out of their sight, despite my beloved's departure from this country.

We met only briefly in a neighboring town upon his return to England from Burma – before he left for America. The inn was quite an unromantic place, I assure you, but it seemed a paradise to us. I will not take the time to write you the details of our exchange, but suffice it to say that your poet of a fiancé would have approved.

Aunt and Uncle missed me, as I was late to dinner, and I have been, for all intents and purposes, a prisoner in my own home ever since.

My own love did have some good news, at least. A distant cousin has generously left him a large house. There was, unfortunately, no money along with the behest, and the residence is in a grave state of disrepair. He at first suggested selling it to fund his enterprises in America, but I have at least temporarily suspended this ambition. We will need a place when we are married – we certainly can't live here alongside so many horrid memories – never mind my aunt and uncle.

And so...I am determined to lavishly spend exorbitant sums of money in fixing up the house he was left. All shall be just to my liking. It will be a great surprise for my love when he returns, and I hope we shall occupy it peacefully and happily once we are wed. I shall write secret letters to drapers and merchants and deplete my fortune so rashly that even *you* would disapprove!

Yours,
H.V.

---

13 February, 1886
Alverton Manor, Cornwall

Vivienne,

I'm certain you've read the papers. You now know that all of my future hopes and dreams have been dashed to pieces. I must have been truly deceived in him all along...that woman – so beautiful with those staring eyes. I cannot doubt that he was in love with her ever since they met in Burma. He wrote of her at the time, but so scornful was his account, I thought nothing of it.

There – my tears are blurring the ink as I write, and I

cannot bear another thought on the subject. I shall have to lock this part of my heart away forever, along with the hope of ever loving another man.

Uncle Harvey and Aunt Bethilde are beside themselves with triumphal disdain. They promptly gave me a list of eligible men they have in mind for me. Men, they claim, who would be willing to marry me, despite my unfortunate engagement with this despicable man.

There – I've set fire to the list, and now the cinders are expunging my writings as much as my tears were. I'll close now. My only solace is in sleep...if it will come.

Yours in despair,
Hattie Vavaseur

Chapter Thirteen

Hattie, bundled in her rosy bedclothes, poured over the letters. The candle beside her bed had burned very low, and she strained to decipher her own young handwriting as the shadows of the deepening night crept in upon her, turning the hue of her chamber from pink to a deep rouge. Indeed, it is a tribute to the fascination of these letters that she did not shiver with antipathy when she wrapped the pink, befrilled coverlet around her shoulders.

The letters were, generally speaking, quite silly, but at least they assisted her in the recollection of her dear, long-forgotten friend, Vivienne. Wispy, flighty, French, and prone to very loud peals of laughter, her schoolfellow had at first been a source of irritation to Hattie when they met.

Thrown together in a shared dormitory at the Château Mont-Choisi finishing school in Lausanne, Hattie could do little to avoid Vivienne's company. Hattie believed the fresh, young French girl to be a shallow and unintelligent creature and had unrelentingly treated her as such. Indeed, Hattie's cheerless upbringing, enhanced by the loss of her parents, had made her cautious with her emotions, which many of the girls interpreted as frigid and aloof.

During one late-night frolic, several giggling young maidens had gathered together to share delectable gossip and raspberry meringues. These romps were the perfect opportunity for the youthful debutantes to share their most recent conquests on trips during the holidays or flirtations carried out by way of letters.

Throughout these exchanges, Hattie had always obstinately remained reticent on matters of the heart. When a fellow student questioned her on the subject, Hattie sternly reprimanded her for such a frivolous inquiry and returned to reading her book.

In a moment of extreme lucidity, Vivienne, who was sitting at the foot of the bed, reached over, lowered Hattie's book, looked directly into her eyes, and flatly stated, "We all know why you can speak French so well, Mademoiselle Hattie Vavaseur. The way you look at Monsieur Pelletier is a *signe révélateur*! How do you English say? A dead giveaway!"

Inexplicably, Hattie and Vivienne became perfect friends from that moment. Vivienne's unique ability to pierce through Hattie's self-imposed reserve created between them a fast and tight bond. Hattie was not naturally constrained, and Vivienne's apparent insipidity was merely an intemperate delight in life and all the joys it had to offer. This delight was secretly shared by Hattie, who had never had the privilege of an environment that would nurture such a gift. Vivienne provided the perfect milieu for Hattie's *joie de vivre* to flourish.

Inseparable from that moment forward, they played pranks together, took punishments for each other, and poured out confidences that will ever be known to none but themselves.

Hattie, transported to her girlhood memories with these letters, was supremely grateful for their restoration. However, an element of doubt still held sway. The lack of recollection of this mysterious man, their engagement, and this apparent jilting troubled her. The French tutor she remembered fully, along with the girlish heartbreak that came when he married the headmistress – a woman a full fifteen years his senior. The fact that Headmistress Ashdown was remarkably plain and tended to belch whenever she spoke became a great source of solace to the youthful, blooming Miss Vavaseur.

All this she could now recall, and yet there was no hint of a memory for her own romantic entanglement. Vamelda had informed her that in this afterlife, a total lapse of memory was rare and even troubling, and the fact unsettled her deeply.

The fascinating letters and the anamnesis that accompanied them had kept her up until the birds began chirruping at the first hint of light. Hattie climbed out of bed and drew back a curtain. A rolling bank of blue-black clouds darkly masked any glimmer of daybreak attempting to reach her windowsill.

Hattie's mind was so distracted with churning memories that she knew sleep would be impossible. Quietly dressing for the day in a plain, lavender-gray frock, she unlocked her door and stepped soundlessly out into the passage. For although she and the master of the house had engaged in one fairly congenial conversation, she was still wary of incurring his wrath by waking him or, indeed, any other members of the household.

Suddenly feeling light as a feather, she glided down the stairs. A youthful sense of freedom and excitement crept into her veins. Her heart seemed to beat stronger with every step.

A trip to the larder rewarded her with a Cornish cream tea – minus the tea – and her hands and mouth were thick with clotted cream. She made her way, still on tiptoe, to the library. Her newfound excitement at the restoration of her memories somehow drew her to the room and made her desirous to inhale the deep, familiar smell of dusky old novels and anthologies.

Just as she was about to cross the threshold, she hesitated. It was as though a hand gripped her heart, squeezing it until she could hardly breathe. The feeling wasn't an unpleasant one, and it somehow propelled her forward.

And there it was, incandescent and glorious...the orb.

Pulsating with vibrant light, the sphere rotated, hovering a full three inches above its silvery stand. Hattie never knew how she made it across the entire breadth of the room – whether she walked or floated. She did know that when her hand reached out to touch the artifact, her entire body was jolted, and for a moment, her own reflection appeared in the smoky glass.

She gazed deeply into the haze. The reflection was so vivid, so brilliant, that her eyes could not focus. Blinking her lashes rapidly, she stared harder still into its depths.

A younger, more vibrant Hattie Vavaseur blinked back at her. Hattie gasped, looked away, shook her head, and refocused. Surely, she was tired...or dreaming. The puzzled expression of this other self matched her own. She wiped her eyes, and the doppelganger did the same. A tilt of the head, the raise of a brow, and, finally, a forced smile completed the little farce.

It was settled. Hattie, inexplicably and, she had to admit, gratifyingly, was...younger. It was not the youth of her days with Vivienne, but yet – a substantial transformation had undoubtedly taken place. Lines still wrinkled her brow, and her hair was gray, not white, as it had been when she died.

Hattie stood there, studying her own reflection in astonishment, and considered. When she had first arrived at the manor, every ache and pain of her old age had been felt – indeed, they were even amplified by the discomfort of travel and the worry about her memory loss.

Somehow, gradually, she had begun to feel better. Her headaches had become less and less frequent. The equestrian walks and hearty food she knew had done her good, but she had no idea that these would affect her in such an astonishing and considerable way.

She was just beginning to admire her brighter eyes and

smoother skin when the thought of her last letter to Vivienne came back to her mind. Her countenance fell with the recollection, and, unconsciously, she began to enact her little habit of rubbing her thumb against her fingertips.

At that very moment, the orb's light suddenly extinguished and dropped back with a crash down into its stand. Jumping back, Hattie tripped over the hearthrug and...darkness.

Chapter Fourteen

A pink hue greeted Hattie's irises when they fluttered open. She knew she must be back in her own room. The groan that escaped her lips was this time not from the color that surrounded her, but from the ache that racked her skull.

Something wet pooled upon her forehead. It dripped down the side of her face in a most uncomfortably sticky manner. Blood. She knew it must be blood. Growing faint again, her eyes rolled toward the back of her head.

"No, you don't," grumbled a voice beside her. "Stay with me, woman."

A deluge of glutinous liquid was lashed upon her. It was freezing – not fraught with the warmth of vital fluids. Opening her eyes once again, she adjusted her vision to view the owner of the voice.

The master of the house sat by her bedside, a large

sponge held awkwardly in one hand. When he came fully into focus, she realized, with relief, that it was not blood, but water. Not very clean or even very soothing, but at least it was water.

He raised his hand and again a rush of liquid poured down upon her face. It ran into her eyes, stinging her sight into oblivion. Sweat must have mingled inside the dish of water in which he soaked the sponge.

She reached up to stem the flow, and in the process, their hands touched. He recoiled; she supposed him unused to contact.

"I'm sorry," she said. "I didn't mean to..."

He shook himself and grunted.

Hattie looked up at him, narrowing her eyes, wondering what could possibly be prompting this unusual kindness. His own eyes darted sideways, and his head lowered ever so slightly. Her feelings were conflicted at this point. Her desire to express gratitude for his kindness collided violently with her eagerness to cease this painful treatment.

Yet another rush of the stingin elixir splashed over her brow, but this time, she clenched her eyes tightly in order to prevent further discomfort.

She remained silent. Straining through her pain, Hattie attempted to look into his face once more. His expression was once again strangely unveiled. So many of her moments with this man were unintentional glimpses into his otherwise indecipherable countenance. He seemed troubled. Hattie, looking upon him, was simultaneously fascinated and fearful. In general, she did not allow herself to feel complex emotions such as this. They made her feel unsettled – out of control. As he stirred, she closed her eyes once again, desiring to avoid a maladroit encounter.

Yet another ichorous waterfall descended upon her brow. Hattie tightened her eyes and mouth more firmly than ever, hoping to prompt his withdrawal by feigning sleep. This was a difficult feat, for the liquid rushed into her nose, and she strained every nerve to prevent a sneeze.

"I'm quite alright," she said, opening her eyes after the last bead of water dripped from her chin. "I think I...I just need to rest."

"Very well, then," he responded, retiring to a nearby chair.

For a very long time, she awaited his departure, but it did not come. Finally, she ventured a covert glance about the room. She was astonished when she perceived him slumped over in his chair, fast asleep.

Hattie quietly attempted to raise herself from the bed. Her head ached awfully, and she wanted nothing more than to slip back down into her covers, but she was desperately thirsty and badly needed a cool glass of water.

As she arose, the bed creaked terribly, and the great noise roused the master of the house-turned-make-shift-nursemaid. His half-opened eyes were red, and he took a moment to adjust them to his surroundings. He grumbled as he awakened, his brows knitting and his face distorted in the petulant scowl of a newly stirred child. His gaze softened as he looked upon her. Hattie thought she even glimpsed the hint of a smile form at the crease of his mouth.

"I'm glad to see you're up," said he.

"Yes, I'm feeling much better, thank you."

Reaching over, he poured her a glass of water from the basin and handed it to her. Not satisfied until she had drained every drop, he watched her closely as she did so. When she had begun to nibble on some slightly burnt toast (another forceful demand on his part), he scowled at her.

A fragment of his ill humor appeared to return as he demanded, "What on earth possessed you to fall over and knock your head in that confoundedly clumsy way?"

"I...I believe I tripped backwards over the rug in front of the hearth."

"How does a capable woman like you manage to trip *backwards*?"

Unsure of whether to be pleased at the compliment or chagrined at his insult, Hattie paused, reluctant to reveal the events of the night before, lest he should think her mad. She studied him carefully and decided that, after all, she was dead, so she had nothing much to lose if he believed her to be deranged.

"It was the orb."

"What orb?"

"The orb in the library."

"What about the bloody orb?" he returned, his anger mounting.

He raised himself from the chair and began pacing the floor.

"It was glowing...and floating."

"What in the bloody hell do you mean, it was *floating*?"

Hattie stiffened.

"I mean that it detached from the stand and hovered above it!"

"I know what floating means, woman! Next, you'll be telling me what the color of the sky is!"

"Speaking of color," Hattie interjected. "My room..."

He cut her short, "Never mind your blasted room! What about this orb? *Why* was it floating and...and glowing? *What did you do to it?!*"

"Absolutely nothing! I merely went to the library and there it was! And when I looked into it..." she paused, uncertain how much she should reveal to him. "I saw myself...myself when I was younger."

A puzzled expression crossed the master's countenance. He stood up and brought his face close to hers. Until then, she had not quite felt the full force of his person. His nose was less than a few inches from her own, and she nearly drew back. In the end, her spirit rose to the challenge, and she stood her ground, albeit she felt a bit woozy in the attempt.

Staring straight into her eyes, he seemed to examine her closely. Defiantly, she stared right back, feeling a thrilling, little butterfly in her stomach as she did so. His amber-colored eyes pierced hers keenly, as if searching for the answer to some long-forgotten questions of the ancients.

Whether or not he found what he was looking for, she did not know. He abruptly sat down beside her on the bed, a bit closer than she would have liked. However, she made no objection, recalling his previous attempt at caring tenderness.

"Once, there was another crystal orb on that mantelpiece. I recall waking up one day as a young man and discovering it there. I cannot recall where it came from or why I found it so fascinating, but I did. I used to go into the library every day. I would take it from that silver stand and hold it in my hand, staring at its depths for hours at a time. In the beginning, it was light and beautiful, but the more years I had it, the darker it became. It turned from purple, to grey, to black...darker with each passing day.

"Although it still held a fascination for me, I felt my very soul pour into this orb. I don't know if it was growing old alone in this gloomy house that did it to me, but all that I can remember about my many years here is wrapped up in that sphere.

"One day, I was in so much despair that I tried to smash it. It was the only thing I could think to do to rid myself of its untenable power over my soul. I pulled back the rug, just where you fell this very evening, ready to bash it to bits upon the marbled tiles. I knew that this would be not only the end of the little artifact, but of myself, as well. I planned to end everything that night.

"I took the crystal, cold as ice, between my heated hands and raised it high above my head, poised to strike it against the stone with all of my might. I felt a hand arrest me on the shoulder. It was Bertram, who stopped me just in time. He said that the object was a priceless artifact, linked to the fate of myself and my family, and that if I destroyed it, I would surely be lost.

"I still don't wholly comprehend his meaning. I placed the orb back in its stand, but I knew that I could no longer allow it to rule my life. I asked Bertram to pack it up and send it away so that I would look upon it no more.

"When it was gone, I felt as though a certain part of myself had been torn away, but at least I wasn't watching my own soul turn to darkness."

Hattie had remained silent during this unexpected outpouring of intimate information. However, at this juncture, a burning query consumed her until she could not help but ask it.

"Where did *this* orb come from, then?"

He started and turned toward her, as though he had forgotten her presence. Again, that piercing gaze met her eyes, and he paused for a little while before continuing on.

"Bertram brought it home the day before you arrived. I

raged at him, as I thought it to be the one I'd sent away. But Bertram, good man, waited patiently until my tirade was done before he quietly informed me that it was nothing of the sort. He felt that the mantelpiece had looked bare since the old one was sent away and merely sought to brighten the place a bit before your coming."

"Ah, I see," she responded.

Without warning, he roared with laughter and slapped his knee.

"Ah, that poor Bertram! He's taken a tongue-lashing or two from me in his time. It's a wonder I get him to stay on. But we do have some good memories, old Bertram and I. He's nothing if not loyal."

Hattie smiled. She was pleased to see that the master of the house wasn't quite so gruff and serious all of the time and that he at least could inspire devotion in his servants. As Hattie well knew, this was no small feat in this day and age.

"*Although,*" she queried inwardly, "*Do servants and loyalties work quite the same here as they do in Life?*"

She shook her head, unable and unwilling to work it out just then. Looking up at him, she noted a grin on his face.

"What is it?" she demanded, unable to prevent herself from a tiny smile in return.

"You just looked like a young miss, thwarted by a difficult sum in school."

Hattie laughed at herself, too.

"I suppose I must have. Everything just seems so... mixed up and confused these days."

"I can agree with you there."

He fiddled with the fringe on the bedclothes as a dark cloud passed over his face once again. Resting his hand absently over the covers, he had unwittingly placed it upon Hattie's, which was underneath.

Her hand involuntarily spasmed under his. The movement seemed to jolt him, and he removed it quickly.

"You should sleep," he said authoritatively, but with a new kindness in his voice. "And rest easy – I shall remove that orb right away, so it won't disturb you any longer."

"Yes," replied Hattie vaguely, and she settled back on her pillows, eyes half closed, until she heard him close the door behind him.

Cautiously sitting up, she tidied herself, changed into her nightdress, and did what she could to clean up the watery mess he'd left in his wake. Smiling a little to herself, her thoughts dwelt on his unexpected kindness and his even more unusual confession about the orb. Amidst all these inexplicable events, one thing was sure – another visit to Vamelda was undoubtedly in order.

Chapter Fifteen

"You've been burning incense again, haven't you, you disgusting woman?" was Hattie's cheerful greeting as she entered Vamelda's shop.

"Only a little to cleanse the soul and the senses. Inhale it deeply, dearie – it would do you some good; I can tell."

A corpulent man in a too-tight suit and too-small spats was thumbing through a book in the corner. He looked up quizzically at Hattie, but, as she did not pay the slightest bit of attention to him, he looked down again, obviously perplexed.

"*Achoo!*" came Hattie's delicate sneeze, in response to the incense agitating her olfactories.

"Bless you, dear," soothed Vamelda.

The man looked up once again.

"*Achoo!*"

"Will you come through?" Vamelda summoned her toward the inner doorway.

"*Achoo!*" Hattie sneezed in response.

The man *in* the corner jumped with each sneeze. Hattie looked at Vamelda inquisitively.

"Oh, yes – he's new," said Vamelda in low tones. "He is still trying to figure out who is dead and who is not. I believe he thinks you're alive, and it's confusing him immensely. It is always rather fun to have a freshly dead one."

"What is his story?" queried Hattie as they walked through to the white room.

"Oh, he believes that he choked on a rib bone at dinner."

"Believes?"

"Yes, but I'm quite sure that he was murdered. Didn't you notice how blue he was about the mouth? He's almost certainly been poisoned."

"Really? By whom?"

"Well, that's the *point*, isn't it, daaahling?"

Hattie chose to move on rather than allow herself to be baited by the medium's infuriating nebulousness.

"Any news for me?" she queried, after a calming intake of breath.

"Well, as a matter of fact, there *was* something here that your nephew mailed to me."

Vamelda began rifling through all of her layers of

scarves and shawls. Very soon, there was quite a heap of them strewn along the table and floor as she searched. All the while, the clairvoyant mumbled to herself indiscriminately. She reminded Hattie of a very lithe and slender bear, pulling out tufts of fur as though impatient to shed its winter coat.

"Ah – here it is!" Vamelda sang out melodiously.

Extracting a small ring from amongst the depths of fabric on her person, she set it on the table. Just then, a tinkle of chimes from the front door clattered in their ears.

"I won't be a moment, dearie!" Vamelda cooed as she whisked her voluminous skirts and what was left of her scarves out the door.

The ring was small – an emerald, flanked by two diamonds and joined together by a band of intricately cast filigree. It was of an antiquated style and quite worn, but it was indisputably beautiful. Hattie reached down and picked up the tiny piece of jewelry to examine it further. Just as she touched it, the orb on the center of the table emitted a small eruption of light. As soon as the light burst forth, however, it was again extinguished.

Arrested, Hattie leaned in for a closer look. Swirls of purple and black within the crystal danced together intimately in the half-light. Unwittingly, she slipped the ring upon her finger – more out of convenience than for any other reason. As she peered in closely, another, more brilliant beam of light escaped from the center, if only for a moment, before being swallowed up in the purple shadows once again.

Fascinated, Hattie reached out and gathered the orb

from its stand. The initial coldness of the sphere turned to warmth and then heat in her hands as the darkness within gave way to a silvery blue. The calescent orb was becoming almost too heated for Hattie to hold. Setting *it* down for a moment, she drew on her gloves, snagging the ring on the material as she did so. Hastily catching the orb up again, she peered into its depths. Two clasped hands appeared – a large one embracing the fingertips of a small one, as men do when bending over the hands of ladies.

"*At least,*" Hattie thought, "*They used to in my day.*"

At that moment, Vamelda and a woman entered the room, but Hattie took no notice of them. She was utterly enthralled in examining the scene displayed within the intricate depths of the sphere.

"Oooo!" exclaimed Vamelda's guest, who turned out to be the lumpy woman whom Hattie had seen at a séance once before. "Just look at *that*! The spirits have been *so* powerful of late – and we haven't even begun our session!"

The interruption caused the apparition within the crystal to disappear.

Without a discernible thought, Hattie straightaway carried the orb across the room and over the threshold. Vamelda and her customer stood in shock; the first lady from seeing her very proper client absconding with a most prized item, and the latter from watching a crystal ball ostensibly float across the room and disappear directly out the door.

"Hattie!" Vamelda shrieked, forgetting both her client's

presence and her usually ethereal manner. "Don't you *dare* rob me of another crystal ball!"

As Hattie made her escape out the front door, she gasped with the thrill of holding the orb in her hands. It was a different feeling entirely from the gentle, fascinating pull of the artifact back at the mansion. She felt a rush of energy that neared hysteria as she held this object. It thrilled every nerve of her soul, simply *willing* her to carry it home.

To her chagrin, Bertram and the green Daimler were not in their usual place directly outside the door. Hearing Vamelda's shrieks grow louder from within the shop, Hattie looked up and down the street, at a loss for what to do. Other than her trips to the medium's establishment, she was vastly unfamiliar with the town of Market Foolsbury.

Shoving the crystal into her bag, she quickly made her way down the street. Hearing the jangling of Vamelda's shop door bells, she darted into an alleyway, hiding in the shadows. Hattie held her breath as she listened to the clack of the medium's Spanish heels on the cobblestones. The footsteps stopped for a moment, just before her hiding place, and Hattie could hear the clairvoyant murmuring to herself. The medium's numerous bangle bracelets accompanied her in musical refrain, tinkling and rattling in empathetic frustration.

Finally, the clattering and muttering slowly moved away in the direction of the shop, and Hattie drew a shaky sigh of relief. She silently acknowledged that she would have to answer to Vamelda at some point for her behavior, but for now, Hattie only knew that she needed to be alone with this orb. Peeking into her bag moment-arily, she discovered that the sphere was still obscured with murky mist. Hattie felt quite wild with the thrill of her small adventure, and the sensations that accom-panied her handling of this object had never before passed through her soul.

Closing up her handbag with the utmost self-control, Hattie determined that she would find Bertram. The drive back to the manor would give her time to think and work out what to do. There was obviously some-thing supremely significant about these crystals, and she wanted plenty of opportunity to unearth the secrets they held.

Brushing herself off delicately, she followed the alley until she emerged on the next street over, startling a sleeping tabby cat as she did so. Turning in the oppos-ite direction from the shop, lest Vamelda should emerge from some back entrance, Hattie made her way down the street.

Oddly, Hattie began to feel faint. Perhaps it was her head injury from the day before, but she seemed to grow weaker with every step. Passing few people, not one of them acknowledged her presence. Indeed, she did not have the energy to feel offended before she realized that they more than likely could not see her.

Just when she was about to give up all hope and sit down upon the very roadway itself, she, with the great-est relief, caught sight of the green Daimler. Stumbling toward it, she wrenched open the door handle. Bertram was fast asleep, with his cap cocked over his eyes to shade him from the sun.

"Vamelda?" he choked, heaving himself to full attention when she unceremoniously slammed the door.

"No, it is Ms. Vavaseur, Bertram. Will you kindly take me back to the manor house?"

"Certainly, madam," he coughed without question.

On their way home, after ensuring that Bertram was occupied with the drive, she peeped into her bag. Those gorgeous, churning hues of violet and ebony mixed together in the most mesmerizing concert; she was convinced that her eyes could never tire of watching their rolling depths.

"Everything go alright at Vamelda's, Ms. Vavaseur?" queried Bertram.

Hattie snapped the bag shut abruptly, startled at his vocalization. Bertram had learned to be respectfully silent during these drives to and from the town and usually left her in total peace. Affronted, she determined to change the subject – her favorite tactic when dealing with too-familiar servants.

"Bertram," she said, a slight shake in her voice that gradually disappeared as she gathered strength in her determination. "I've been meaning to ask you. Any chance of those mirrors being reinstated? I've had a very distressing afternoon, and I am most put out that I am unable even to make myself tidy!"

"I'm very sorry, madam, but the master…"

"Don't you give me that claptrap, young man. I saw you only the other evening shining the mirrors in that odd little closet."

Bertram nearly swerved off of the road at this juncture, and Hattie was hard-pressed to maintain both her balance and decorum as he straightened the car out once again.

"Bertram!" she shrieked.

"Terribly sorry, madam," he apologized, removing a handkerchief from his pocket and dabbing at the beads of perspiration that stood out on his forehead.

They continued in silence for a short time, and Bertram seemed to mull a thought over in his mind.

At last, he let out a long exhalation before he said, "You might as well be told, madam."

"Be told what, exactly?"

"You may, perhaps, realize that I, too, have passed...to the other side?"

"I...I suppose I hadn't thought of it," she said slowly.

He paused again before continuing, "It is tradition, you'll remember, to...cover the mirrors of the household when someone has passed? To prevent their souls from being trapped, you know."

"A very silly superstition, I always thought," Hattie returned, tossing her head.

"A very necessary one, unfortunately, madam. You see, I'm afraid it's true. For a time after one passes, a mirror can indeed trap one's soul. And if that mirror is broken...well..." he paused, as if unable to continue.

"It distresses me greatly, madam, that you should have been in such close proximity to those mirrors. I have been dead a very long time, so they no longer affect me, but *your* passing over is still so fresh...I implore you to be careful."

"Why wasn't I informed of this danger immediately upon my arrival?" demanded Hattie.

"We don't often tell new souls – for many reasons."

"Reasons such as?" Hattie queried.

"I have heard tell of souls seeking to *h*arm other souls. Some even attempt to end this stage of existence by misguidedly trapping themselves. Others still have difficulty coming to grips with their new reality and might look upon their own reflection quite by accident."

Hattie, aghast at this new, vital piece of information, remained speechless as they pulled through the front gates and up to the manor, whe*r*e the master of the house stood – silhouetted in the doorway.

Chapter Sixteen

The master of the house bowed deeply as Hattie alighted from the car.

"I'm pleased to have met you at this opportune moment. I was just going in for dinner," he said nervously.

"Oh, yes?" Hattie returned, clutching her bag closely.

"I...I was hoping you would join me?" he stammered, hopefully.

Hattie was astonished. Up until now, she had invariably taken her meals in solitude.

"I suppose – yes," she faltered.

Upon seeing his visage fall slightly, she amended her statement: "Why, of course."

His brow cleared, and he made a little bow.

"Although, if you wouldn't mind," Hattie continued, "I would just like to go upstairs to...to change?"

Her knuckles were white with the grip she kept upon the handles of her bag. He stood aside, allowing her to pass.

"I shall await your return in the dining room, then," he stated.

With a sprightly and slightly desperate dash up to her bedroom, Hattie swiftly closed the door behind her. Turning, she surveyed her quarters to try and discover some secret and secure hiding place for her prize. Her eyes rested on an all-too-frilly sewing basket that was dusty with neglect. She opened it, drew out the tissue that lay on top, fetched a shawl from the wardrobe, and, wrapping the orb carefully, placed it hurriedly inside. Dragging the basket toward her bedframe, she shoved it as deeply as she could underneath the frills of the valance. Dusting her hands off satisfactorily, she began to prepare herself for dinner.

Hattie's host smiled warmly at her as she entered the dining hall, and he even proffered her a seat next to him. It was such an alteration from his usual attitude that she felt quite at a loss for an appropriate response. Even the lines of his face seemed to have softened considerably, and his usual scowl had very nearly absented itself from his countenance.

"And how was your trip to town? Did you complete all of your shopping successfully?"

He looked directly into her eyes as he questioned her – an act that always made Hattie uncomfortable. Especially now, she felt her cheeks burn with the knowledge of the artifact that lay quietly tucked away in her room upstairs.

With an indiscriminate vocalization, she did not disabuse him of his assumption. Meditatively, she fell into a brown study, and they continued their meal in silence.

With the scrape of his knife across his plate, Hattie's nerves grated excruciatingly, drawing her out of herself. His eye was upon her.

"Do you find the town...pleasing?" he continued, almost desperate in his endeavor to hold her attention.

This time, she managed a nod, but no sound passed her lips.

He then attempted to broach a subject that they had discussed with fervor a few nights before during their literary discourse. He was rebuffed by another taciturn response from Hattie.

As a result, his words from that point on became more impatient and less kind. Soon, he was as reticent as she. It was as though his icy veins had begun to melt with the warmth of her company, when suddenly a winter frost had blown in and killed all that had begun to bloom.

As the pudding passed in silence, Hattie's mistake began to dawn upon her. Embarrassedly and half-heartedly, she made an effort to regain their former footing of moderate amicability.

"Bertram is a very good driver," she said inanely.

She was too late – he had withdrawn too deep into his sullenness, and she was met with no more than a grunt.

The clatter of their plates became as deafening as though an entire host of company was dining amongst them. As the meal ended, they arose from their seats, and Hattie assumed that they would transition into the sitting room or library, giving her another chance to set things right, but he merely nodded his head and began to retreat from the room without her.

Regretting more than ever her reserved distraction, Hattie arrested him by the arm as he was about to pass through the door.

He did not draw back; he only held perfectly still as she said, "Dear sir, please forgive my taciturnity this evening. I have not been quite myself."

"Madam..." he began.

A long pause ensued as he stared down at her small hand on his arm.

"Madam..." his tone was softened, and she removed her hand disconcertedly at the fleeting allure of his deepened voice.

Misunderstanding her withdrawal, he stiffened once again.

"Madam, I would that you could make up your mind about this house!" he yelled violently as he exited the room.

Hattie stood there, flushed with hurt and anger. Her momentary lapse in vivacity did not merit this behavior. If he was incapable of showing some clemency, well, then – he was a lost cause, indeed. Coupling that with his bizarre mention of the house, her frustration reached a tipping point. Did he believe her to be in pursuit of the procurement of his home? The man must be mad.

In her puzzlement and chagrin, the thought of the orb had entirely slipped Hattie's mind for the moment. Instead of retiring to her room to stare into its depths as she had previously planned, she crossed through to the breakfast room. Flinging the French doors wide, she strode through onto the green. Excessively distressed by his odd behavior, she desperately needed a walk to clear her head.

Pacing the length of the green, the lowering sun enveloped her in an evening glow. Her eyes narrowed in thought. Why was this man forever swinging on a pendulum of extremes? At times, he was intelligent and courteous; at others, rude and almost deranged. Hattie had, until now, vaguely believed that it was *he* that kept her prisoner here and commanded her to be taken on these strange visits to Vamelda's. She only now realized that he must be utterly ignorant of these appointments, as was evidenced by his remarks about shopping in the town. Hattie simply couldn't comprehend his role in this bizarre adventure of her afterlife.

Seething with a bubbling turmoil of emotions, she moved about the garden, unconsciously breaking off branches with her skirts as she traversed to and fro.

Gradually, she calmed the violent agitation of her soul. At last, she relieved her tormented frame with a deep inhalation of the thick, evening air that was pregnant with the heady smell of summer blossoms.

Within the dusky light, she stared out across the lawn and watched the trees as a mad, wild, lonesome wind burst through the leaves, reminding each of them that they might easily be plucked from safety upon their mother branch at any moment. The tirade was soon followed by a sweeter, warmer, almost reluctant breeze that reassured the tiny foliage. The leaflets seemed to cower in fear at the first, then dance with joy at the second.

Just then, she caught a glance of little Teddy running through the orchard, a mound of green apples spilling from a makeshift receptacle he had made by folding his shirt over upon itself. At the sight of him, Hattie smiled and then sighed.

She vaguely wondered what she had made of the time she spent during her life. The recollection of years spent in abject loneliness shadowed her mind.

Her thoughts wandered. Broken memories drifted as she attempted to recall any good deeds that would somehow merit a reward in the afterlife.

Despite her wealth, Hattie had never been one to give money to any ladies of the neighborhood that came rattling their charity boxes. Nor could she be conned out of her coins by street urchins. Instead, Hattie often listened to servant and church gossip, learning of those whose needs could be met by some subtle act of kindness.

Had her neighbors known of these acts, she might not have grown quite so lonely in her advancing years. Strong in her convictions and stern in her sense of propriety, she had always spurned all attempts at friendship, believing them to be made out of an unwelcome sense of pity. According to her acquaintance, Ms. Vavasuer had always held her head very high. Consequently, the fullness of her soul had been kept stringently secluded and guarded.

Only now did Hattie begin to think that she may have missed something truly beautiful in life. As far as she could remember, she had always pitied those that suffered with the burden of a marriage or children. In the past, Hattie felt grateful that she had never met with such intrusions into her life and heart.

Now, an overbearing wistfulness enveloped her, covering all of her fears and antagonism with a bright shade of blushing charm that attracted her immensely. Where had this desire been in life? What was this longing that overtook her soul so painfully, yet alluringly, now?

One would have thought that it was the mislaid memory of her lover that had spurred this drift into lost regrets and vanished wishes. It was, however, the sight of little Teddy that had led her to these thoughts. If she had but fostered a child in life, perhaps the ache of these lost treasures might not now sting so very much.

While her mind was adrift in this abstraction, she hardly noticed when a man came stumbling through a patch of rosebushes. The sound of his scrambling had barely caught her ear, so it was to her great surprise when the blue-lipped man from Vamelda's shop spilled out at her feet.

He struggled into an upright position, much bedraggled. His clothes torn and his face scratched, he hardly made a pleasant sight for Hattie to take in at that crucial moment. She scowled dreadfully at him, but he did not notice, as he was attempting to make himself presentable.

"Oh! It's you! I mean...well, you *can* see me, can't you?" he queried, almost tremulously.

Hattie very nearly affected not to hear him, merely to be rid of him, but she could not in all good conscience dismiss him so uncivilly, particularly as the man seemed to be in great distress.

"Can I help you, *sir*?" she asked coldly.

"Why, yes, you can, I think," he said, smiling at her brightly. "You see, I desperately need your assistance in the matter of my death."

Chapter Seventeen

As the man began to speak in full sentences, Hattie realized that he was American. His loud checked suit and the brightly colored ribbon that adorned his boater hat should have been a good indication. She thought only young men wore boater hats, but she accepted it as solid fact that Americans never quite knew how to age with grace. This man was middle-aged, at the very least, and too far past his prime to be wearing such garish garments.

Hattie strove to temporarily suspend her preconceptions and made a real effort to listen to this man who was in such obvious trouble.

"Vamelda –" said he, straightening his tie. "Vamelda tells me that I've been murdered. It seems that I need somebody to help me find out who did it. I took right to you when I saw you in her shop. Particularly when you made away with that nice, little bauble, I thought, 'That's the gutsy kind of gal for me.'"

"I hardly *think*, my dear sir, that I can be of any assistance to *you*."

Hattie rolled the phrase over her tongue as though it were drenched in lemon sauce. She resented this reminder of her questionable behavior and was none too keen on his familiarity, either.

"I can offer you a great deal of money...er...I suppose I can't anymore, but if there is anything you want, I would absolutely do it for you! You have my word on that."

As she currently happened to have the higher ground on a little hill, she put all of her effort into peering down her nose at him.

Willing him to feel every ounce of her moral superiority, she said, "I do realize that Americans think they can solve every little problem by flashing about a fistful of banknotes, but that is *not* how we do things over *here*."

With a deft swish of his wrist, the man swiftly removed his hat from his head, which was very nearly bald – only just crowned with little tufts of hair about the ears. Unfortunately, he seemed to have made a desperate attempt at taming this fluffy plumage with some sort of sickly looking paste.

Hattie, momentarily distracted by this troubling sight, did not at first notice the man's utterly abject expression. Holding his boater in both of his hands, he looked up at her so pleadingly and apologetically that she began to feel a familiar pull of sympathy.

"I apologize, my dear lady. Do forgive me. This entire experience has been so distressing, and I..."

Glistening tears welled up in the man's eyes, and Hattie, whose own afterlife ordeal had been so troublesome, was softened considerably. Her heartstrings were already raw with her evening musings, and this man had caught her in the perfect storm of emotions to elicit some kindliness from her usual rigidity.

Noting the poor man's blue, trembling lips, Hattie sighed in final surrender, "Well, I can't very well help you tonight, young man. It's getting very late."

"Young man? Well, I'm blessed!" he said, slapping his knee with his hat in delight.

Ignoring his sudden burst of misplaced joviality, she continued, "Let's go and see Vamelda together tomorrow. What is your name, young man?"

"Mr. Several Carrington. 'Carri' to my intimates."

"Well, *Mister* Carrington," Hattie over-enunciated the appellation, unwilling to be categorized as something so scandalous as an *intimate*. "Until tomorrow, then."

She watched his retreating figure as the night closed around him.

***

Hattie was out in the garden with the bright spring sunlight the next morning. The night before, it had been far too late to make any headway with the orb – her candle had been too short to allow her to study it for any great length of time. This morning, she wanted to have a full stomach of hearty food and a breath of fresh air to en-sure that if her vision in the orb was repeated, she could rely on its reality with some confidence.

As she rounded a corner and surveyed the beautiful, wild scenery, she failed to discern an essential feature of the landscape: the master of the house, sitting on a stone bench. Hattie's small shoes crunched on the gravel underfoot as she passed near to him. She might have remained completely oblivious to his presence, but for a linnet that chose to stretch its narrow wings to the sky and glide toward her.

Hattie followed the flight of the little bird, envious of its freedom and agility. Narrowly missing a nearby tree, it alighted atop a rhododendron behind which the master of the house was ensconced. She was fully wrapped up in the amusing habits of the feathered little creature, which were very charming, indeed. It was peeking in and out at her from behind a billowing blossom, appar-ently intent on determining whether she was friend or foe.

As the little linnet flitted away, Hattie caught a stern eye studying her through the branches of the bush. She stepped back in alarm as she recognized the master of the house. Feeling absurdly abashed at first, she soon gathered her fortitude as she realized that *he* was at fault for not making his presence known.

Her scowl brought him out of hiding.

"Good morning," the words seemed to rush out of him as he stumbled to his feet.

"Good morning," she returned coldly.

"Who was that man?"

His abrupt manner was not cold, but his voice sounded strangled, as though he was attempting to harness some raw emotion.

Hattie was confounded – her thoughts wrapped up in the orb along with their current antagonism.

"What man?" she queried, looking vaguely about them.

"The man you were in the garden with last night. This very garden. Near this very bench."

"Were you spying on us?" asked the affronted Ms. Vavaseur.

"Of course not!" he spluttered with rage. "I merely looked out of my window to see a man on *my* property, speaking with *my* guest, without *my* foreknowledge or permission. I believe I am still the master of my own estate. Simply because you're thinking of purchasing it doesn't mean that I don't still have the right to know who trespasses upon it – particularly if those persons are men with pasted hair in checked suits that are far too tight for them!"

A ripple of laughter escaped Hattie's lips. His accurate description of poor Mr. Carrington, coupled with the absurdity of his obvious and unaccountable jealousy, tickled her sleeping sense of humor.

"What?" he asked.

The master of the house's face, which had turned to a purple rage, softened a bit at the sound of her laughter.

"What is it?" he demanded, though not unkindly.

"I'm sorry that you weren't informed of Mr. Carrington's arrival, but it can't be helped. He's to accompany me to the village this morning, and I'll be sure to introduce you before we leave. He's merely a new acquaintance I met through a mutual friend. I know nothing about him, except that he's desperate to solve his..."

Hattie paused, unsure of how to phrase Mr. Carrington's untimely demise. Did this, the master of the house, know of his own death? Or was he mortal and strangely gifted, as was Vamelda? It was odd that she hadn't dwelt on this concept before. It didn't seem important, somehow, whenever his manly and sometimes abrasive presence entered a room.

"Yes?" he prodded.

"A mystery. I offered to help him."

"Oh, I see. And is there something about this man that...that *attracts* you? He seems a very bad lot to me."

"He's quite harmless, I assure you. You'll see that for yourself if you agree to meet him."

He pondered the opportunity with furrowed brow.

"Very well," he responded. "I shall meet you both in the drawing room, whenever your guest arrives."

He turned to enter the house.

"A moment, sir," Hattie said, placing a hand on his arm.

As the last time she'd touched him, he froze.

In the present instance, however, some strong emotion within him made him tremble momentarily as his face looked down upon hers.

Hattie, far too busy organizing her thoughts, did not take notice. By the time she looked up at him again, his face was composed – the emotion displaced.

"You spoke of purchasing this house. Is that why I'm here?"

She nervously rubbed her thumb and fingers together, as was her wont when in an uncomfortable situation.

"Heavens, woman – it was *your* idea!" His temporary flash of anger softened as he looked down at her. "You may, of course, take as long as you need. Far be it from me to rush you. Taking on an estate is a grave responsibility, and I don't wish you to do it hastily. I have no heir, and therefore this estate must pass into steady hands if it is to survive."

All the while, he stared at her hands with a softened expression. Hattie looked at her own fingers, curious about his point of interest.

"I assume you have someone to whom you intend to leave the estate?"

"Yes," said Hattie, absently, "My nephew…"

However, her attention, too, had turned to her hands.

It was miraculous. The age spots were gone. The wrinkles and lines had softened.

"How curious," she said aloud.

When she looked up, the master of the house had left her, and her words had fallen empty upon the morning breeze.

Hattie felt her waist. It was decidedly firmer and larger. Hattie had never been a small woman until age's tight grip had shrunk her frame. Again, she looked down at her hands. The nails were less yellowed – less ribbed. The knuckles were smaller and, as she moved them, not quite as stiff.

It was yet another mystery to add to the long list of puzzling questions she had for Vamelda, but for now, she reveled in her newfound youth. She began by stretching her fingers. Then she lifted her arms high above her head – a feat she hadn't accomplished in years. She bent over, and although she didn't quite meet her fingertips to her toes, she was doubtlessly more limber. A thought struck her, and an energetic, mischievous glint in her eye reappeared after years of absence. It made her entire face come alive as she looked out across the windswept lawn.

Clearing her throat and straightening her dress, Hattie began to run – a little tentatively at first, but faster and faster with each step did she go. Laughter rushed through her lungs and up into her throat. A thrill of untethered freedom swept through her frame as she took leap after leap.

Without warning, her foot caught on a little cavity in the ground, her ankle twisted, and she came crashing to the earth. It did not hurt much, and she remained grounded as the sky began pouring rain. She looked up into the darkening clouds and laughed and laughed.

She felt foolish, but not in the way that most people blush with embarrassment. Hattie felt gaily, happily foolish, in the way a child does when playing an impish prank. It was supremely silly of her to run. More ludicrous still that she should attempt it in heels. She was breathless - quite heaving, in fact, but she felt so remarkably liberated from her old, frail frame that she did not care.

Limping back to the manor, she hobbled upstairs to her room. As she changed, she felt how tight her clothes were. If her afterlife figure were anything like her middle-aged mortal one, she'd need larger dresses. Hattie entered the hall and was about to return downstairs, when suddenly, she recalled the orb.

Narrowly avoiding the maid, who was walking down the hall with a pile of bedclothes, Hattie stepped swiftly back into her room. Locking the door, she pulled out the sewing basket. The orb was still there – a little clearer and a little less dark than before, but still swirling with depths of shadowy hues.

Once again, it warmed at her touch. As Hattie stared into its wondrous expanse, a new vision – as vague as a memory – began to unfurl. A long rowing boat appeared within the hazy wafts of smoke. She could just make out a group of young men pulling at the oars, and she watched intently as one of them dove into the purple murkiness. Then all vanished into swirling obscurity once more.

A knock came at the door. Hattie quickly wrapped and

replaced the orb into the basket, again stowing it in her hiding place beneath the bed.

Chapter Eighteen

It was the maid again, who had apparently disposed of the bedsheets and was now back to request Hattie's presence in the drawing room. She followed the young woman down the hall, then left her to her duties. As Hattie descended the stairs, she could hear the boisterous voice of Mr. Carrington and the low grumble of the master of the house. She hurried her step, worried that some disagreement might erupt and hoped that her presence might avert it.

Entering the drawing room, she was surprised to perceive that the two of them were getting along very well, indeed. The master's fears seemed to have been assuaged by her words of the evening before, and, hopefully, the innocently jovial manner of Mr. Carrington.

"Yes, and then the gypsies sent me off with a bag of wild mushrooms and a beautiful, new coat!"

The rumble of polite laughter softened as Hattie walked through the door. She merely nodded at the master of the house but extended a warm hand of welcome to Mr. Carrington.

"Thank you for coming to fetch me," she said. "Are you ready to depart?"

"Why, yes. I've my car here. It's a bit old-fashioned, but I simply can't give her up, even though I'm no longer...er...working."

"You're retired, then?" queried the master.

"In a manner of speaking...yes."

Mr. Carrington's eyes drifted toward Hattie's inquiringly. She subtly shook her head, signaling to him not to speak of the afterlife.

The master saw the exchange and stiffened his heretofore relaxed posture.

"Exactly how did the two of you become acquainted?" he asked abruptly. "I can't imagine that you run in the same social circles?"

Mr. Carrington began to bluster, unsure of his footing.

"Oooo...ahhh..." he said, incoherently.

"Through that mutual friend I mentioned," Hattie quickly interjected. "We're going to visit her now."

"Oh, yes? And who is *she*?"

"Well, she's quite an interesting character. I'm not certain you'd approve," responded Hattie, lightly. "She happens to be the village soothsayer."

"Does this woman have a name?" returned the master.

"Vamelda...Vamelda..." Hattie trailed off, realizing that she did not recall the medium's surname.

"Anstruthers," kindly interpolated Mr. Carrington.

The master's eyes widened. He seemed unable to quite process the information.

"*That* woman? She's been trying to snake her way into this house for years. The servants have turned her away more than a dozen times – not to mention that blasted, impudent Bertram keeps trying to get me to see her. I won't have her in this house, and be sure you tell her so!" he raged.

"We wouldn't dream of inviting someone here that would make you feel uncomfortable," Hattie said soothingly. "She's merely an amusing acquaintance with whom we like occasionally to converse – for a little variance of company, you understand. Neither of us considers ourselves dabblers in the occult. We merely find her diverting."

The master opened his mouth, but, looking at Mr. Carrington, shut it again.

After what seemed like an eternity of silence, Hattie said, "Well, we must be going."

"I hope you enjoy your visit, then. Don't let me keep you," he returned with just a hint of bitterness.

He gave Mr. Carrington his firm hand, and as he passed Hattie, he paused and took hers, as well. He bent over it, his lips hovering so closely to her skin that she could feel his breath upon her knuckles. A little thrill flowed through her. She withdrew her hand quickly, before he could feel her tremble.

Why would her flesh (if she could call it that) react in such a way? It wasn't as though she found this man kind...or even handsome, if matters of the body were of any importance in the afterlife. She dismissed it as nervousness and continued down the hall and out the front doors on Mr. Carrington's proffered arm.

The drive was pleasant. Hattie made no move to inquire after Mr. Carrington's life. She felt that it was an immense mistake on this man's part to enlist her help. Hattie rather hoped to transfer his interest in her to Vamelda, who could, perhaps, find some relative with whom he could converse through the clairvoyant, as she had done with her nephew.

Hattie's reserve didn't impinge upon Mr. Carrington's joviality. He began chattering away at her, regaling her with tales of his life. It seemed he had begun as a rather indiscriminate salesman and, by virtue of his product, had made himself quite a fortune.

"That, along with one or two little bequests to my humble self for services rendered to illustrious clients, and Mrs. Carrington and myself were made quite comfortable – quite comfortable, indeed."

Hattie was surprised to hear that the man was married. She politely inquired after his wife.

"Oh, yes. She's still alive, but she's in America. I don't believe Vamelda could convince her to come all the way over here. She was a skeptic of all things mystical."

At this point, Mr. Carrington gave Hattie a sideways glance as if gauging her reaction.

"She'll get the surprise of her life whenever she passes... which I hope is a good, old age – I really do."

Hattie nodded, as he seemed to be expecting an answer.

"Yes, I want my dear Mrs. Carrington to be able to enjoy the finest things in life. She always loved the clothes and the jewels and the fine houses. When I met her, I had already made a tidy sum, but she helped me perfect my product, and we did even better business together!"

The man had gone quite starry-eyed: "She's quite a woman, is my Mrs. Carrington."

He sighed and wiped a tear or two from the corner of his eye.

Hattie, uncomfortable with this flow of emotion, inquired, "What was the product that you sold?"

Again came that sideways glance, and Hattie worried that she had offended the poor man by passing over his obvious grief.

Mr. Carrington withdrew a checked handkerchief from his pocket that matched his suit to perfection and blew his nose into it rather noisily.

Stuffing it back into his breast pocket, he replied, "It was a little tincture of my own invention. It helped take simply *years* off of my clients. You can imagine that it was particularly popular with the ladies."

At this moment, they arrived at Vamelda's door. Hattie graciously accepted Mr. Carrington's hand to help her out of the car, and they walked into Vamelda's shop together.

A noxious smell greeted them as they moved through the doors. They found the great oracle sitting in a chair in the outer room, her feet plunged into an open sarcophagus that was filled with some indeterminate liquid. Vamelda was indulging, rather sloppily and very passionately, in a bunch of large, dusty grapes. Not bothering to select them individually, she was holding the entire bunch in her palm, sucking them off lustily. Simultaneously, she was loudly humming a jarring, tuneless ditty. Obviously lost in her own, innocent pleasure, she did not seem to hear the tinkle of her shop's bells.

All of Hattie's senses convulsed with revulsion at this sickening combination, and she made a little, choking gasp. Vamelda sat up, sloshing what looked like onions and rose petals from inside of the sarcophagus, where she'd been soaking her feet.

"Darlings!" she sputtered, a mouthful of half-masticated grapes spilling from her lips. She smiled brightly at them both, a smidgen of grape skin clinging to her teeth. "It's these frightful callouses, you know. I tried Gets-It, and it didn't do a thing, so I went back to my time-tested remedy."

She gestured vaguely toward the sarcophagus.

"Do the ancient Egyptians have something to...um... curse them off?" Mr. Carrington politely inquired.

"Oh, heavens, no! What put such a ridiculous idea into your head? What have *onions* and *roses* to do with the *Egyptians*?"

A screech of laughter erupted from the occultist's lips, along with a few more pieces of grape and a dainty snort.

Without bothering to pat her feet dry, Vamelda led them to a heavy brocade curtain, dripping the putrid-smelling petals and bits of onion behind her bare feet. Sweeping the curtain aside, she revealed a small, rounded door. She deftly removed a tiny key that jingled from one of the many bangles that adorned her wrists. She fiddled with the lock a bit, but finally, it turned, and Vamelda opened the door.

Hattie didn't quite know what to expect of this new, heretofore unseen apartment. It turned out to be Vamelda's kitchen, which was, in many ways, much more frightening than the outer room. It was quite cramped and very dirty. Floored with what at one point must have been black-and-white tile, the white was now somewhere between a dull grey and a mild beige. Scarves, beads, food, and wine glasses were intermixed in brazen confusion.

Vamelda seemed not the least bit embarrassed as she drifted through the untidy disarray of used teacups and discarded oyster shells. It smelled of fish and cinnamon – not a particularly pleasant combination, unfortunately for Mr. Carrington and Hattie.

The former didn't seem to mind, but the latter, already slightly nauseated from the smell of the footbath, pulled out a handkerchief to hold over her nose. Hattie stepped tentatively over the piles of dishes and she knew not what else, trying not to breathe in the malodorous contents of the room.

The medium led them through to the end of the kitchen and out the back door. They all descended a flight of wrought iron stairs that were painted thickly black more times than anyone could ever count, and Hattie found herself in a small courtyard that could almost be called charming. It was covered in flowers, secluded, and had a lovely creeper growing on the deep, russet-colored bricks beneath her feet, but Vamelda's influence could be felt here, too. Half-transplanted potted plants, broken gardening trowels, packets of spilled seeds, and the inevitable scarves made it lose some of its appeal.

Vamelda perfunctorily brushed the seat of a patio chair that was nearly indistinguishable from the surrounding ivy that crept over the wall. The medium vaguely pointed Hattie toward it. Mr. Carrington chivalrously cleared another two chairs and drew one forward for their hostess.

"Tea?" Vamelda queried.

Mr. Carrington's cordial assent contrasted starkly with Hattie's hesitant nod. Vamelda disappeared into the house once again and returned with a tray of mismatched teacups and a few broken biscuits.

Hattie took a reluctant sip of what turned out to be surprisingly excellent tea and settled a bit more comfortably into her seat.

"There," stated Vamelda. "Now that we're all comfortable, and there is *no* chance of you disturbing my clients *or* stealing precious property..." This last phrase was accompanied by a disgruntled glance toward Hattie. "We can delve into all of the glorious details. Have you any idea who the murderer is?"

Chapter Nineteen

Mr. Carrington gave an awkward cough at Vamelda's abrupt transfer to the delicate subject.

"I...I swear on my wife's life that I can't think of a single soul," he said stoutly.

Vamelda looked expectantly at Hattie, her eyes blinking rapidly.

Hattie was affronted: "How on earth should *I* know? I've only just met the man. The only person I've heard him speak of is his wife."

Vamelda sat back, slurping her tea with gusto.

"Has either of you thought that *she* might be the culprit?"

Tea spluttered from the little man's lips. He turned away, applying a handkerchief to his chin. When he turned back, tears had filled his eyes. Sorrow poured over his face, from the top of his bare forehead to the tips of his chins.

"There is no way on this earth that my dear Mrs. Carrington could be responsible! She loved me too, too dearly. We were...ahem...*are* twin souls! Made of the same cloth, as it were."

Despite his protestations, Hattie caught onto Vamelda's idea. A rich man with a beautiful wife...

"Are you certain?" queried Hattie. "Did you never suspect that she could, perhaps, be acting a part? You did tell me that you've become a very wealthy man."

"Even so, I was well on my way to making even more money. We were building an empire together, so killing me would only cut her off if she was at all mercenary. However, such an accusation is simply preposterous. Mrs. Carrington would never...no, *never* dream of doing me any harm."

A few tears dropped down onto Mr. Carrington's checkered pants.

"I'm so sorry, Mr. Carrington," inserted Hattie. "I did not mean to injure you. I merely thought that at times, when couples spend time apart...well, *love* can grow apart, as well. If you were traveling a good deal for your business..."

"They say that poison *is* a woman's weapon," continued Vamelda.

"It makes complete sense," Hattie was growing warmer with their advancing theory. "You did say she was beautiful, Mr. Carrington?"

Hattie's eyes began to sparkle, although she didn't know it. There is nothing like the thrill of a mystery to take an individual out of their own troubles.

The little man had been blowing his nose once again into his checkered kerchief, but when he looked up, his face was contorted with outrage.

"How *dare* you? How *could* you bring such allegations to her doorstep? She was everything to me! I worked each day to ensure her comfort and happiness! There is no scenario I can imagine where she would ever consider doing such a thing!"

Both of the women fell silent. Lost in the fervor of their speculations, they had forgotten that a human soul with very real and poignant feelings sat between them.

Hattie excused her behavior a second time: "I do apologize, Mr. Carrington. I've gotten quite carried away. Of course, we must trust you to know your wife best."

"Thank you, dear lady," said the man, abruptly cheerful once again.

His emotions seemed to change as quickly as a butterfly kisses the flowers from which it draws nectar. His tears were dried in an instant, and a wide, satisfactory smile spread over his face.

"Have you any living family we could consult, Mr. Carrington?" Hattie inquired gently. "Vamelda made contact with my nephew, and he has been most helpful."

The little man shook his head so vigorously that the tufts of hair on either side of his head stood out a great deal farther than usual.

"I'm afraid Mrs. Carrington is all I have now, and we know she won't believe any of this...she would call it 'nonsense of the afterlife,'" he replied.

"I *do* so want to help, Mr. Carrington, but I'm not quite certain how I can go about it."

Hattie turned to Vamelda.

"What can we possibly do? Travel to America? Interview witnesses?"

Vamelda let out a harrumph of exasperation.

"And how would you go about that, my dear? Would you like me to buy a boat ticket for a *ghost*? I have tried that a time or two, but it never works. You spirits are all the same...so difficult! I went to all the trouble of purchasing tickets, but when it came to proving their existence, they refused to show themselves! It damaged my reputation severely, I can tell you."

"Vamelda, I..." Hattie tried to ask a question, but the medium's exasperated flow continued without pause.

"Even if you were able to leave this place...what would you do? *Haunt* them into confessing?" She gave a shrill laugh, accompanied by her signature snort. "No, it must be a *living* person that discovers what happened to poor Mr. Carrington."

"Besides," the medium disclosed, "Your soul is bound to that house, you know...at least until you've resolved your past. Bertram's allowed to take you on these little outings, but not too often or for too long, or your soul begins to fade. You're fading a bit now, in fact, sweetums."

"What?" gasped Hattie, surprised. "Is that true? I must stay near the house?"

"Why, yes, my dear sugarplum. I should think it was obvious. And yet...perhaps it's not the manor, after all," Vamelda sipped her tea dreamily. "Perhaps...it's the resident inside it?"

She raised her eyebrows inquiringly.

"What do you mean?" squeaked Hattie.

She was afraid that if she moved even an inch that she would completely evaporate.

"Maybe not, then, my dear. I'm always looking for romance where perhaps I shouldn't."

"You are quite mistaken there, indeed. The man's been nothing but a brute to me ever since I arrived," mumbled Hattie through gritted teeth, as she continued to sit perfectly still.

Vamelda tilted her head and eyed Hattie scientifically.

"As much as I would like to witness a complete corporeal waning, I believe we'd better hurry you along home."

A very pronounced "Ahem!" came from the corner that contained Mr. Carrington.

Both of the ladies had once again forgotten the man's presence.

Just then, bells jangled in the distance.

"I won't be a moment, dearies. I wasn't expecting anyone, so I'll just see if they can make an appointment to return at a later time."

She left the two souls sitting in silence. Hattie felt great discomfort and kept delicately arranging the hem of her cuffs in a meager attempt to appear occupied with minimal movements. Mr. Carrington was sulking in the corner and fiddling with the ribbon on his hat. Just as Hattie was about to break their mutual reticence with another apology, a dirty, white cat jumped down upon her lap and began grooming itself with great enthusiasm. Hattie tried to push the unkempt feline out of her lap, but it gave a short hiss, then continued to lick its fur even more vigorously. Haughtily ignoring all of Hattie's attempts to unseat it, the cat began purring loudly, tucked its head beneath its tail, and fell asleep.

Vamelda reentered the room.

"He's here, my darlings! The answer to all of our prayers! Oh, I see you've met Pimsie."

"Can...can it *see* me?" inquired Hattie, nervously giving the creature a nudge.

"Why, of course she can, my dear. Cats, dogs, horses, babies...they can all see into the spirit world. Why else would horses be so skittish when nothing is there? Why would babies coo at the spot just past your ear?"

"Oh, I see," responded Hattie, thinking of her experiences during her life when this had occurred.

"That's all very well," said Mr. Carrington, "But you did

say that someone is here that could help us?"

"Yes, that's right, now, isn't it, Sweetie Pims?" the medium said, awakening the cat with an expertly placed scratch behind the ear. "This way! We must have an impromptu séance right away!"

She draped the white cat around her shoulders like a fur stole.

Leading them through the chaotic kitchen, she locked the door behind them as they entered the outer room. A rather nervous-looking young man stood near the front of the shop, hat in hand, his eyes darting about at the conglomeration of terrifying objects that surrounded him.

Hattie at once recognized her nephew. His apprehensive manner and obvious ineptness had her wondering how he could possibly be the answer to anyone's prayers.

Still, she followed the medium, who began her occult theatrics by summoning them all into the inner room with a, "Let us begiiiin the séaaaance!"

Chapter Twenty

"But won't I waste away?" Hattie said nervously as they entered the stark chamber.

"Oh, no," replied Vamelda, under her breath. "Not now that your nephew's here. These ties we have during life, whether with mortals or with places, always lend a strengthening power."

As Gerald passed the medium into the room, she arrested him by placing a flattened hand against his chest. She pointed at him straight between his eyebrows, making the poor lad go slightly cross-eyed. Then, with the same vermillion nail, gestured to a chair seated opposite her own velvety throne.

Gerald, his hat crumpled nervously in his hands, wobbled over, knocked-kneed, and seemed grateful for the proffered seat.

Vamelda worked her usual tricks with the darkness and flashing lights until the young man looked as white as a ghost himself.

"Your *auntiiiiieee!*" she moaned. "She is in *diiiiire* need of *fuuurther assistaaaaance!*"

"Well, I have here, in fact..." Gerald reached for his pocket.

"Hush, now! Do not speeeak! Her spirit is very-very-very neeeeaar!"

Vamelda fluttered her eyelids closed and stretched her arm out to where her crystal ball usually stood on the table.

When her thin fingers found nothing but air, she cracked a sliver of an eye open and said, "Your aunt has been very diiiificult of late."

"Oh, I say, I am sorry," returned Gerald.

"*SIIIILEEENCE!*" the medium shrieked.

Gerald relapsed into nervously crumpling his already disheveled hat.

"Let me see," continued the occultist.

She began waving her arms mystically in the air, as though trying to grasp onto some unseen spirit that was hovering upon the ceiling. Breathing in deeply and momentously, Vamelda's eyes shot open. With a surreptitious flick of a switch, she shone a light directly into the striking blue of her irises, illuminating them with an eerie hue.

The effect was so great that even Hattie was quite taken in by the performance. Recalling herself, she looked over at Mr. Carrington, who had a bemused look on his face.

In an unnaturally monotone voice, Vamelda spoke without taking a breath: "You must travel to America. You must seek out anything you can discover about your aunt's fiancé."

Hattie started at this. She hadn't told Vamelda...ah – it came to her. The devious woman must have read the letters from Vivienne before handing them over to Hattie.

"Righto, but I do have..." said Gerald in a meek voice, reaching for his pocket once again.

The clairvoyant rushed on, "You must also seek out one Mrs. Carrington of...of..."

"New York City," delivered Mr. Carrington, promptly.

"New York City, New York," repeated Vamelda. "You must discover everything you can about the death of her husband. This you must do and not fail us."

The soothsayer ended her little charade by standing up to her full height, shaking her arms up and down from the floor to the ceiling, and letting out what sounded like an ancient war cry of an indeterminate nature.

Gerald had tipped his chair back onto two legs in shock, but the lights soon flickered on to a warmer, mellow glow, and Vamelda sat down gracefully as though nothing out of the ordinary had happened.

Taking a moment to collect himself, Gerald finally replied shakily, "Sure...I'll play gumshoe. Dear old Aunt Hattie left me enough cabbage for a boat trip out to ye olde New York City. I'll track down this dame for sure –

you can bet your buttons."

"Your dear auntie will be most grateful. You can be sure to be blessed with many healthy children..."

"As for her fiancé, I have here..." the young man reached for the third time into his pocket, but Vamelda paid him no mind.

"*Yeeeaas*! Many healthy, happy children, for whom you will be a guiding example of *fatherhooooood*!"

"Oh, for heaven's sake!" broke in Hattie. "Can't you see my nephew is trying to show you something, you fool of a woman?"

She marched over to the table and withdrew the item in question from Gerald's pocket. The young man jumped back, fully tipping his chair over as he watched what turned out to be a piece of paper floating beside him in the air.

"Oh, no," he said, practically choking on his own words. "I'm not about to burn my peepers on *this* mumbo-jumbo again. I've been laying off the giggle water and everything, just so I'm certain I'm not sloshed and see-ing things."

With that, he shoved his rumpled hat onto his head and fled the room.

"Send me a telegram!" Vamelda said cheerily, waving him out the door.

Hattie stood up the chair that her nephew had over-turned in his frightened haste and sat down upon it. She stared intently at two faces on a slip of paper.

One was an immensely beautiful, sophisticated-looking woman in a long, fashionable gown. The other...it was her own face – the face of herself at perhaps the age of nineteen or twenty.

"Why, it's a newspaper, by golly!" said Mr. Carrington who was looking over her shoulder.

Hattie hardly noticed his exclamation as she gazed steadily into her own youthful eyes. Looking herself up and down, she noted that the clipping had been torn very neatly at her right elbow. The tip of a man's shoe was visible next to the hem of her dress. Most of the page was taken up with photographs and half of the words of the article were missing where the page had been ripped. Almost in a fever, she began to read the partial sentences that were left:

ENGAGED TO MISS H. VAVASEUR, HEIRESS OF ALVERTON
MANOR, CORNWALL. THE MATCH
A YEAR. HE HAD KNOWN MISS CAMPBELL IN BURMA,
WHERE HE WAS STATIONED DURING
NDER THAT HE WAS ENTRANCED WITH THE FASCINATING
YOUNG WOMAN. THE MURDER
ITH HER IN HER DEFENSE.

That was it. The only other line was under the photograph of the exquisite woman:

MISS L. CAMPBELL, PHOTOGRAPHED OUTSIDE OF THE COURTROOM IN AN
ELEGANT TAFFETA GOWN, MADE UP IN HER SIGNATURE PINK SHADE.

Hattie put the article down. "*Pink...*" she thought, "*PINK.*"

She turned the newspaper clipping over to see if she could glean any more information, but it was merely an advertisement for "Dr. Falliere's Flesh-Food," touting the benefits of increased weight for women.

Turning it back over, she stared into the eyes of the breathtaking beauty who seemed to have charmed her former lover right out of her arms. She had suspected as much when she had read the last letter to Vivienne, but the mention of murder shed quite a different light on the entire situation.

After reading and rereading the clipping until she had practically memorized each word, Hattie at last looked up at Vamelda. The woman was cleaning her long fingernails with her teeth – or perhaps it was the other way around? Hattie wasn't certain. She was also astounded at – and grateful for – Vamelda's eerie moment of clarity as the medium had allowed her time to read the article undisturbed.

Looking behind her to see Mr. Carrington's reaction at the clipping, she realized that he was gone. She swept the room with a glance, but the bright-checked suit and boater hat were nowhere to be seen.

"Oh, yes, sugarplum. He left. After he saw the clipping, he mumbled something about a 'moment of privacy' and said he'd wait for you in the car. May I see this fascinating little tidbit, then?"

Hattie handed over the tiny slip of paper that seemed to hold so much.

With several gasps and groans that were not wholly merited by the minuscule amount of information contained therein, Vamelda gave it back to her, exclaiming, "Another murder! How absolutely, divinely juicy! We shall have to wire Gerald about this the moment he arrives in America."

Chapter Twenty-One

Excerpt from the journal of Gerald Warburton,
nephew of Hattie Vavaseur

May 6, 1927

I must say, the journey here has been ever so ripping. On the boat, I danced twice with Miss Julia Favorleigh and thrice with her sister, all the while talking nonsense, but neither of them seemed to mind. I had no idea that fulfilling a behest of my beloved auntie would be so enjoyable. America is before me, with it's lovely, wide-open spaces and even wider-eyed Betties. At least, that's what all the boys at Cambridge used to say.

I never thought I'd fall in with this spiritualism mumbo-jumbo, but that Vamelda has got it right on the money. She knew of the time I fell and broke my arm and told my auntie a whopper about how I was bravely rescuing a bird from its nest when really I was trying to take the bird *out* of the nest. Aunt Hattie always could see right through me, and now, even from the grave.

I shudder to think that she could be here, in my small cabin. *Right now.* What do spirits do when you're bathing? Turn politely away? One can only hope!

I am to communicate with Vamelda via telegram. The young lady in question that I am to interview resides in the sparkling metropolis of New York City.

Trixie was none too happy about my traveling overseas, but I asked my old chum Gunther Hendrickson-Smith to look after her. He'll take her to all the dances I can't and shows she's longing to see. I gave him plenty of dough, so she'll be well taken care of. He can always wire for more if her tastes extend to the extreme, as they have been recently.

It's late, and I must be up early for a stroll on deck tomorrow with the lovely Miss Favorleighs.

- *G.W.*

Telegram from Gerald Warburton to Vamelda Anstruthers

May 13, 1927

Have arrived in New York. *Stop.* The merry widow here. *Stop.* Spending husband's money on all and sundry. *Stop.* Not my husband her husband. *Stop.* Have put up at the Ritz not that grubby little hole in the middle of nowhere that you forced me to book. *Stop.* Awaiting further instructions. *Stop.* - *G.W.*

Telegram from Vamelda Anstruthers to Gerald Warburton

May 15, 1927

Received your telegram from NYC. *Stop*. Make friends with merry widow. *Stop*. Find out how she is handling her husband's demise. *Stop*. Would like to know her state of mind, etc. *Stop*. How is the weather there – it is dreary here. *Stop*. Aunt says to stop wasting money on inane details in telegrams. *Stop*. No shorter. *Stop*. No shorter. *Stop*. Oh sorry darling it was your aunt telling me to make the telegram shorter. *Stop*. Have a lovely time in New York, and be sure to eat a delectable hot dog for me. *Stop*. - V.A.

Excerpt from the journal of Gerald Warburton, cont.

May 17, 1927

By golly, that Mrs. Carrington is a ripper! I don't care if she is a bit older, she's the goods, by jingo. Those fiery eyes that see right through to one's skivvies. Whew! A boy like me can get into some hot water there, as sure as moss grows on trees.

I don't think she'll ever have me, so it's as well that I'm stitched up together with my old Trixie. I ain't no cake-eater, but I came close last evening!

I put on my glad rags for a night at the theatre, hoping to catch another glimpse of the woman. I've met her at a few dances and dinner parties, and I couldn't stay away. I'll admit that the stage canary held no interest – all I could stare at was that Mrs. Carrington in the box across from me. She was glittering with gems from head to foot, but she didn't need them for any red-blooded man to see that she's quite a beaut.

I went outside during the interval for a gasper, and what

do you think? She was there. All elegant with furs and diamonds. She lit up the alleyway like fireworks, let me tell you! She bummed a cig from my deck, and you've never seen such a dainty, elegant little thing.

We bumped gums about this and that until we heard the bell. I was about to offer my arm to take her inside, when she was right there beside me. I've never smelled anything so sweet. Wrapping her fur stole around my neck, she pulled me in for a kiss!

I was tempted to the limit of my manly abilities, but I politely declined. I pulled away and lammed off the moment I could, making my way to the nearest speakeasy to tip back a few.

I'm not sure if I can keep my head straight around this dame to even ask questions about her husband's death. I am flattered, but I need to stay faithful to Trixie. Was ever a man in such a predicament as me?

- G.W.

Excerpt from the journal of Gerald Warburton, cont.

May 23, 1927

I gave myself a week to cool off after that close call with Mrs. Carrington. I must, however, do my duty by my dear, old auntie. She did keep the wolves from my door, especially after she kicked off and left me those gobs of money.

I called Mrs. Carrington up on the blower and invited her out for a chew at the Astor. She graciously accepted with that melodiously haunting voice of hers. We met, and she was dressed in quite a number that made every man in that place stare. I couldn't believe that she was meeting with me and had to pick my jaw up from the floor when she actually sat down at my table.

We talked of this and that, and I finally came to the subject of her husband. Tears welled up in the poor dame's eyes as she spoke of his horrible death. Heart attack, she said. He always would eat extravagantly, it seems. I put my fork down right away, I can tell you. Scooting over to the seat next to her, I quite literally let the little woman cry on my shoulder, even though it was a new suit. When she stopped her sobs, I found that the material had no tears upon it – the divine Mrs. Carrington even *cries* delicately!

I can't help but want to protect her from the wide, bad world and all that is in it.

- G.W.

Telegram from Gerald Warburton to Vamelda Anstruthers

May 24, 1927

Mr. Carrington not murdered. *Stop.* Couldn't lay off the meatballs and cream soup. *Stop.* Mrs. Carrington a charming woman. *Stop.* Will focus on finding more about Aunt Hattie as soon as. *Stop. - G.W.*

Telegram from Gerald Warburton to Vamelda Anstruthers

June 1, 1927

Tell Trixie it's all off. *Stop.* Can't do it myself. *Stop.* Better coming from a woman. *Stop.* Going to marry the lovely, wonderful, beautiful Mrs. Carrington. *Stop. - G.W.*

Chapter Twenty-Two

"Oh, that horrid boy!" exclaimed Hattie, who was having difficulty controlling her temper. "He's behaving atrociously! He knows perfectly well that this trip wasn't a pleasure cruise. We're trying to solve a murder!"

She was in Vamelda's kitchen, which had become slightly tidier after some rather severe nagging on Hattie's part. The telegram felt like acid in her hand, so she dropped it on the table. Vamelda's white, furry cat promptly jumped up and sat upon it.

"Get down, you horrid thing," Hattie continued, nudging the pet with a teaspoon.

Pimsie wouldn't budge but instead began batting happily at the spoon. Hattie, frustrated, let the utensil clatter to her plate, which frightened the feline into jumping off of the table, spilling greasy crumbs all over the telegram as it did so. She brushed the piece of paper off and picked it up again, reading it through for the seventh time.

Vamelda continued drinking her tea...or slurping it, rather, as she was wont to do.

"Darling," she said calmly. "What did you *expect* him to do? Mrs. Carrington sounds like a *very* attractive woman. Her husband's fortune is utterly massive. What could she do but live the high life in New York City? *I* would. You can't blame a lady for enjoying her freedom – particularly when she's receiving so much attention from wealthy dandies such as your nephew."

"But I *do* very much blame my nephew for falling in love with her. All he'll tell us is that she's wonderful, marvelous, and couldn't possibly commit murder. He's supposed to be engaged to that Bertha creature."

"Trixie," Vamelda lazily interrupted.

"Bless you," returned Hattie, handing her a handkerchief. "And although his original fiancé's manners left something to be desired, I'd much rather he be wed to her than to a probable murderess!"

"Yes," Vamelda said dreamily, spreading jam atop a scone that was already dripping with cream.

Hattie was eyeing her actions disapprovingly. A Cornishwoman through and through, it was burned into her that the only proper way was to place the jam on the scone first. Watching Vamelda do the opposite nearly drove her to distraction.

"I would burn right through your money, too," continued Vamelda, taking a generous bite, heedlessly allowing the cream to dribble down her chin. Her next phrase was hard to distinguish between the jam and scone that squelched between her teeth: "You did have quite a lot of it."

Hattie rapped the table sharply as she raised *her* voice, "Don't *you* become greedy, now, Vamelda."

The occultist shot up straight, nearly choking on her overly large bite of biscuit as the tea things rattled around in an inelegant dance before her in response to Hattie's near-violent knocks upon the table.

Hattie stood up and began to pat Vamelda on the back as the medium continued to spew bits of scone and clotted cream all over the table.

"What is our next step, do you suppose? More telegrams? Do we send reinforcements? What about Bertram? *You* obviously can't go."

"Why not?!" demanded Vamelda. "I'm very fond of New York."

"I need you here. *I* can't leave...and I can't manage poor Mr. Carrington by myself. He'll know about his wife's engagement to my nephew soon enough. This entire ridiculous situation is going to make it very awkward for me. I simply can't handle his weepy eyes and heaving sighs all on my own. Besides, between you and Gerald, you'd spend my entire fortune within a week, I dare say."

Vamelda, only just recovered from her coughing fit, soon launched into another, this time expelling the tea she'd taken to soothe her throat.

"I have it!" said Hattie after another round of energetic back-patting. "We'll send Penelope."

"Trixie!" the medium managed to squeak out between coughs.

"Yes," Hattie continued, thoughtfully. "How soon can you summon her?"

The clairvoyant at last calmed her throat and was able to take a full breath before she responded, "She's knocking about the countryside in some house or other at a weekend party. Her mother was in to visit just the other day. I'm sure I can get hold of her somehow, sugarplum. Don't you worry about that."

The medium began to suck the cream from her fingers, one by one, from the base of each knuckle all the way to the tip. Hattie looked away, disgusted by this complete lack of manners.

"Ah, New York City. I should so love to visit again," the medium sighed.

Pimsie chose that moment to drop into Vamelda's lap from a shelf above, knocking down a few cookbooks that narrowly missed her head as she did so. The clairvoyant didn't even flinch as she dreamily stroked the purring feline.

"However, I suppose you are right, my darling. Trixie *would* be the best option to win your dear nephew back from that woman."

A male voice called out from the front room.

"Oh, bother," moaned Vamelda. "Just when we were getting so nice and comfortable."

She upended the cat, who at first looked disgruntled but soon after seemed to pretend, like those of his kind, that jumping onto the floor was entirely his idea. He began licking his back in good earnest, twisting his neck around until he looked like some grotesque circus creature. Hattie looked down her nose at him, and their eyes locked. He winked at her for just a moment before raising his tail up in the air and walking proudly away.

Vamelda soon returned. "It's that magnificent Bertram here to take you home."

"You will tell me as soon as you've heard anything from Trixie?" Hattie queried, looking earnestly into Vamelda's eyes. "Oh, I simply can't call her that. What was her Christian name? Beatrice? Offer to finance her travel expenses. We'll need to ensure that she's comfortable...*and* well dressed if she is to stand a chance against this apparently supremely fashionable Mrs. Carrington."

Vamelda waved a hand before her face as if dismissing these details as a cloud of irritating gnats.

"Let me know when you've been successful in sending her over, will you?"

She placed the telegram in her handbag and snapped it shut. After collecting her shawl and bidding Vamelda an unconsciously warm farewell, she allowed Bertram to accompany her to the car.

Hattie tried to relax as the warm wind teased her by pulling at her hat. Lock after lock of hair divorced itself from the pin that had heretofore held it tightly in place. After attempting to painfully jam the pins back into her scalp, she finally gave up the battle and removed pins and chapeau, letting her long tresses stream out behind her. With no mirrors in the car, Bertram couldn't see what she was doing, so she unashamedly ran her fingers through the tangled locks until it flew about her face in wild abandon. Within this moment, she temporarily relinquished the anxieties that clouded her mind. The joy she felt in such a moment was almost complete.

Closing her eyes, she imagined herself free from worry and care – she conjured up in her thoughts the afterlife she'd always expected. Most of these fantasies were vague and usually included perfectly-proportioned people, adorned in shapeless, white robes, and quite possibly winged. She realized, though, that with each generation, a new idea of bodily perfection cropped up. Firmly deciding that heaven should contain all shapes and sizes, just as earth did, depending on the individual's ideals of perfection, she still relished the thought that her body was steadily growing younger.

Inexplicable though it was, she was grateful for the renewed energy and strength that she had discovered. There were no more splitting headaches, no more creaks and groans from her wizened joints, no more awakening in the early hours of the morning with the inability to fall back asleep.

Instead, she was filled with a youthfulness and fortitude that rivaled even her best middle-aged years. No sickness kept her from her beloved pastimes. She feared no looming injury from a fall off of a horse or down the stairs. Where her strength of body was concerned, she felt only an exuberant, infatuating peace that she had never before experienced. However, the joy she felt in this newfound physical liberation was short-lived, as her mind fell back upon her present worries.

Hattie had faithfully studied the orb whenever privacy would admit, but, to her great chagrin, it had yielded no further visions. Disappointed in this, as well as her nephew's stupidity, there were even more troubles that pressed upon her soul.

The master of the house had withdrawn from her company entirely these past weeks. No longer her dinner companion, no longer her intellectual rival, she had spent her days largely in the company of Mr. Carrington. By turns, she would soothe the little man's fears about his murder and listen to him regale her with stories of his early days as a traveling salesman. He could prove to be a very charming companion, but she could tell he was irritated whenever they spoke of his wife, so she, as often as possible, gave the subject a wide berth.

Delicately, she had inquired of the servants after the master of the house, but they had responded in vague and even frightened terms, leaving her saddened that she was not even provided the opportunity to try to charm away some of his displeasure. Well, perhaps not "charm" at her age, but at least attempt to rekindle their friendship on a more solid footing.

A small part of her feared that her daily interactions with Mr. Carrington were the source of the master of the house's absence, but the deep independence of her soul rebelled against what she could only guess was his punishment for her behavior. Defiantly, she agreed to meet with the former salesman day after day, refusing to give in to the master of the house's sulky and childish behavior, if that indeed was his intent. Mr. Carrington would often call for her in the morning, and they would walk about the lanes near the estate, visit Vamelda, or simply drive aimlessly in the countryside. As the mansion was not her own, her insurgence did not quite extend to inviting Mr. Carrington into the house.

Reflecting on all of this, Hattie was decidedly surprised to see the very man who was invading her thoughts walking about on the grounds as they turned into the drive. Waving the Daimler down, the master of the house walked directly in front of the car and commanded Bertram, with a gesture, to stop.

Chapter Twenty-Three

As the tires crunched to a halt on the gravel, Hattie nervously attempted to tidy her hair. Just as the master of the house came around to her door, she successfully fastened her hat atop her pile of curls, hoping against hope that the brim would cover the imperfections of her hurried coiffure.

As he opened Hattie's door, he greeted her with a wide smile, which unnerved her, particularly after their last interaction. Although she never knew what to expect with this man, she felt uneasy in this new twist of emotion. He seemed almost giddy, and his broad, engaging smile made her quite breathless.

The wrinkles at the corners of his eyes and the way his full lips stretched over his fine, straight, white teeth made him suddenly seem remarkably handsome. The tips of his wavy, grey locks had darkened to tinges of deep auburn. He reached for her hand to assist her out of the car, and she gave it without thought.

"Welcome, dear lady," he crooned at her, bending over her glove. "I was hoping you would take a walk with me about the grounds."

Hattie inclined her head and half-curtseyed – the social convention automatic in her movements. Turning away momentarily to straighten her skirt and make one final adjustment to her hat, she kept a wary eye on the master of the house, suspicious of this unusual greeting.

They began to walk down the drive toward the house as Bertram pulled away. Although their shoes were grinding noisily, the silence between them was by far louder. Hattie bent down to loosen a pebble that was stuck in her heel, and as she rose up again, her sleeve brushed against his, quite by accident. The touch seemed to awaken him out of his nervous reserve.

"A few weeks ago, I fear I did not make your friend feel welcome whilst he was in my home," he spoke in a deep, smooth, though hurried voice. "I shall make a better effort to do so in the future. Please accept my apologies."

"Um...yes," faltered Hattie, unable to place a finger on his motives.

"Any friend of yours is of course welcome at any time. He was a most interesting little chap, and I hope to see more of him whilst he remains in the neighborhood."

"Thank you," returned Hattie, still bewildered.

"I have been a most negligent host for these past weeks. I come into these fits of dark thoughts at times, and I cannot seem to shake them from myself. I have spoken of a similar time before – you remember?"

Hattie nodded her assent but made no reply. She had no wish to condone his behavior, but she also did not want to seem unfeeling, so she firmly pressed her lips together to avoid a rejoinder that might injure them both.

"Yet, I have determined within myself that these battles with my inner demons will no longer take possession of me. I must overcome them, and now seems as good a time as any to wage a war against these base feelings."

He had stopped at this juncture and had begun fingering a little, budding leaf upon a tree that lined the drive. Turning, he looked down into her face, and she rewarded his determination, openness, and humility with a tender and encouraging smile.

"I am certain you will be successful. A strong-minded, intelligent man like you has endless power to accomplish all he puts his mind to."

Seemingly bolstered by her little speech, they began walking together again. His step was lighter, and he seemed to leave the weight of his past behavior behind him. They turned to the gardens on the opposite side of the house where she had never ventured before. There was a small kitchen garden at the end of a long, grassy pathway.

The air was heavy with the heat of the bright, orange sun that shone upon them. They took their time walking between the rows of neat vegetables, listening to the busy hum of the lazy, summer bees. Hattie removed her gloves as she bent over to test the ripeness of a blackberry, and, pulling it easily from the vine, savored the juices as the little pockets of delicious sweetness broke within her mouth.

Soon, given their environment, they began a light discussion of husbandry. As a somewhat inane and passionless subject, it was the perfect segue into their usual scholarly banter, somehow.

As their exchange turned to more interesting subjects, she was reminded of his philosophical fascination. When he chose to, he could magically weave a captivating thread that could take them everywhere from mythology to music to metaphysics. Lost in the depth of their conversation, Hattie hardly noticed when another pebble that she'd unknowingly collected in her shoe began to make her heel smart. Working its way into a most uncomfortable position, she abruptly cried out in distress just at the peak of an intellectual mountain they had climbed together. She was forced at this juncture to hobble over to a nearby bench in a most ungainly fashion.

Embarrassed at her outcry and her unrefined gait, she felt even more disconcerted when he bent over her feet and began to remove first her shoe, then the errant pebble. He turned away at what must have been a most displeasing smell, and Hattie couldn't help but realize the ludicrousness of their situation. How could they fly to such great heights on the wings of ideology, then come crashing down to the mundane act of a malodorous foot and a pebble in her shoe? Her sense of the ridiculous bubbled over into a stifled burst of laughter.

He looked up, startled. For an uncomfortable few moments, he stared piercingly into her eyes as she attempted to repress her amusement. A wash of tenderness and longing overtook his features, and Hattie blushed, looking away embarrassedly as her giddiness calmed in his relentless gaze.

The master of the house quickly replaced her shoe and stood before her. Covering her small, trembling hand with his large, warm one, he assisted her from her seat with a gentle but firm pressure.

Somehow, her other hand found his, and he steadied her as she stood. As he gripped both of her palms in his, she felt almost forced by his very proximity to look up into his face.

In a deep, low, sweet voice, he related, "It is true that I have difficulty keeping the demons at bay. I am not familiar with the sound of laughter...but I do know that when I hear *you* laugh or when I look into your eyes, I feel...I feel..." he faltered.

Drawing her closer to him, Hattie felt one of his hands release hers as he encircled his arm about her waist. Her free hand drew up to her throat in an act of feminine protection. His face was inches from hers now, and she couldn't look away from his magnificent eyes.

Hattie couldn't recall ever seeing such thrilling passion in anyone's eyes before. Every ounce of her was trembling – almost frightened. His gaze shifted to her lips, and for one, horrifying yet elated moment, she thought he was going to kiss her.

Completely unconsciously, the thumb of her left hand began to rub over her fingers in the suspense of the moment. The movement must have shocked the master of the house back into reality as she watched his eyes focus on her hand. Relinquishing her from his grasp, he clasped her right hand in both of his, bent down, and kissed it so warmly, she almost wished he had pressed those lips to her own.

Without a word or a backward glance, he left her there in the garden – flushed, bewildered, and alone.

Chapter Twenty-Four

"You rea*lly* don't *un*derstand what I've been *through*!" cried Trixie, sobbing into a garish handkerchief. "The *a*trocities I've faced at the hands of that horri*ble* wo*man*!"

Hattie, Mrs. Bothell, Vamelda, and Trixie were all gathered around the table in the séance room. The weeping Trixie blew a very wet nose into her even wetter kerchief. Hattie noted the wide difference between the spurious sobs that this same young lady had affected at her funeral and this sincere lament, laced with unctuous bodily fluids.

"It all star*ted* when I *ar*rived in *New* York. I made my way to Ger*ald's* hotel. He was shocked to see me, of course, but he started *crying* right away. He knew he'd done me wrong, poor lamb. I don't *blame* him in any of this. He was just a sim*ple* boy who didn't know what *to* do with *him*self and all that mon*ey* and *a*ttention."

To her chagrin, Hattie also observed that Trixie's way of

emphasizing peculiar syllables had not left her during her travels.

The distressed young lady wrapped her furs around her comfortingly.

"It was that e*vil* wo*man* who got her claws stuck into him from the mo*ment* he *a*rrived. I still don't *under*stand what he could be do*ing* for his aunt that would in*volve* such a hor*rible* crea*ture*."

"There, there, dearie," consoled Vamelda, patting her hand. "Never mind all that. Just tell us what happened next."

"Well," the fractious woman continued between sobs, "It was like this. Ger*ald* was go*ing* to a din*ner* par*ty* that eve*ning*, and he rang up the host to say he'd be bring*ing* me *a*long. He was *su*pposed to meet Mrs. Car*ring*ton there, and I *wanted* him to meet her, alright. He promised to break things off and let her know, straight and true, that he was all-in for *me* and *not* for her."

"We *a*rrived, and she made for him right off. To think that *I* could be thrown over for *that kind* of woman! Nobody's disputing the fact that she *is* beautiful – if you like that obvious sort of beauty. I thought I was looking very fine myself, in my new gown, but she acted as though I wasn't even there! She took his face in her bony, little hands and laid one on him, right in front of me! I was hopping mad, I can tell you!"

As Trixie became more passionate whilst she retold these events, her attempt at affecting a superior accent all but disappeared.

"She tried to take Gerald's other arm and join the rest of the company, but I stood my ground and refused to let him move on with her. Mrs. Carrington broke away eventually and tried to laugh it off, but I could see by the look in her eye that she had it in for me. I've seen the same look from plenty of dames who've set their cap at Gerald since I landed him."

At this juncture, Hattie wanted to protest such casual language when speaking of the holy state of matrimony, but she remained silent for the sake of hearing the remainder of the tale.

"During the rest of the dinner party, Gerald only paid attention to *me*. He had gone back on his word once, and he wasn't going to do it again, he told me. Try as she might, that money-grubbing woman couldn't get him to give her a second glance. We did *try* to enjoy ourselves, but she was flirting with some duke or other until she made an utter spectacle of herself. Gerald became quite red in the face as he heard her go on."

"Serves him right, the two-timing cad!" interjected Mrs. Bothell, who was drinking in every word her daughter spoke with the gusto of a gossip columnist.

Trixie allowed herself a deep, shaking breath before continuing: "When we were about to leave, Gerald went to fetch my wrap. As he came back to me, *that woman* also walked out of the coatroom, bold as brass. I'd no idea that she'd sneaked in after Gerald. All evening, she'd been draping herself over that poor duke!"

"Your mascara, my dear," Vamelda gently nudged a fresh handkerchief into Trixie's hand.

"What? Oh! Yes." Trixie dabbed at her eyes.

Unfortunately, her attempts to wipe the black stuff from her face did more harm than good. It gave her the look of a buskin mask, rather than a tender maiden in distress.

"I was awfully worried that she'd snagged him again, but he came up and whispered, 'It's over,' as he slipped my wrap around me. By golly, I can tell you I *was* relieved! She looked daggers at me as she passed, but then went on flirting with the duke as though nothing had happened."

Trixie seemed to have been calmed momentarily with the thought of her beloved's stalwart manner, but then, an "Awowowowow!" made the other three ladies in the room jump as one. Trixie had let out another burst of mournful wails.

Despite Trixie's generally crass language and rough manner, Hattie was beginning to feel that this seemingly shallow young lady might actually have sincere feelings for her nephew.

"But then...but then..." Trixie went on, shivering all the while. "It was that night. I was all tucked up in my hotel room next to Gerald's when a knock came at the door. It was a present with a note that read, 'No hard feelings.' I opened the little box, and it was an expensive cold cream that I've been *dying* to get my hands on. It's made *only* in Paris, and I'd told Gerald that I planned to get some on our honeymoon, so I thought it was from him, but...but...just *look* at me!"

It was true that poor Trixie's face was not only covered in blackened trails of mascara, but also bloody pustules that made her look quite horrific. Reddened and sore, it looked as though she'd had quite an adverse reaction to the cream.

"I've always warned you that your vanity would get the better of you, Trixie!" her mother reprimanded.

"Oh, shut up!" Trixie spat back at her. "You were always hounding me about improving my complexion! I would never have touched the stuff if *you* hadn't told me my natural coloring was patchy!"

The women had both stood up and were looking at each other like two tigresses fighting over a carcass.

"Well, there's nothing to be done about it now," soothed Vamelda. "So you believe that it was the devious Mrs. Carrington who poisoned your face cream?"

"Of *course* it was! And Gerald's been blamed! Oh – I don't know *what's* to become of him. All I can think of is him rotting away in prison or destined for the hangman's noose, when really I know it was *her* who took revenge on me for stealing him back again!"

Hattie agreed with her nephew's former fiancé. First Mr. Carrington's poisoning...and now Trixie's face cream. It was too much of a coincidence to be dismissed.

As Trixie had used up all of the dry kerchiefs available to her, she began to dab at her eyes with the tablecloth.

She turned to Hattie and said remorsefully, "I'm ever so sorry, Ms. Vavaseur, that it turned out like this. I would have done everything I could to make your nephew happy if we'd been able to get married. He was a perfect lamb – I often told him so."

"And *you* led him to the slaughter!" shouted Mrs. Bothell, interrupting her daughter.

The women leveled looks at each other that could have killed, had they not both already been dead.

Hattie gently touched Trixie's elbow in a rush of sympathy after Mrs. Bothell's spiteful outburst.

"There, there, my dear. I'm certain you did your best. Gerald never *could* behave himself if some wolf, like this Mrs. Carrington, got their claws into him, and they *always* sniff him out. I don't exactly blame the wolves, either. He's such a foolish boy, with that sheepish face and docile manner you mentioned...the wolves simply can't help themselves."

As Trixie seemed somewhat mollified by this overture, Hattie went on, "There's nothing to blame yourself for one bit. Just you take yourself off with your mother here and try to forget everything that's happened. I do hope that someday, you can find happiness once again."

As the two Bothell women gathered their things, they argued and spat insults at each other all the way out of the shop, so Hattie had little faith that true happiness was in Trixie's foreseeable afterlife.

The two remaining ladies moved to the kitchen to discuss everything that had transpired.

"This confirms all of our fears, wouldn't you agree,

Vamelda?"

The medium nodded in concurrence as they settled in for their traditional cup of tea.

"Whatever am I going to say to Mr. Carrington? He won't be easy to convince, despite all of the evidence against her," Hattie deplored.

"I'm simply at a loss, my dear sugarplum," Vamelda returned. "I really haven't faced such *denial* before. Customarily, my murder victims know quite well who did them in and want me to deal out justice as though it was a tray of fairy cakes. That's simply *not* my line, I always tell them."

She paused thoughtfully, then went on: "If only I could speak with Mrs. Carrington in person, perhaps I could convince her that *a terrible calamity will come upon her if she does not confess.*"

During the last part of her sentence, Vamelda's voice had trailed off into the low moan that she used with clients, rather than the sprightly voice that she'd gradually fallen into the habit of using whenever Hattie was present.

"We *should* send someone to post bail for my nephew until the trial...and we'll need them to hire a good solicitor, as well. We must send someone trustworthy...and *soon.*"

Vamelda brightened up at the suggestion of sending someone to America. She was busily collecting her scarves about her and smoothing her hair while Hattie spoke on.

"If only we knew someone sensible..." Hattie became lost in thought.

Vamelda cleared her throat and continued patting her hair expectantly. When Hattie took no notice, she gave up the unspoken hints and oozed out of her chair. Kneeling by the kitchen fireplace, she began to rake up the coals. Soon, the flames were crackling merrily, and Vamelda roasted some cheese on toast. She offered a bit to Hattie, who absently picked at the sticky mess as she struggled vainly to work out a solution.

"Well," Vamelda said at last, hurt by the absence of an offer to travel to America, "Since you obviously *still* don't believe that I could be of any help, I *do* have someone in mind that I could possibly persuade."

"Excellent!" said Hattie, relieved.

She finally took a hearty bite of the repast, which suddenly seemed delicious as her worry over a solution was slightly mollified by Vamelda's suggestion.

"I'm not certain you'll like her, however," Vamelda said, a hint of unease in her voice as she absently selected a stray string of melted cheese from her lip and fed it to the cat, who was curled up on the hearthrug. "You can be so picky, at times. Even *I* had the feeling that you didn't like me during our first few meetings...but that's quite impossible, isn't it, my dear sugarplum?"

Hattie tucked the last little morsel of toast into her mouth to avoid a smile.

Chapter Twenty-Five

Hattie coughed somewhat dramatically. Behind a cloud of murky smoke, cigarette after cigarette was lit, sucked, then extinguished much too quickly. Hattie looked at the guest from toe to top. A pair of neatly polished Oxfords peeked out from beneath well-tailored, pinstriped pants. Next came a matching suit coat and vest that were both a bit broader across the chest than they strictly should be. Lastly, a sharp-jawed face that was hidden partially by a swankily-tipped fedora completed the look of the newcomer. A knot of curly hair tied at the base of the neck and the full, feminine mouth were Hattie's only clues that this friend of Vamelda's was, indeed, a woman.

"No need to look so shocked, old dame," said the personage behind the blanket of vapor. "*I'm* the one who can see ghosts. I could be looking at you with every bit as much disgust as you are at me."

Hattie unsuccessfully attempted to soften the expression of consternation that she could feel had formed upon her features. She even tried a little half-smile of polite welcome.

"That's better, m'dear," said the lady. "At least you gave it a good old try. That's more than most."

They were in the outer room of Vamelda's shop, and the woman began shoving knicknacks aside, helter-skelter, so she could drape her arm more comfortably over the mantlepiece.

"I usually won't even try to help spooks. Luckily for you, Vamelda here uses her powers for good. I mostly just try to avoid you lot," said the woman, lighting another cigarette.

"That's perfectly ridiculous, dear. You've helped me so many times," contended Vamelda.

"Only because *you* helped get *me* out of that asylum. My family already thought I was crazy for dressing like this," she said to Hattie, with a sweep of her hand across her manly suit. "Top that off with a steady stream of ghosts and talking to people nobody else can see, and you've got a certifiable loonie on your hands."

"Nonsense, darling. It was a simple matter of pulling a few strings and hosting a handful of séances with the right people. If only you would come over to my way of thinking, you could be my assistant or set up your own practice! You merely have to play to peoples' pre-conceived *notions* about communicating with the dead, rather than just speaking to them rudely and outright, as you've been known to do."

This was the clearest Hattie had ever heard Vamelda

speak. The medium's voice, filled with practicality and sense, was not ethereal nor musical, as was her wont with individuals other than Hattie. She even detected the slightest hint of Cockney that had previously never appeared before during their sessions. Hattie suspected that the no-nonsense attitude of this newcomer was the reason.

"Now, Vamelda," the woman said, "You know I'll have no truck with you and your wispy ways. It's not straight shooting, and I don't like a bit of it. I know your heart's in the right place – most of the people you help can't even pay you since they're dead, but I simply cannot pretend to be someone I'm not."

Hattie cleared her throat. From the look of consternation on Vamelda's face, Hattie feared that the conversation was about to become heated and uncomfortable between the medium and her guest.

"Aren't you going to introduce me to your *interesting* friend?" Hattie tried very hard not to emphasize the word "interesting," but years of strait-laced British decorum made it a herculean task.

"Syd," responded the woman.

"Florence Sydbury," interjected Vamelda nervously, throwing a glance between the two ladies.

"Ugh! Don't use my full name. It reminds me too much of the institution! I've always been Syd since I was a little girl. Besides, how could they expect me not to want the freedom of a man when they always treated me like a boy, anyhow?"

"I shall call you Miss Sydbury," said Hattie forcefully.

Syd looked her over appraisingly, "I'll settle for Miss Syd if you'd like," she rejoined. "But only because I've taken a fancy to you. I quite like your long hair and the brazen way you let it blow about during car rides."

Hattie was astonished. She had believed that no one had been able to see her brief, exultant break from convention.

Reddening, she had a feisty retort on her lips when Vamelda interrupted the two with a raspy, "Now, now."

Standing, Vamelda tucked her scarves away as she moved between them, as though the act would cut through the tension.

"Let's not get into an argument before we've had the chance to become properly acquainted, my dearest darlings," she mollified. "Hattie, I truly believe that Syd can help your nephew in his sad predicament. She's remarkably clever, and, like me, can communicate with the dead, as you see."

Syd began to fiddle with an Egyptian curio as she said, "I'm not like Vamelda, you know. I won't do things without proper compensation."

"As you see, she also has the advantage of being deliciously level-headed," interrupted Vamelda, attempting to ameliorate her friend's brusque, if honest, behavior for Hattie's benefit. "What do you say?"

Hattie eyed the newcomer suspiciously. She still did not like the way the woman was dressed or her abrupt manner, but she was desperate. Her nephew was being held for a murder she knew he didn't commit – she had little other recourse.

Vacillating momentarily on how to respond, Hattie settled on reserved politeness: "Vamelda and I would be very grateful for your assistance in this matter, Miss *Syd*." She emphasized the sobriquet with obvious disdain. "We *can* offer you some generous compensation. My nephew is quite the foolish little believer in Vamelda's methods, so I'm certain we could settle on something that would accommodate your needs once he is free."

"I'd be very grateful, Hattie," Syd returned roughly. "Money is hard to come by when your family practically disowns you, so I'd appreciate the help. I get little enough from shooting competitions. You know, England would have won the 1920 Olympics in marksmanship if only they'd let women compete."

Once again, Hattie tried not to look appalled, especially as the woman extracted a neat, little revolver from her waistcoat. With a flick of the wrist, she detached and spun the cylinder, feigned an aim at some distant mark, and then placed it back in her vest, all before Hattie was able to blink.

"This job, then. What, exactly, do you have in mind?" said the markswoman.

"Well, it might prove very dangerous," said Hattie, once she was able to catch her breath.

"As you can see, I am prepared for a bit of danger. Would love it, in fact. Life in the Cotswolds has gotten a bit tiresome. I was thinking that a trip to London would slake my lust for adventure, but America will be just the ticket," she smiled broadly, and her heretofore hazy eyes gave just a hint of a sparkle.

Squaring her shoulders as though a soldier in full uniform reporting for military duty, she faced Hattie. "Just what would I be up against? What do you need me to do?"

Taking it in turns, Hattie and Vamelda explained the entire situation, from beginning to end. Syd took it all in stride. Her only emotional reaction seemed to be during the most distressing points in the story, when she would light yet another cigarette although a halfway-smoked one was still upon her lips.

"Any details you can gather about Mrs. Carrington's past or her motivations would be greatly appreciated," concluded Hattie. "You'll need to ingratiate yourself with her crowd. From what I know of human nature, you should be somewhat of a novelty, so you may be able to play that to your advantage in these American, high-society circles. I hope I have not offended you by saying so?"

"Not at all. It's a pleasure to have my eccentricities touted as advantageous. Go on," Syd replied, mirroring Hattie's businesslike manner of speaking with just a hint of amusement.

"Good. That's settled, then," said Hattie, nodding with satisfaction at Syd's logical view of the matter and choosing to ignore the sly smile that played upon the newcomer's lips. "You fully comprehend what is needed by way of my own strange situation, as well?"

"Indeed. You have my deepest sympathies. Extreme lapse of memory is something I've never come across before...with the exception of one person, of course."

Hattie's curiosity piqued, she turned to Vamelda in excitement.

The medium seemed to be preoccupied as her eyes intently followed the pathway of a spider crawling skittishly across the floor. Just as Hattie was about to draw breath in further query, she perceived Vamelda ever so slightly shake her head at their guest.

Frustrated by this action, yet determined to pursue the subject, Hattie barreled on: "I recall that you hinted as much to me when we first spoke about my memory loss."

Vamelda made no response. Turning to Syd for some confirmation of this disclosure, Hattie found the adventuress seemingly enraptured with the gilded emblem that was inscribed upon her box of matches.

Exasperated at this unified wall of silence, Hattie refused to be repressed.

"I can see that you're reluctant to divulge further information on the subject. Vamelda, don't you think that this would be the time to speak of such things? Perhaps this parallel situation Syd mentioned could bear some light!"

"Oh, my dear. You quite mistake Syd!" fluttered Vamelda. "She was merely speaking of the *general* memory loss that occurs to all that have passed onto the other side. Some cases are more severe than others, but of course, everyone is so unique, it wouldn't be fair to compare various conditions!"

Standing, Vamelda made quite a little show of straightening a few books on the shelves, handing one or two to Syd as she did so. Exasperated, Hattie scoffed at the pair of them.

"Come now, Vamelda. You can't expect me to believe such nonsense when Miss Syd has just said..."

Hattie looked earnestly at the woman's face, hoping to elicit some acknowledgment of her previous statement.

Syd turned away from her and began to closely scrutinize a large tome that Vamelda had placed in her hand. Having examined the same volume herself, Hattie knew that Syd was only feigning interest, as the woman was perusing the Arabic writing from left to right.

"Very well," sighed Hattie, extremely dissatisfied with their mutual response. "Keep your mysteries to yourselves."

Internally, however, she resolved to have the truth of the matter sooner or later.

Chapter Twenty-Six

Syd sailed on *The Knight's Wonder* the very next day. It was difficult to book a first-class passage on such short notice, but a little hint of wealth and family proved to do wonders. Syd's family was well-connected, and her surname still carried some weight, albeit Syd herself was no longer considered a member of the family – a fact, she told Vamelda, that she took pains to conceal in this instance.

Hattie was nervous for the woman...she felt her own fate really lay in this stranger's hands. Syd assured Hattie that she would do all in her power to save Gerald and bring the true culprit to justice, whether it proved to be Mrs. Carrington or not. All Hattie could do was wait.

In the interim, whilst expecting Syd to land in America and send news, she very pleasantly spent her afternoons in the company of the master of the house, and, frequently, Mr. Carrington. The little salesman had at first been very concerned with this new murder, but still refused to believe that his beloved wife could have anything to do with such dastardly and, in his mind, unwomanly deeds. The subject was rarely touched upon from that moment forward, although whenever in his company, the back of her mind was always clouded with concern and sympathy for this poor, gullible man.

However, his stories were quite a pleasant distraction for both Hattie and her host. The little man regaled them with tales of his travels – interesting people he met...curious accidents that befell him....kind strangers along the way. Hattie was utterly fascinated by him. Living, as far as she could remember, a very narrow kind of existence, each story became a full and wondrous chapter in her imagination. His loud, yellow-checked suit became a token of adventure whenever she saw it crossing the lawn to knock on the breakfast room doors.

Sometimes, his familiarity even led to his abandonment of niceties, and he would climb in through the low windows at the front of the house – a feat unappreciated by Hattie's host. Each time Mr. Carrington sauntered in that way, a dark furrow would cross the master's brow, but it would soon conscientiously clear if ever he caught Hattie looking at him with a firm, if slight, degree of consternation.

A complete transformation had taken place within the master of the house – particularly his behavior toward Hattie. He took pains to make her comfortable. He was solicitous of her tastes in food, her need for a shawl in chilly weather, and, especially, her selections in reading.

Mr. Carrington was indeed charming and fascinating, but to the master of the house, she felt a profound, exceptional pull. He rarely made her laugh, as Mr. Carrington did nearly every day. However, there was something sincere about the master of the house that almost explained his gruffness upon their first few encounters. She knew now that he was privately suffering under some great sorrow, which, like an animal, made him fiercely protective of its open wounds, lashing out whenever someone came near.

Hattie understood this kind of pain. She'd experienced much of it in her life, but women are trained to pass through trials differently than men. She did not condone nor excuse his behavior, but rather attributed it to the breakdown of society where the sexes were concerned. A good woman has often attempted to remedy this black, gaping hole, but womankind should certainly not be the sole antidote to this all-encompassing illness.

Often sighing when these thoughts came upon her, Hattie sincerely wished that he had been different upon their first acquaintance. A myriad of barriers that even now kept them from expressing their innermost thoughts could have been avoided – for Hattie had begun to hope that there was something more than friendship springing up between them.

It was absurd, of course, at her age. Whether it was the loneliness of her life or the ludicrousness of her situation, she did not know, but the sentiment that had begun to blossom within her, she found disturbing. Not only was she entirely uncertain of his return of these feelings, but she felt foolish – out of control. Society dictated that it was the man who must display his desires first. Woman's sole power lay in the acceptance or denial of such overtures. Although Hattie's logic rebelled against this primitive, patriarchal practice, she nonetheless bowed to it as a matter of course. It was merely the way things had always been, and she could see no path past the custom. She nonetheless could not help but acknowledge that her soul gravitated to him as her thoughts did to the orb hidden in her room, which, incidentally, remained as blank as Hattie's memory.

When the master of the house left her breathless with his lips nearing hers, she had not known the depth of her affections as yet. Gradually, in the days that passed and with his unveiling and winning personality, she had let her heart be undone little by little until she knew it was his.

However, despite his renewed friendliness, she could detect no further romantic inclination on his part. It must have been loneliness or a burst of extraneous feeling that had led him almost to kiss her, for since then, he had made no attempt at an embrace – passionate or otherwise.

Always a gentleman, their interactions had been continuously pleasant, yet strictly platonic. His solicitousness of her comfort could lead him indeed to fetch a shawl for her, but never to place it upon her. It would compel him to walk with her in the garden, but never to lend her his arm. Mentally, he was warm and interested. Physically, he was stiff and distant.

Yet Hattie could not dismiss her growing affection. Just as she studied the orb for visions every night, she studied his face each day to determine some magic within.

Neither canvas was opened to her.

There was only one thing to be done, then...but did she have the strength to do it?

Hattie had been in the library – often her favorite haunt on any given afternoon that was not taken up by Vamelda or Mr. Carrington. The rain drizzled outside as though the angels of the heavens were lazily dripping water from their fingertips...as if they did not entertain enough celestial fervor to punish the earth with an outright downpour.

A book was lying unread in Hattie's lap. Absently, she traced an embossed illustration of a medieval dragon with the tip of her finger. Weaving in and out of the strange undulations of the drawing, she pondered all of these thoughts, particularly dwelling on the question as to why the orb would no longer provide her with visions.

Lost in a brown study, she didn't hear the master of the house enter the room, but she was not at all startled when she saw his strong, firm hand rest on the edge of the chair in which she was sitting.

"Are you contemplating the moral dignity of the scullery maid or the quality of your luncheon repast?" he inquired, looking down at her with a slight twinkle in his eye. "I've found that the secret lives of servants and the state of my stomach are the only two things really worth a solid, studious think."

"Nothing quite so pleasant – I assure you," returned Hattie. "Although I shall be sure to file that away in my memory for future reflection."

She longed to continue their banter, but she had come to a resolve. It was going to be difficult, and she wasn't quite sure of his reaction, so she had undertaken to execute it with determination as quickly as possible.

Clearing her throat as more of a hesitation than for the tonicity of her vocal cords, she began, "Sir, I truly appreciate your generous accommodations in these peculiar circumstances."

Catching her formal attitude and playing along with just a hint of a smile, he responded, "My dear lady, it has been a surprising pleasure. I..."

Hattie cleared her throat again, cutting off what she assumed was to be a rambling of polite banalities. Wrapped up in the seriousness of her task, his nuanced flirtation was lost on her.

"However, I have been an inconvenience to you for long enough."

She now glanced up into his face and thought she read an odd mixture of fear and relief. The memory of their near kiss made her falter momentarily, curious about his innermost thoughts.

Hattie was about to continue, but a further study of his countenance revealed that he looked even less careworn than on that near-fateful afternoon. Many more lines of his face had been smoothed, as though by a painter's brush – particularly the scowl that usually lived in a state of constancy between his brows. These slight changes had come upon him gradually, but today, they looked even more pronounced. Slightly preoccupied with this transformation, she endeavored, with difficulty, to continue.

"I intend to take full possession of the house as soon as it is beneficial for you to vacate it," she finished hurriedly after the pause.

A shadow of the scowl returned at her words.

"Very well. I shall have Harold look for new accommodation immediately."

He looked slightly troubled as he spoke the words, but she pressed on, eager to suitably conclude the details before her own emotions beset her. If he wished to sell her the house and move onto whatever plane of existence he desired, now was the moment. She could at last begin a new life...well, *after*life...free of distractions. Free of his moods. Free of his soulful eyes. Free of the anticipation of that kiss...

Hattie found herself examining his mouth distractedly, so she straightened herself up, shaking her head a little as she did so. He had been pouring out a stream of conventional details about the arrangements that would need to take place for the transaction to occur.

"Whatever you desire, of course," she responded haltingly, quite unsure of his meaning and distracted by her own thoughts.

"Thank you," he said, covering her hand with his. "I hope this will be a happy home for you."

It was the first time they had touched since that nearly wonderful moment in the garden. Hattie, a little breathless with the mental and spiritual struggle in her soul, arose, and the book in her lap fell to the floor. It splayed open to a chapter of Shakespearean excerpts.

Bending over, he picked it up, and, glancing at the title, he read out Sonnet 29 before handing it over to her:

"When, in disgrace with fortune and men's eyes,
I all alone beweep my outcast state
And trouble deaf heaven with my bootless cries
And look upon myself and curse my fate,
Wishing me like to one more rich in hope,
Featured like him, like him with friends possess'd,
Desiring this man's art and that man's scope,
With what I most enjoy contented least;
Yet in these thoughts myself almost despising,
Haply I think on thee, and then my state,
Like to the lark at break of day arising
From sullen earth, sings hymns at heaven's gate;
For thy sweet love remember'd such wealth brings
That then I scorn to change my state with kings."

Blushing over the contents, she quickly took and shut the book.

Pondering for a moment, he said, "I've often thought my own situation relates perfectly to that particular sonnet, although I don't have the luxury of a 'sweet love.' If I had, however, I am confident that I would not then, 'change my state with kings.'"

Her cheeks burned even deeper with the knowledge that she, too, had been thinking of the master of the house whilst he read it aloud. Embarrassed by the connection and determined to keep her thundering heart in check, she nodded to him curtly and bade him good-night, leaving him to ponder her news and his feel-ings...whatever they might be.

Chapter Twenty-Seven

Hattie was wandering through a darkened shadowland. Her feet were bare and pale on the soft, pine-needle-strewn path of rich dirt beneath her. She could not feel the prick of the needles, only delicate touches of the soft, springy earth. Almost floating, each step was a leap of a hundred feet before she touched down once more. Through the mist, she heard a voice calling to her from far down the deep, forest path. Batting away at the fog that began to engulf her, she tried to catch the voice with her hands, knowing it had taken physical form in a bright, glowing orb. Through the greyness that surrounded and almost oppressed her, the light waxed luminescent and more distinct with each bound. Warmth and shining brightness began to envelop her, lifting her soul, until she was nearly blind with the lustrous radiance of the object. She was reaching out to grasp it, the voice becoming more distinct as each finger stretched to its zenith...

"Wake up! Wake up! *Will* you wake up? Why is it that the

dead are always so much more difficult to rouse than the living?"

Vamelda's voice entered Hattie's dreams. Hattie awakened, feeling groggy and muddled.

"What is it?" she yawned grumpily.

Rubbing her eyes like a small child and leaning up a bit, she realized that Vamelda was sitting on her bed, hovering over her. The medium's owl eyes were wide, supplicating, and full of an almost tangible fear.

"We must be quick! Teddy sneaked me in at the back. The master of the house isn't terribly keen on me, darling."

Teddy, who was standing behind the medium, lazily biting his fingernails, touched his cap, and winked at her.

"Why didn't *you* send for *me*, then?" queried Hattie, her wits gathering at last.

"There wasn't time!" Vamelda said, breathlessly. "Something's happened."

Hattie sat up, and, taking Vamelda by the shoulders, pushed her gently but firmly off of the bed.

"We cannot know...I do hope nothing serious...but it *must* be if she's flitting," continued Vamelda, only slightly more erratic and incoherent than usual.

However, Hattie intuitively knew that something truly was amiss.

"Good heavens, woman. Tell me what it is!" she cried.

"It's dear, sweet Syd," responded Vamelda.

Hattie thought that any word but "sweet" would describe Syd, but she let it pass, more interested in the tidings Vamelda had come to share.

"Go on," Hattie encouraged.

"We've had a telegram. The poor, dear sugarplum...I just *know* she's in trouble."

The abrupt, "*Cough, cough,*" of a voice interrupted them. Hattie looked around the room. The cough was far too deep to come from little Teddy, and she had been looking at Vamelda when she heard the sound, so it could not have been her. As Hattie surveyed the room, however, she could discover no fourth personage. Disconcerted, she looked quizzically back at Vamelda, but Hattie's look was lost on the woman. The clairvoyant was completely and distractedly wrapped up within her own world in a paroxysm of distress. Hattie, eager to learn more of Vamelda's worry, dismissed the sound as one of those household noises one sometimes hears.

"Well, tell me what the telegram said, then, if it was so important!" Hattie ordered.

"I can't imagine what she's doing. There must be something...some transitioning period, otherwise..."

"*What did the telegram say?*" demanded Hattie stringently.

Vamelda, who had been worrying the rosy fringe on the bedstead, looked up with a more than usually vacant expression on her pinched face.

"What? Oh...I have it here, somewhere."

Rifling through her heavy shawls and endless scarves, Vamelda eventually pulled out, from unbeknownst whereabouts, a crumpled, yellow, stiff paper. Hattie caught it up immediately and began to smooth the folds.

Just as she was about to read it aloud, once again, a mysterious, "*Cough, cough*," was heard from the recesses of the boudoir. Hattie was less inclined to dismiss it as the groanings of an old house and immediately straightened to full attention.

"Vamelda! Teddy!" Hattie hissed, "We are not alone in here."

She raised her voice, "Hello?"

The closet door of the artificial rose-festooned wardrobe creaked open.

"I apologize," said a smiling Mr. Carrington as he mincingly stepped out of the wardrobe. "I seem to have lost my way through this wandering house."

"And you ended up in *my* wardrobe while I was *sleeping*?" she challenged.

Hattie and Mr. Carrington stared at each other, a flash of bad temper caught between them. After some minutes of silence, the latter turned away momentarily, coughing into a handkerchief. When he faced Hattie once again, he seemed to have recovered himself.

"Rather a fascinating contraption, that," he said, swinging the door of the wardrobe open wider. "You see, it's a portal to this adjoining bedroom. I found myself lost, and, mistaking the door on the other side for an exit, I stepped through. My wife, Lydia, had a similar one installed in our home. Very convenient between husband and wife. As I was coming through, I heard the dulcet tones of our talented medium, Vamelda."

He bowed politely in her direction, "When I realized my mistake, I did not wish to disturb you, so I was going back from whence I came, but I, unfortunately, inhaled an overpowering cloud of dust as I brushed against some old suits, coughing as I did so. The scent of mothballs is quite strong, you see," he finished, brushing himself off histrionically.

Hattie thought that there was something a bit different about Mr. Carrington's manner this morning. Whether it was his embarrassment at being caught in exploring the house or something quite apart from that, Hattie could not tell. The little man was always polite and affable, but he seemed to be reigning himself in today...or was it the opposite? Either way, Hattie didn't entirely believe his story.

She vaguely wondered if his behavior pointed to a romantic interest in herself. After all, the man sought her company nearly every day. True, this venture through an adjoining room was not a very gentlemanly way of going about courting, but allowances were often made in her day for Americans. Still....Hattie did not quite like it.

As though waiting for the moment when all of the adults were distracted, Teddy took this opportunity to lift the bottom of Hattie's bed covers and release what looked like a wriggling salamander into the depths of the bedclothes. Hattie caught what had transpired out of the corner of her eye. Although she had not much experience with children, she resolved not to react when she felt the slimy thing touch her bare leg. Instead, she reached down to prevent it from exploring any further up her nightgown, grasped it around the belly, then calmly handed it back to the culprit in question. Mouth agape, apparently at the lack of entertainment he had anticipated, he hurriedly stuffed it down his trouser pocket.

Without even acknowledging Mr. Carrington's presence or the scene enacted with the rapscallion Teddy, Vamelda stood up and bent over Hattie, demanding her attention.

In a strangled voice, she said, "This is *important*, Hattie Vavaseur! Syd is *flitting!*"

"Oh, dear!" said Mr. Carrington with a horrified air.

"What on earth do you mean, Vamelda?" asked Hattie, taking the woman by her arms and shaking her slightly.

The tone of the medium, rather than their male interloper or the juvenile truant, was what concerned her now. Vamelda's icy blue eyes brimmed with tears, altering them to the purest lavender.

"There must be something horribly wrong. I keep seeing Syd! Here! In England! There's been a terrible accident. She fell onto the subway tracks...she thinks she may have even been *pushed*. She *says* she's making a recovery, but then *why* do I keep seeing the dear thing?"

Hattie looked down at the paper before her with trembling hands.

Telegram from Florence Sydbury to Vamelda Anstruthers

August 23, 1927

Hot on trail. *Stop.* Discovered a name connected with Ms. Vavaseur. *Stop.* Reggie. *Stop.* Was on my way to appointment with Mrs. C. when pushed onto subway tracks. *Stop.* Scrambled up just in time. *Stop.* Broken leg, but recovering well, so not to worry. *Stop.* - *Syd*

As if by magic, the shadowy figure of Syd's face appeared opposite Vamelda's worried countenance.

"Hullo, old thing," it said.

"Syd! What on this very earth, darling?" Vamelda replied.

Hattie was in complete astonishment at this apparition and remained speechless, falling back upon her pillows.

"Or rather," continued Vamelda, "I supposed you might not be on earth if I can see you! But I suppose even the dead are really still upon the earth, just not in the same realm. I..."

"*Vamelda, dear!*" the disembodied head continued, becoming more clear. "I simply haven't got time for this! I have no intention of hanging about while you ramble on with every thought that pours out of that wooly head of yours! Listen to me. I've got something to tell you."

The apparition flitted in and out of focus for a moment,

and Syd's voice crackled like a poor radio recording.

"I...it's...my hotel room...smoke..." there was some rattled coughing, and Syd's face disappeared for a moment.

"Syd? *Syd!*" cried Vamelda.

She reappeared.

"Don't let them fool you!" she cried, obviously distressed now, abandoning her usual, careless manner. "You've been duped!"

The spectre flitted out again, then back.

"It's HIM. *They* did this to me! Warn Hattie," she was weakening. "It's Lydia. *Don't trust that man.*"

And then she was gone.

Slowly, Vamelda, Teddy, and Hattie all turned their heads toward Mr. Carrington.

Flushed and visibly angry, he spluttered a bit, and then said, "You couldn't think...there's no possible way...there are *so* many Lydias in the world."

For a moment, Hattie suspected Mr. Carrington of coming off as rather disingenuous, and she puzzled over it briefly. However, it soon passed as she justified this feeling with the idea that he was beginning to come round to the possibility that his wife wasn't the pure, noble creature he'd believed her to be.

She shrugged off her doubts as she said, firmly, "Mr. Carrington, you *must* come to terms with the fact that it's entirely feasible that your wife is perfectly capable of doing grievous harm to those that get in her way.

Syd went over to America and made an appointment to speak with her. Your wife, guilty with the knowledge that she murdered you *and* Miss Bothell, made arrangements to be rid of her."

Mr. Carrington's face momentarily contorted with rage, and he turned from the six eyes that were so earnestly studying him. Teddy soon sauntered over and touched him on the arm.

"It's alroight, sir! Don't be too troubled in your 'eart about it. Alluvus 'as 'ad loved ones 'oov disappointed 'us. Me own father used ta get right riled up at me and gimme a lickin' when he was in his drink."

The salesman's back stiffened for a moment, but then he looked down into the boy's innocent face. He put a small, plump hand on Teddy's head, rifling his hair a bit.

"Thank you, m'boy," he said and sighed.

Vamelda began violently sobbing and wailing.

"They all get wots comin' to 'em in the end," Teddy continued. "Me pap died o' the drink a few years atter me. I still goes and visits 'him sometimes. He can't leave the ditch 'ee died in, you know. He still tries to take a snatch at me when he's in a foul mood, but I keeps me distance. I 'xpect it'll be the same for your missus. She won't be h'able to getcha, once she passes ova."

Mr. Carrington sighed and looked at the two women. A small smile crept across his face for a moment, and he shrugged his shoulders as if to say, *I don't like it, but you've convinced me at last.*

Silently, he and the boy left the room – Mr. Carrington's arm draped over Teddy's small shoulders while Teddy, ever the rascal, silently transferred the errant lizard from his own pocket to his companion's.

While Hattie dressed behind a screen, she and Vamelda spoke of what had passed. Hattie allowed herself a small smile when she heard a faint cry from down the hallway and knew that Teddy's wriggling pet had caught the attention of Mr. Carrington.

"What do you think of this 'Reggie' Syd mentioned?" questioned Vamelda musingly as she waited for her friend.

"I'm more concerned about the man she told us not to trust." Hattie said, frowning.

"Well, at least we know it cannot be Mr. Carrington. If he was very wicked during life, he would be confined to the space where he passed," Vamelda informed her.

"I'd gathered that from Teddy's stories about his father," said Hattie defensively, her forehead moodily creasing a little between her brows.

"Perhaps this 'Reggie' could be your long, lost fiancé that we read about in the newspaper!" continued Vamelda dreamily.

This, too, had entered Hattie's mind, but then she guiltily recalled Syd's more pressing troubles. Wrapping up the wrath she felt toward herself, she unleashed it upon her friend.

"Vamelda! We have a *much* more essential dilemma to

think of! Besides, this 'Reggie' could have been anyone...a lawyer, a distant relative, or even a *shoemaker*, for all we know!" she waxed furious in her projected self-loathing. "What should we do about *Syd*?"

"Oh, I wouldn't worry about that. I have a feeling just here," Vamelda pointed to her abdomen, "that she'll be quite alright now that she's spoken to us. I'm certain she'll telegram to us as soon as ever she can."

"Only moments ago, you seemed quite at the end of your rope, Vamelda!"

Hattie felt a mixture of exasperation and relief.

"Yeeeeaaas," said the clairvoyant, stretching out upon Hattie's bed and giving a great yawn. "It's something we mediums get a feeling for, you know. Syd *was* in danger, and I *was* quite distressed there for a moment – I have only ever *heard* of flittings, you know. It was quite a distressing thing to *experience* one. I shall have to see if I can use that in my practice somehow..."

Vamelda trailed off, quite possibly dreaming of inventive ways to coax coins from her patrons with this new knowledge.

Coming to herself, she said, "Don't worry, my dear sugarplum. I *know* Syd is going to be ab-so-lute-ly fine."

Hattie fiddled with her final button and came around from the screen. Seeing Vamelda's recumbent posture, combined with the fact that the medium was once again using her customary, honey-sweet sobriquets, settled Hattie's fears.

"Well, you're the expert in these matters, I suppose," Hattie said, reluctant in the admission. "What are we to do now?"

"Oh, we shall carry on," Vamelda said, waving a wispy hand lazily in the air above her.

Hattie, although rattled from their experience, nevertheless felt compelled to do just that.

Chapter Twenty-Eight

For the next few weeks, the back of Hattie's mind prickled with the anticipation of any news from America. However, she did, for once, follow Vamelda's advice and thoroughly occupied herself in the interim. Most days were spent closeted with Harold, the butler, as they began making arrangements for her to take possession of the manor.

As Hattie would be forced to stay close to the house for the foreseeable future, she reasoned that she might as well make the best of it and begin making adjustments to her liking. She intended to divest the entire house of the select pieces that had so disgusted her when she first came. All of the antlers and stuffed game must go first, followed by the large-scale, heavy, plain wooden furniture that she could easily do without. The rose-colored room – her own room – would, of course, be completely stripped. She'd discovered some old, green damask hangings and bedding up in the attic that were still in very good condition. They were just to her taste, and she ordered them to be beaten and washed. Eventually, they would be hung in her room.

Harold proved to be a most intuitive and pleasant companion for such matters. She found herself speaking freely to him, and his responses, though always respectful, were friendly and invaluable.

One day, they were clearing out the library. The master of the house had made his selection of various precious titles and left the rest to be sorted through by her. Harold, eager to dust this section of the manor that had been, at the master's insistence, neglected for years, was ready enough to assist Hattie in her endeavor.

During their times together, a question began to grow in Hattie's mind. This man – the master of the house - who was he? She yearned to discover his identity – if only to whisper his name to herself, alone, under the cover of darkness and seclusion in her room. Heretofore, she had never been brave enough to confess that she was not in possession of this simple fact, but the time had come when she felt sorely pressed to learn and then to bask in the comforting connection of his name upon her lips.

Deciding not to waste this comfortable opportunity to make inquiries of the helpful butler, she began, rather haltingly in her nervousness, to broach the subject, "Tell me, Harold: You're aware of our...unique circumstances?"

"Of course, madam," Harold responded, ever politeness itself. "The fact that we have passed on to...shall we say...another frame of existence?" he intuitively concluded.

"Yes, thank you, Harold." Hattie was excessively relieved. "Why do you, then, continue in this servitude, if I may ask?"

She did not want to imply that this afterlife was some form of punishment, but she was curious about the inner workings of what determined his unusual fate.

"The master was very good to me during my lifetime. A select few of us volunteered to help him. He has been unable to...accept our current fate and...and move on from Life. Bertram, Teddy, and a few others banded together to attempt to assist him, but our efforts have so far proved fruitless. We did try to reason with him, but he refused to accept the truth of his death. We were especially afraid after an incident with a particular orb."

Harold broke off abruptly, blushing at his own effusiveness. Hattie sensed this and came to the realization that there should be no social barriers in this afterlife. His embarrassment at addressing a supposed superior so freely and at such length was merely a force of habit.

"When he tried to smash the orb and end his existence, you mean?" encouraged Hattie.

Harold visibly started at her nonchalant statement of the facts.

"Yes – I am shocked that you learned of this, madam," Harold said, the surprise fully apparent in his voice and manner.

"Your master told me of it several months ago," she said.

"That is very interesting indeed, madam," he said, mulling over her statement for a moment.

"Well, you must understand that ever since then, we've been reluctant to reintroduce the subject. We hoped that he would come to terms in his own time," he concluded.

"Perhaps this selling of the house will be just what he needs to help him evolve into a more rational state of mind," said Hattie logically.

"Yes, hopefully, madam. We are all quite unsure about where he came up with this scheme of selling the house, but we are indeed very hopeful that it means he is preparing himself to *move on*."

"I certainly hope the best for him – for all of you," said Hattie pleasantly.

"Thank you, madam," Harold said, once again stiffening to his usual, slightly obsequious attitude.

"I expect you should call me Hattie," she said, reaching over to shake his hand warmly. "At least, when we're not in front of your master."

Harold returned her pleasantness with a wavering grin.

"It's so pleasant to have another comrade in arms, so to speak. As he confides in you so freely, perhaps you can have an influence over him that none of us have been able to achieve."

She smiled a little, thinking of her interactions with the master – their spirited conversations, their brief near-caress...

Harold continued, "When the master first came to the house, he was merely depressed, but then as time went on, his sadness turned into frustration, and frustration to rage. He began to hate this house and everything about it. He began to make alterations that baffled us."

"Such as?" encouraged Hattie.

"Well, for example, the door was originally a very nice shade of green. In a fit of frenzy, he had it painted white. I cannot tell you how many coats of paint it took to block out that shade. Since then, he has grown listless with the upkeep of the manor, and it has unfortunately begun to decay. Then, there was your..." a slight pause, "...the room you've been staying in, madam. He had it all redone in pink. Simply awful, we thought it was and curious that he took such an interest in that particular room, but he insisted on every shade of green from this house being taken away."

"How very curious, indeed," said Hattie.

Internally, she considered her own aversion to pink and vaguely wondered how people came to these inexplicable quirks of character. In her moments of self-reflection, she knew that she had avoided the color, particularly out of rebellion against her Aunt Mathilde, whose favorite shade was a sickly rouge. The hue often reminded her of the horrible abuses she suffered at the hands of her aunt and uncle. Never physical, of course, but emotional – pressing her almost to the point of insanity.

Hattie knew that continuing the antipathy into adulthood was foolish, but she simply couldn't seem to overcome it. She had often tried to plant the occasional hollyhock or primrose in her flower garden, but she would always pull it up in a fierce fury a day or two after it had blossomed. Each time the shade crossed her vision, an insult, a disparaging comment from the couple that reared her would come back to her mind, and she would be filled with a pain so deep-rooted, it was immensely satisfying to tear away the tendrils of each tender plant.

Understanding a little more about her past, she now knew that Miss L. Campbell, who had ostensibly stolen away her fiancé, also always wore pink. This, of course, gave her even more reason to abhor the ghastly shade.

Lost in thought, Hattie had been kneeling over a caseful of curios, and, rising, dusted herself off, both physically and mentally, brushing her hair out of her face as if the action simultaneously removed the cobwebs from her mind.

Just as she did so, she noticed a long lock of black hair intermixed with her grey curls. She pulled it away from the others, imagining it to have escaped from some decorative, Victorian mourning piece. But as she tugged at it, she realized that it was attached firmly to her scalp. Quickly, she pulled out her tight curls, held fast by bobby pins, one after the other. Each lock streamed around her shoulders, blacker and darker than the last. She could hardly believe her eyes. Her brittle, stiff, grey curls had vanished. Every strand had turned to the luscious, black color of her youth. She ran her hands through it, finding a girlish pleasure in twining each spiral around her fingers. Laughing aloud, she swung it about her shoulders, glorying in its luxuriousness.

A deep, full laugh echoed behind her. She turned around, and the master stood in the doorway, beaming down upon her. Harold was nowhere to be found. Blushing visibly, Hattie quickly began repinning her curls.

"It's perfectly lovely hair – nothing to be ashamed of," said the master.

Hattie was speechless, a little affronted, and a bit flattered. She decided to throw caution to the wind and let the pieces she'd started to coil unfurl once more.

Smiling, she said, "It *is* rather nice, isn't it? I despaired of ever seeing it quite this way again."

He had moved closer and made as though to touch the flowing strands but stopped himself abruptly. Instead, he reached up to his own hair.

"Nothing like this ugly, old mane," he said with a tug at it.

Hattie pulled her hair back and tied it in a loose knot at the base of her neck. She had momentarily longed for his touch – to feel his fingers intertwining themselves amongst her curls as she had done. As she tucked each lock away, she simultaneously attempted to tuck away her feelings for the man before her.

Looking down bashfully, she said, "I don't find you ugly."

"You don't?" he said laughingly. "I can't say I approve of your taste. I'm a very cantankerous, unprepossessing, old specimen, to be sure."

"I have always felt that what makes a person attractive

is the strength of their *moral* character. I can be quite the cantankerous old lady as well, you know, but I do feel that a person should always try to do what's *right*, and *that* is what should make them appealing to the opposite sex more than anything. I'm sure I'm very old fashioned for saying so, and my nephew wouldn't agree with me at all."

"Oh, yes. Your nephew. You've mentioned him before."

"He's actually sort of a nephew by adoption – a cousin's son. I don't have any brothers or sisters. He's my sole heir – there's nobody else to leave my money to."

"You must invite him for a visit soon." With a wry smile he continued. "I suppose you already have one planned. I'm forgetting that this will be your home soon."

"A visit may prove rather difficult," said Hattie.

Then she stopped herself short, recalling what Harold had said about the master of the house not accepting the fact that he was dead.

"Why is that?" he asked politely.

Quickly thinking of an excuse that was closest to the truth, she replied, "He's...he's in America, taking care of some business for me."

She had no wish to enter into the specifics of her nephew being held on trial for murder.

"I spent a good amount of time in the Americas. It's a difficult country, but a chap *can* learn to enjoy himself there."

Hattie raised her eyebrows archly.

He spluttered a bit, "I only meant that...well, making one's way in the world can be very difficult – and that one can meet very interesting people if one has a mind to."

Hattie moved closer to him. He seemed, in this moment, a bit vulnerable...approachable.

"I'm certain that you made quite an impression on the ladies over there. As I said, you're hardly as unsightly as you think."

She raised a hesitant hand to his forehead as if to lightly smooth the wrinkles that had appeared above his furrowed brow. He steeled himself as if for a blow and nearly flinched at her touch, but the wrinkles relaxed as her fingertips lightly caressed his temple.

Hattie thought, for a moment, that his eyes revealed a flicker of elation. Returning his gaze with a hint of brazen tenderness, she felt a small twinge in her stomach.

"*No*," she thought internally. "*I* cannot *allow myself to feel this way again*."

But as she cautioned herself, her heart rebelled against her head, and she allowed herself one fleeting moment of hope.

Yet...Hattie knew that she must stay determined. She took the only action she knew would quell the warmth rising within her, so she passed him swiftly by and left the room.

As though dreaming, Hattie walked up the stairs to return to her room, lost in her own thoughts. She passed

Harold, who was assiduously cleaning a tableful of silver in the hallway. Pausing, she absentmindedly selected a candlestick and halfheartedly began to shine it with a nearby rag.

Harold was prattling on about the various pieces of silver and their value when Hattie realized that she had not yet obtained her object: discovering the name of the master of the house.

Throwing a sidelong glance at Harold, she interrupted his chatter with an abrupt, "What is your Christian name, Harold?"

"Albert," he responded, not missing a stride with his impeccable training as a butler. "I'm happy to be called 'Harold,' however, until the master is able to come to terms with his...*ahem*...situation."

"I shall indeed try to keep to Harold as I mentioned before, so as not to arouse suspicion in your master," she responded confidingly.

Setting the candlestick down and choosing a vase, she felt she'd reached an appropriate enough segue.

She broached, "Speaking of names, what *is* your master's Christian name?"

"He has forgotten it, you understand, but in life, he was known as Reginald Llewelyn Tenbury."

The silver vase Hattie had been holding clattered to the floor. "Did you say *Reginald*?"

"Yes, madam. I mean, Hattie, madam," Harold responded, a bit awkward in his attempt at discarding the title.

"Excuse me," Hattie hastily placed the now-cracked vase on the edge of the table and rushed down the hallway.

Opening the door to her partially stripped bedroom, she paused for a moment to think what she'd done with the telegram she'd received that fateful morning when Syd was flitting.

Pink flounces and bows and bedclothes and coverings lay in chaotic piles throughout the room, resembling a wild, rosy, jungle. Sorting through the chintz and lace, she came up with nothing. Suddenly, she remembered – she had placed it under her pillow, and now, with the bed coverings completely stripped by the maid, she'd no idea where it had got to.

She tore through this mound and that, feeling a strange sense of satisfaction as she imperiled pile after pile of pink tapestries, curtains, and coverings.

At last! She espied the dull piece of yellowed paper underneath a particularly flamboyant rosette and took it up immediately. Tearing it slightly in her eagerness, she reread the missive, addressed to Vamelda.

"Hot on trail. *Stop.* Discovered a name connected with Ms. Vavaseur. *Stop.* Reggie. *Stop.*"

Hattie didn't bother reading the rest of the telegram. It fluttered to the ground.

Reggie. Short for Reginald.

Could it be that her fate was tied up with this man's during life? That strange cloud that came upon her when she thought of her early adult years almost seemed to clear a little now. The darkened image of a man in the orb...not unlike the build of Mr. Tenbury.

Hattie felt an irresistible desire to once again peer into the depths of the crystal ball. Flattening herself on the floor beside the bed, she fished under it for the sewing basket. At last – there it was, behind a trunk. Pulling it out and kneeling before it, she began sorting through the buttons and needles and folds of material, feeling for the precious orb.

Her search complete, Hattie sat back on her heels, sweat beading on her brow.

The orb had vanished.

Chapter Twenty-Nine

After bringing the maid to tears, Hattie was satisfied that the girl was not complicit in taking the orb. As far as Hattie could make out, she was an honest girl who had been cajoled by Teddy into helping out at the big house, and, in return, he had promised to cease acting as the resident poltergeist in her family's home.

The poor girl's father had been driven to distraction with the amount of nighttime moanings and missing sweets that Teddy had inflicted upon him. The moanings were simply an aftereffect of consuming the sweets, but that didn't make it any less unpleasant for the girl's family.

"I don't 'ave to be here! I was enjoying my time perfectly well without this to deal with!" the girl sobbed. "I don't know 'as I've always been a good girl and done wot's right. Per'aps I led that nice p'liceman along a bit when really it was the milkman I was after, but there's not a blemish to my name, and that's a fact!"

She rushed out in a flurry of tears, her apron flung up over her head.

"*Well,*" thought Hattie, "*I can easily do without her. I'll enlist Harold to help me cover her absence for the few days that Mr. Tenbury remains here.*"

Harold, although curious about the artifact Hattie was looking for, was of no help, either. He *had* been in the room a few times in the last weeks, helping to dispose of the heaviest bedroom draperies. However, his kind manner and innocent expression relieved Hattie of the suspicion that he could have absconded with her precious object.

Eager to determine her precise history with the master of the house, Hattie felt that the orb would provide the solution. She longed to plumb its depths – to view once again that personage who plunged into the water. Could it be...her Mr. Tenbury?

Hattie tore the house apart, covering her feverish search for the orb with excuses for readying everything for the master's departure, but it was to no avail. Harold had searched Mr. Tenbury's room, as Hattie did not feel comfortable looking there herself. The only two rooms left were the library and the mirrored room. The former, she had neglected as she and Harold had, in her mind, already thoroughly gone over its contents. The latter, as it threatened her very existence, she avoided at all costs. However, as she could think of no alternate hiding place, she elected to give the library one final examination.

Checking in desk drawers for secret compartments, lifting the cushions of the furniture, and even crawling up the chimney, Hattie was unsuccessful in her quest. As she dusted the soot from her dress, she espied a large pile of less-beloved volumes that she had intended to place in a portmanteau the day before. The antique trunk was gaping open in the center of the room, as if it were some mystical animal waiting in eager anticipation for its dinner.

Hattie sighed, giving up her pursuit and instead resolved to finish her neglected task. Bored with the undertaking and frustrated in her fruitless search, she began cavalierly tossing the books, one after the other, into the willing receptacle. Slipping from Hattie's fingers in her haste, one volume knocked against a corner of the portmanteau. A letter written on thick ivory paper fluttered out of its pages and down onto the bare wood floor.

Spying the name "Reggie" scrawled across the top of the missive, Hattie's curiosity got the better of her, and she momentarily chose to neglect her more virtuous duties in order to satisfy it. Catching it up, she began to read.

As she perused the epistle, Hattie's cheeks flushed in embarrassment and vexation.

It read as follows:

15 January 1886

My Dearest Reggie,

When last we parted, it did not sit right with me the way your eye flashed in anger at me. I'm certain we can clear up this little misunderstanding. You know I only have a heart for you. Every other man pales in comparison. Your strong, stern countenance quells me. Indeed, I would never dream of taking another man in place of you. I would sooner kill another man than have you believe that I could be unfaithful to you. Come back to me, my darling beloved, and let us never be parted again.

Come and see me tomorrow evening. Come late and alone. I long to be in your embrace – your lips and body against mine. I shall wear that new tea gown that everyone has been raving about...so much more intimate for our activities, don't you agree, my darling?

Come to me soon,

Your own,

Lydia

Hattie crumpled the paper in a paroxysm of anger. Disgust rankled in her soul. Lydia. Lydia Carrington. The woman had known Mr. Tenbury in life, then. He mentioned before that he had spent time in America. What was it he had said?

"A chap can learn to enjoy himself there."

If this immoral note was any indication, it seemed he had enjoyed himself *very* much, indeed.

Ashamed of her feelings, Hattie berated herself thoroughly: To *think* that she had allowed her heart to be turned toward this man, when all the while, his loose morals and depravity during life made him completely unworthy of her affections.

Another thought caught at her mind like the unpleasant sting of a wasp. Syd's warning had been clear: Lydia and *a man* were not to be trusted. Wicked idea, but...could it be *her* Mr. Tenbury? If he was wrapped up in the arms of this disgusting woman who invited men into her apartments and did not hesitate to plot against and even murder her enemies...

What on earth was she going to do? Hot tears welled up in her eyes, temporarily blinding her as she stumbled up the stairs and to her room. Fortuitously, she met no one. She couldn't have borne to have any servant or the master...*Reggie*, as he was so scripted in the letter, view her in such a state.

Hattie flung herself upon her still-stripped bed, allowing the wretched anxiety of the last weeks to flood through her, wrenching her very soul. She had not cried like this since she was a child – giving way to the shudders of disconsolate emotion that swelled to passionate sobs.

Outside her window, a murder of crows departed swiftly from their branches, sending shrieks of alarm out into the mist. A mortal farmer boy passing the house walked just a bit faster on his shortcut home from the fields, as he, hearkening to the eerie sobs and erratic behavior of the birds, for the first time gave credence to the ghostly rumors about the abandoned, old mansion.

A soft knock came at Hattie's door, which at first she did not catch. Too wrapped up was she in her despair that she did not perceive the man who entered the room and stood over the bed. It was not until he laid a warm hand upon her back that she became aware of his presence.

Promptly sitting up and hastily wiping the tears from her face, it became clear that her visitor was none other than the man who stood foremost in her thoughts: Mr. Tenbury. His arm was enveloping her, a hand brushing the tangled hair back from her face.

Hattie smacked away the tender caress and forced his hand from her waist.

"How *dare* you touch me!" she rasped, her voice nearly absent as a result of her lamentations. "And how *dare* you enter this room without my permission! I should have known. I should have guessed from the very moment I entered this house that you were such a villain! It's *you* who has stolen the orb! It's *you* who has conspired against poor Syd and dear Mr. Carrington! It's always been *you*!"

Reginald had drawn away from her and stood up from the bed, taking a step back with each castigation she leveled at him. He was now almost at the door but made no move to depart completely. Hattie expected a torrent of rage and defense to fly from his lips, so she was intensely astonished when instead, a look of deep sorrow and confusion crossed his face. This unexpected absence of his usual temper merely spurred her on to further accusations.

"Do you deny it? I see by your looks that you do not," Hattie lied, hoping to trap him with an assumption of guilt. "Where have you taken the crystal? I *will* have it from you! And I *will* have you answer for your atrocities, along with that horrible Lydia woman! But first –*give me the orb!*"

The master of the house no longer looked like the mighty beast of a man she'd first encountered. His face had turned white and wan, his hands hung limply at his sides, and his mouth was open at a grotesque angle. He suddenly looked more like a corpse than anyone Hattie had encountered...either living or dead.

"Did you say...*Lydia*?"

His voice was quiet, weak, and hesitant, like a small boy who has just mustered the gumption to say his first bad word aloud.

"Yes, Lydia. Your criminal cohort, your lover in life...*Lydia Carrington*."

"I know no Lydia Carrington, but there was...there was, I think, a Lydia in my life."

He looked as though he were about to be sick as the name once again crossed his lips.

Hattie took in his words with no less anger than the letter she'd read.

"Oh! Well, then that clears you of at least *one* crime. If you did not know her when she was married, then at *least* you didn't help to murder her husband," she spat with venomous sarcasm.

"Of *course* I couldn't have helped to murder her husband." He clutched at his abdomen as he cried, "*She* murdered *me*."

Chapter Thirty

The two people stared at each other – anguish and astonishment illustrated in varying lines upon their faces.

Quivering with all of the power she could muster, Hattie challenged him, "I thought you didn't know you were dead. All this time…"

Reginald stumbled across the room, feeling for the back of a chair to steady himself. He seemed hardly able to muster the strength to face it forward before tumbling into it.

"I…I've only just realized, but I don't understand. I'm dead. I am *certain* that I am dead. I remember her sinking the knife into my flesh."

He tore open his shirt, exposing his muscular chest. The wounds he spoke of were there, open and gaping as he felt for them with his fingertips. Blood began to flood from the gashes as he touched them.

"How is this possible? I remember watching myself in that coffin. She came in pink...she always wore pink. Even at my funeral, she made a sensation. That's why this room..." he gestured toward the piles of rosy fabric. "The color has always haunted me, but I...I never understood *why*."

"Lydia..." he almost spat the name. "She came to the house where they laid me out for my funeral, laughing at my corpse as soon as she was left alone with me. She told me of all her plans for the future – how she would kill and kill again to achieve her evil ends. When I first met her, she was driven by jealousy and hatred. There was something about my life that she wanted," he paused, gasping for breath as the lacerations poured forth his life's essence.

"It can't be! I cannot make sense of it. I have already felt this pain. I died *before* from these very wounds!"

Grasping fistfuls of his own hair on either side of his head, Reginald moaned. Then, shaking, he removed his hands from his head, seemingly surprised by the wetness that had transferred itself upon his scalp. He held the sticky mess of vital fluids before his eyes. They filled with terror as he watched drop after drop fall to form a distorted pattern upon the carpet.

"I...I've been living in this world, thinking I was still alive...left all alone in this huge, empty house, never realizing...never remembering...until now. Until *you*."

Eyes ablaze, he looked up at her, and even now she felt the sway of his heart over hers. It seemed an age as she battled within her soul. Torn between her newfound distrust and his mental and physical anguish, she tee-tered as though on a precipice overlooking an ocean of grief. Should she take the plunge into his world of tormented waves? Was this man, his eyes looking hungrily into hers, worthy of her sympathy?

"Please…" he pleaded, reaching out to her, his hand trembling with the effort.

This entreaty – almost a prayer – pushed her over the edge. She held her breath for a moment before she made her decision, as though preparing herself for the leap and all that would follow it.

Mercy prevailed.

Looking around the room, she discovered a bedskirt upon the floor. Tearing it to use as a makeshift bandage, she crossed over and knelt before him. Helping him sit up a bit, she began to wrap the wound in an attempt to staunch the crimson flow. Taking his hand in hers, she wiped away as much of the blood as she could with a remnant of the cloth.

As she completed the tender act, he hesitatingly reached out to caress her chin, then drew her face up to his. They kissed, tentatively at first, then with increasing fervor as their bodies melded together in a single passionate embrace.

Until that moment, Hattie did not know what ardor lay latent within her spirit. It was as though she had gone through life as a mere bud, and it took his touch for her soul to blossom fully, unfurling petals of exquisite intensity – at last giving them living breath in the warmth of the sunlight.

Alas, the blood of his wounds interrupted this ethereal moment. Seeping through his bandages to her clothes, the shocking dampness led Hattie to break away, albeit reluctantly, from his embrace. Feeling the sanguine fluid permeate her dress, her momentary elation gave way to the practicality of the gruesome reality before her.

"Your wounds. We must get them tended to. Let me call Bertram."

"No," he said firmly. "I need only you."

He held her wrist, pulling her back to him, but released her in a convulsion of pain.

"I'm a horrible nurse," Hattie returned glibly. "I've never had the patience for it. And we've no idea how this..." she gestured to his chest, "...can affect your...existence. It's imperative that we contact a personage with knowledge of these matters."

"Who could possibly...?" Reginald queried, but Hattie interrupted him.

"I know just the woman, but I can't very well help you to her establishment all by myself. Bertram or Harold will be able to assist you much better than I can alone."

"Is Bertram...?"

"Yes," she responded to his vague query. "We are all of us dead. Me, Bertram, Harold, even little Teddy."

"Teddy? That little scamp of a boy who's always leaving frogs and snakes in my writing desk? Good heavens! I have a good deal to catch up on about how this afterlife functions."

A smile crossed his face for a fleeting moment before it was once again contorted with agony.

"Where will you take me, then?" he inquired.

"Vamelda...the local medium. She'll know what to do," Hattie said. "Let me..."

"No!" Reginald cried, "Not that miserable woman!"

He reached out for her as she stood, but was unable to hold her back as the blood began to flow more freely.

"That witch is more liable to kill me all over again than to heal me," he said sardonically.

Reginald fell back with rattling lungs after the effort of his outburst. Hattie bent down again, pressing both of her hands more firmly on his chest until the blood flow alleviated a little, and he was able to take a full, deep breath.

"Vamelda is what she says she is," Hattie explained. "She's a mortal medium who really can communicate with all those who are dead. I can't begin to tell you how helpful she's been."

"I don't believe in all of that nonsense," he said as stoutly as he could under the circumstances.

"You're going to have to believe in it now, Reginald Tenbury," so stern was she in her rejoinder that he was quelled.

"Yes, perhaps she might exaggerate her powers here and there," Hattie resumed. "I, too, was skeptical in the beginning. You must trust me, Reginald. It's really quite straightforward. Vamelda is very practical and quite a savvy businesswoman. She simply likes to put on a bit of a show."

As Hattie waxed stronger in her explanation, she was surprised at her defense of this woman that only months before had been the bane of her existence.

Hattie's mind caught on a thought that would prove the truthfulness of her assertions.

"She really is the genuine article, as is evidenced by the fact that you have spoken to her!"

Hattie nodded her head in triumph, sure of the persuasiveness of her argument. Reginald's countenance softened, and he seemed slightly mollified as he listened to his newfound love.

"But can she be trusted? A woman who willfully deceives the world around her cannot be the individual to help me with such a predicament as this, can she?"

At that point, the blood had fully soaked the bandage, turning each rosette, along with the surrounding cloth, to a deep scarlet. Hattie reached for the bedskirt and tore off another strip. Reginald winced as she made him once again sit up so that she could wrap the cloth more tightly about his chest.

Looking down upon the rosy fabric, a weighty thought planted itself in Hattie's mind. Standing up, she bustled about the room, ostensibly to collect more material to use as bandages, but in reality, Hattie was seeking out a particular article that would confirm or refute the suspicion that began to grow in her thoughts.

As Reginald did not yet seem convinced of Vamelda's legitimacy, Hattie simultaneously pursued her attempt to convince him as she searched.

"I'm certain Vamelda will have some knowledge that can assist you. The woman might seem like a swindler, but she has a good heart. In fact, one particular friend told me that she often works for individuals who have passed on, but who have no money at all."

Ah – there it was, in the drawer of her bedside table. Folding the item and placing it in her bosom, she turned back to Reginald. He looked into her face as though searching for some assurance of her declarations. He must have found it there, for he nodded and motioned toward the door.

"I shall be as quick as I can. Just you rest there, now," she said.

Passing another soft and swift kiss on his full lips, Hattie rushed out of the room in pursuit of Harold and Bertram.

Chapter Thirty-One

Dashing down the staircase, Hattie encountered Harold midway.

"He knows," she told the butler, "And he's injured."

Searching her face and reading the urgency and depth of her words, he bounded up the stairs to his friend and master.

Hattie needed to find Bertram herself. She wanted his advice as to whether it was indeed the best idea to take him to Vamelda's straightaway. Bertram was industriously polishing the Daimler just outside a front window. Hattie unlatched and threw up the sash, then leaned out to speak with him. Just as she did so, in the autumnal dusk, she thought she saw a dark figure dart behind a nearby bush but reasoned that it must have been an animal or the shadows of the evening playing tricks on her agitated mind.

Upon hearing Hattie's news, Bertram dropped his rag and polish immediately and rushed inside. Hattie, seeing what she thought was a brownish or yellow-ish something or other again behind that same bush, stayed for a moment longer to squint into the fading light. But no – she could see nothing, and she had more important things to worry about than creatures of the night.

Hattie hurriedly closed the window – forgetting, in her haste, to latch it. Returning to the staircase, she met the two men, who were struggling to support a limping Reginald between them. The sight would jus-tifiably send many people into raving hysterics. Hattie, miraculously, was able to keep her calm – but only just. With the movement of being transported, the ragged and soaked cloths had fallen from Reginald's wounds. Hattie could not help but stare in wretched alarm at his bare flesh – ripped and torn as it was. Could it be that further injuries had manifested themselves since she had first bound them?

Once their patient was deposited in the back of the car, the two faithful servants climbed into the front seat while Hattie allowed an exhausted and pale Reginald to rest his head upon her lap. Bertram began driving at breakneck speed to the occultist's.

Reginald's breathing was growing labored, but he man-aged to mutter, "Since you left me, I've recalled add-itional details about the end of my life."

Despite Hattie's insistence for quietude, he continued to speak.

"I knew Lydia when I was stationed in Burma during the war. She wanted me...wanted me badly, but I knew she was corrupt to her very core. The things she used to write to me sometimes. Disgusting. No man or woman should ever read those words of filth. As an officer, you make many of these casual acquaintances. Women you mildly flatter or are expected to dance with, out of politeness to their family's breeding or their father's position. It was during an officer's ball that she first began to tell me of strange things. We'd met a handful of times before, and she had made no secret of the fact that she doted on me.

"At first, I took it as a schoolgirl's sentimentality and chose to ignore it. However, that night at the ball...her words turned strange and savage. She told me that she could see – nay, speak with the dead. I, of course, had heard of such things. Conan Doyle was always a great purveyor of séances, and though I have always been a fan of that great man's work, I gave no real credence to the idea of spiritualism. Young ladies at that time often expressed an interest in these matters, but the subjects of which she spoke at first baffled, then worried me.

"She began by saying that the room around us was filled with people who had come to the most grisly and un-speakable ends. With each rotation around the room, her descriptions became exceedingly gruesome. Next, she turned to even more sinister subjects. She spoke of her desire to one day have the power to rule the dead – to become their queen, and that I was to be her co-hort in the darkest of deeds. She desired to bend all who knew her to her will and claimed she had the means to accomplish such wickedness. It was unfathomable at the time. I now recognize that her intentions were dark, bitter, and loathsome, but back then, I put them down to a misguided bid for attention, or, perhaps, a streak of madness."

Reginald shuddered and coughed, while Hattie, desiring still to quiet him, was also nearly paralyzed with fascination and horror at this grisly tale.

He continued, "Despite her youth, she tried to seduce me, but her multiple attempts were fruitless. I had no desire to possess her as she did me. Soon, the war was over, and I was to return to England. She came to my chambers one night, in a last endeavor to have me, but I fully and publicly rejected her, calling upon my compatriots as witnesses. Shamed and shunned, she swore in her wrath to have her revenge on me.

"I believed the entire repulsive affair to be over, but nearly a year later, I encountered her again in America when I traveled there to make my fortune. We met at a party. My endeavors for financial gain had been relatively successful, and I was welcomed into circles of wealth and station. Lydia always made a sensation wherever she went with her beauty and charm. Laughing our previous encounter off as though it was an excellent joke between us, she seemed to feel no opprobrium for her previous behavior.

"She was very much changed. The dazzling life of high society had seemed to shift her lust upon mortal riches. She flirted and flattered and was admired and pursued. Relieved, I relaxed in her company, believing her former behavior to be but an aberration, brought on by imprudent youth and the chilling effects of living in a country ravaged by war.

"However, my belief was imprudent, to say the least. One evening, as we were thrown together once again as partners at a dance, she confessed her love – nay, obsession – for me. Taking advantage of the privacy afforded by the waltz, she also set before me a plan to marry and murder a wealthy man of our acquaintance. I was to help her carry out the horrible deed. It was as though the very voice of hell spoke through her delicate throat, and the dance became one, not with a debutant, but with a demoness. It was only then that I understood that she was not only fully deranged but dangerous, as well."

Again, Reginald's body convulsed, but his weakening voice spoke on: "Her lust was set toward me, but I wanted none of it. My heart was protected by...by..." he stopped abruptly, furrowing his thick brows until they almost touched one another.

"It's hazy, at times, but there was something that kept me safe from her enticing magnetism. Something..." he broke off.

"Lydia was certainly very beautiful, and many were won by her charms. She must have mistaken my natural, brooding nature for something more fiendish, believing me to be the ideal confederate for her immoral deeds. Nevertheless, my soul was wholly repelled by her. I was shocked to my very core with the words she had poured forth upon me that evening. As she neared me for a kiss, I shoved her small frame fully from me with all of my strength, and she fell across the floor. I must have hurt her, but in that moment, I had no feelings of pity for her. I left her there in the middle of the crowd, with no thought of the consequences that might follow."

At this point, Hattie's hand retreated to where she had stowed the item she had found in the room before she went for help. Her very being trembled with the knowledge she believed she possessed. Taking out the newspaper clipping, Hattie partly unfolded it and held it before Reginald's face. His eyes widened in recognition and terror as Hattie's suspicions were confirmed.

"It's her, isn't it?" she said in a low voice that sounded much calmer in her ears than she felt. "'L. Campbell' is what the caption says. I suspected it to be her when you spoke of her unparalleled beauty and what it says about her signature color – pink."

"Yes," he said slowly. "That's her. Lydia Campbell. That's the woman who murdered me."

Hattie put away the newspaper clipping. She had been careful not to reveal her own photo, uncertain whether or not a further shock would make his situation more dire.

Reginald, wrapped up in his own tale, did not ask where she had discovered the newspaper clipping.

The memories seemed to rush through him in a flood of emotions: "I withdrew myself fully from society, but I heard through mutual friends that Lydia had begun to carry out her heinous plan. She delicately and deftly wooed the wealthy gentleman in question. He was easily won by her wit and willfulness, and they were soon engaged. As their nuptials neared, I felt it my duty to warn this man of her wicked intentions. At my wit's end, I dashed off a hurried note to him, requesting an audience that evening, and I received a brief note in return, stating that he would be expecting me."

A fit of coughing interrupted his narrative, and blood from his overtaxed lungs splayed upon Hattie's cheek. Quickly wiping it away so as not to distress him, she listened on.

"When I arrived at his apartments, however, I found only *her*."

Hattie gasped in astonishment.

Reginald, lost in retrospection, merely continued, "They'd already been married – secretly – that very day. Lydia was stunning in her ivory bridal gown that matched her pale skin to perfection. You'd mistake her for any happy, young wife, flushed with the glow and excitement of her wedding day. She was very charming as she led me through their apartments to what I thought was his study, laughing and chattering all the while – once again making a jest of all that had previously transpired between us.

"It was no study that she led me to, but his bedchamber. He was lying dead on their marital bed – shot through the heart. Shocked, I stared for a moment as she pressed something into my hand. It was a revolver. I dropped it immediately and turned toward her.

"She smiled wickedly at me in the shimmering candlelight. 'Now,' she said, 'I'll have my revenge upon you. *You'll* be blamed for his death. A jealous rage, I'll tell them. You came in, frenzied with the desire to prevent our wedding night together, and I lashed back with the only weapon I could find.'"

Reginald touched at his wounds, "Swiftly, her arm darted out and pierced me with a small stiletto knife. The puncture was deep and effective. I staggered in reverse, crashing into a glass case of curiosities. Dusty specimens of butterflies, birds, and bones fell about me. I felt amongst them for some sort of weapon, and my hand landed on the revolver once again. Blindly, I pointed the gun at her and pulled the trigger, but all that came to my ears was a vacant click. The gun was not loaded.

"'You fool!' she raged at me, 'You think I'd be senseless enough to give you a weapon you could use against me? No...you will die slowly and at my own hand. Perhaps I cannot have power over you in life, but in death, you will worship me.' Her eyes as luminescent as the steel she gripped in her fingers, she leaped toward me.

"Defending myself, I imagined that I could easily overpower her slight frame, even with my initial wound, but that night, she possessed a maniacal force. It felt as though all of the demons from the underworld were on her side, forcing me to the floor as she plunged the dagger repeatedly into my body."

He winced with pain, the memory seeming to awaken the depth of every wound.

"Shhhhh," soothed Hattie, now horrified by her macabre curiosity that had allowed him to continue in this vein for so long. "We're nearly there. Try to rest if you can."

She planted a tender kiss on his lips as though to seal

them shut. Looking up at her gratefully, he closed his eyes and took a long, deep, rattling breath.

A few more minutes and they pulled up to the medium's shop. Bertram and Harold once again hoisted Reginald up, helping him limp inside. Hattie did not expect Vamelda to be present downstairs at so late an hour, so she was not at all surprised to find all of the lamps in the outer room unlit.

Feeling around for some matches that she had in other visits observed on a table near the door, she set one alight, the diminutive glimmer flickering as lustrously as the small hope of Reginald's salvation. Hattie paused for a moment, waiting for both the flame and her heart to settle into something solid enough to chase away the eerie shadows that Vamelda's odd curiosities made on the surrounding walls. Twisting the knob of a nearby lamp, she set the wick aflame, sending a ray of light through the gloom.

What she perceived in the half-light made her lose her breath.

There, in the far corner, sat Vamelda, bound by hand and foot, a gag in her mouth. Her head was drawn back, exposing her long, goose-like neck, while a beautiful, ethereal woman held a gleaming knife to the medium's throat.

Chapter Thirty-Two

"Lovely to see you again, Reggie," said the woman, flashing a dazzling smile at him.

So casual and charming was her manner that you would have believed her to be hosting a society dinner, rather than threatening an innocent woman with imminent death.

"How long has it been?" she said nonchalantly as she looked him over appraisingly. "Too many years. The afterlife hasn't been kind to you...but we'll soon remedy that."

The woman's golden hair was fashionably cut in the style of the day. It glistened lustrously in the lamplight. Her features were full and symmetrical. Her large, green eyes were done up perfectly with that smoky look that only Hollywood film stars could achieve. Her high cheekbones needed no counterfeit rouge, for they glowed with the blush of youth. A rosebud mouth completed the breathtaking loveliness of the woman. Any painter would have gone hungry for many a meal in order to secure such a muse.

Hattie had her suspicions of the woman's identity, but as the light flickered upon her duskily pink ensemble – flawlessly crafted to exhibit her exquisite frame – Hattie knew precisely who it was.

"Lydia Carrington," she said decisively.

The woman turned supremely disdainful eyes on her. Hattie could have been a spot of mud on her shoe.

Reverting her attention to Reginald, Lydia continued, "I easily discovered your little plot, Reggie. I met that foolish Gerald Warburton in America. So easy to dupe, and I very nearly pulled the same trick on him that I played upon that rich American we both knew. Such a simple plan. I have, of course, moved on to grander ambitions, but old habits die hard...and when there are so many willing subjects, it's almost impossible to resist."

Reginald looked puzzled. Hattie knew he had no idea what Lydia was speaking about.

She longed to illuminate him, but Lydia went on: "I was interrupted, however, by that blasted Trixie woman. I had to alter my plan a little, but I got my revenge on her, anyhow. In the meantime, I was able to swindle a lovely, young duke. 'Easy pickings,' as they say. He turned over all of his money to me without me having to marry the buffoon."

She shook her golden head in triumphant exaltation.

"I don't really need the money...but it's always nice to know I can keep my hand in while I'm pursuing other, more worthy intentions. Especially after having been thwarted by someone so tawdry as that little Trixie creature. It all came right in the end, though, didn't it?" she smiled luxuriously.

However, as Lydia gloated in her exploits, Bertram had been slowly passing the weight of Reginald over to Harold. Silent as a predator stalking its prey, he had begun to move stealthily toward Lydia.

Unfortunately, in his endeavors to gain ground in the shadows, he brushed against a scarf that festooned a nearby lamp. Hattie saw it catch upon a button of his coat, and she held her breath in anticipation of what soon followed. As the butler moved forward, the scarf wrapped about a relic, then sent it crashing to the ground in his wake.

Lydia flashed her vibrant eyes from Reginald to Bertram.

"Ah-ah-ah!" she warned in heightening tones of sing-song as she pressed the knife more forcibly against Vamelda's throat.

A tiny droplet of blood trickled down into the clairvoyant's collar.

"Not another move out of you, my good man. And yes, I can see you. Reggie should have guessed by now, but I do have the same gift as your little friend here."

She smiled warmly down at Vamelda, as though she was about to take a satiating bite out of her.

"I can see everything that she can see – and more if I have the right tools. There are certain objects in this world that enhance our abilities, you see. Crystal orbs, for instance. Mediums are very fond of using them, although most of them haven't a clue why they're so beneficial. A person's soul is intertwined with relics such as that," she stated matter-of-factly.

"And I want *yours*."

She turned her gleaming emerald eyes once again upon Reginald.

"I've always wanted you, body and soul, and now I shall have you completely to myself. I regret what transpired between us all those years ago. I've come to realize that I've only known true passion once – for you."

Her expression was hungry and almost desperate for a moment.

"Yes, at the time, I took my revenge, and I was immensely satisfied when completing the act. But then…after I'd lost you…"

Something near pain crossed her features, but then she straightened herself, and they hardened once again into vicious lines.

"Well, an attractive woman is always allowed her fickle ways, you know."

With a vain little shake of her head, her hair fell in an even more attractive pattern around her cheeks. She smiled confidently, as though she knew the power her beauty could invoke upon those that surrounded her.

"Now…which of you is going to turn over that orb?" she said with conviction.

The woman dominated the room, leaving no time for anyone to answer her.

"I need it for *us*, my love...I once thought you were lost to me forever, but now I know that you still can be mine – that we can be together as I've always longed for. Soon, you will long for it, too."

Her eyes were commanding – confident in his return of her affections. However, Reginald made no move to answer her, and his eyes were filled with all the hatred he could muster in his weakened position.

"No?" Lydia's forehead barely made a crease as she widened her heavy eyelids to stare at him. "There *was* always something in you that I did not quite like. Some bend toward goodness and honor that is complete foolishness. You will come to know it as folly, too. I simply need your orb *and* that of your former fiancé. Could this be she?"

With a slight, almost listless motion of her knife-weidling hand, she gestured toward Hattie, her lip curling back to show exquisite, white teeth.

"No, there is no possible way you could prefer *her* over *me*," she looked Hattie up and down appraisingly. "That small frame, that black-as-coal hair. I can admit that she has some charm in those almond-shaped eyes. She might even be a bit intelligent by that look she's giving me, but she is nothing compared to my beauty, you must admit."

Hattie, wounded as any woman would be under such an onslaught, looked at Reginald to see the effect these words would have upon him. He never removed his eyes from Lydia's face. The blood draining from each lineament by the moment, he became as pale as his shirt was red.

"No answer, my darling?" she shrugged. "It is of little consequence. You *will* help me find the orbs...or *this* one dies."

She pulled Vamelda's hair back until Hattie could see the blue vessels of the medium's throat throb with the strain.

"You've no reason to doubt my intent. We both know I'm capable of, and, indeed, have easily done, much worse."

At that moment, Reginald lunged toward her, curios crashing from shelves as he shoved them aside to get to this woman. Surprised, the knife dropped from her hand, and she stepped back, suddenly cowering in the presence of this massive beast of a man. Reginald's palms were reaching around her silken throat, about to crush it, when his palms passed through her as though mere wisps of smoke.

Fear had flashed in Lydia's eyes momentarily, but then she laughed wildly in relief.

"So! You've spent all this time believing that you're alive. You've learned *nothing* about the rules of the afterlife!"

Reginald looked down at his hands, disbelieving. He made another desperate swipe at his nemesis and caught nothing but vacant air. Then, grasping at his own wounds, he collapsed on the floor at Lydia's feet.

Laughing in triumph, she bent down to clasp the knife once again, but as she did so, a small figurine of an Egyptian goddess struck her hand, causing the blade to clatter to the floor a second time.

Lydia looked up, astonished. Hattie had already hurled another figurine at the evil woman's head and struck her on the face.

A small red blotch was beginning to appear on her porcelain cheek when Hattie took up a large, weighty tome to fling at her. Backing up against the wall, this time Lydia was struck in the shoulder, and she clasped at it in breathless pain.

Objects, books, lamps, and scrolls flew across the room at the woman. Hattie's rage had been set afire against this wicked temptress.

Whilst Reginald had been unsuccessfully attempting to overpower the woman, Hattie had recalled her struggle with Vamelda over the light switch, as well as her ability to remove the orb from the medium's stand. The dead might not have the power to affect living beings, she reasoned, but they could undoubtedly influence material matter.

Hattie's torrent of curios was unrelenting. Soon, Bertram and Harold joined in. Lydia skirted the room, avoiding the largest of the objects until she reached the doorway.

Turning back with savage and violent fervor, she screamed, "You *will* be mine, Reginald Tenbury!"

The two men heaved a bookcase that crashed toward

her as she attempted an escape through the doorway. By the time the dust and splinters of wood had settled, Lydia had vanished.

Chapter Thirty-Three

Hattie rushed over to the now-unconscious Vamelda, who had fainted and slumped to the floor, unnoticed, at some point in the struggle. Calling for smelling salts or spirits to revive the medium, Hattie saw Bertram rush to the kitchen. He returned with a small bottle of gin. Vamelda was unresponsive both to nudges and the calling of her name.

Hattie did see a bit of an eye flutter open, which promptly closed tightly again when the handsome Bertram drew near. Hattie mercilessly slapped the clairvoyant into sensibility, correctly surmising that Vamelda was overdramatizing her temporary lapse of consciousness for the chauffeur's benefit.

When the medium was willing to admit to at least a partial alertness, a tender Bertram took the occultist into his arms and gently nudged a bit of the spirits through her quivering lips.

Allowing the attractive chauffeur to lift her to her feet,

Vamelda leaned on him for support as she summoned them all to her kitchen. Sitting around the table and in the window seat (there was a shocking scarcity of chairs for them all), Harold made some strong tea as they exchanged frightened and exhausted looks with one another.

Hattie felt she must take charge. Vamelda seemed in too weakened a state, despite her theatrics; Bertram was solicitous of the occultist's welfare; Harold was busying about the kitchen; Reginald was grunting quietly in pain.

"We're in need of a plan," Hattie began abruptly. Turning to Vamelda, she said, "What do you know of this woman in your sessions with Mr. Carrington?"

"All I'm aware of," said Vamelda, gasping a bit between sips of gin. "Is that the poor man absolutely adores her. He speaks no ill of her."

"I can see why," interpolated Bertram, "She's quite a stunner."

A quiet shriek erupted from the reclining Vamelda.

"But *evil*. Absolute evil, of course," he rejoined.

Vamelda gave a little sigh of relief and settled more deeply against his chest. He grinned up at Hattie and winked at her with roguish and dancing eyes.

He always did have a bit of a cheeky side, Hattie remembered. She now recognized him as the same Bertram she'd known as a child. He had been a groomsman in the stables during her youth. As they'd both aged and with the advent of motorcars, he had gradually transitioned into the household chauffeur. She remembered that he had passed away several years before Hattie's own death. Somehow, she knew that it was the same man, but with his youth restored.

Filled to the brim with questions, Hattie made a swift detour, "How is it that Bertram was able to help you just now when Reginald couldn't touch Lydia?"

"Oh, my deeearr," Vamelda returned breathily, "The dead cannot *harm* the living, they can only *help*. No one is allowed tooooaaaahhh!"

The last word ended in a substantial wail. Vamelda pointed melodramatically at Reginald, whose hands had moved from pressing against his abdomen to reaching for a cup of tea. They were covered in blood.

"How is this possible?" the medium cried.

"We hoped *you* would know," returned Hattie, moving over to Reginald and pressing a tea towel against his wounds.

"Oh, you poor, dear sugarplum!" She looked with pity on the injured man. "The only time I've seen wounds this raw are when a subject has just passed over. You'll recall Mr. Carrington's blue lips when you first encountered him in my shop? Having just been poisoned, he still felt the effects of it until he fully accepted his fate. At that point, people generally tend to begin healing...and not just with wounds or illness, but age, as well. You'll note that Bertram and Harold are both in their prime of life, although they passed on when they were quite aged. Bertram's especially turned out quite nicely, I've always thought. I've seen photos of him in his youth, and he wasn't nearly this handsome."

Vamelda caressed the butler's face, absentmindedly staring off into a corner of the ceiling. As one, they all turned to observe the object that the medium was looking so intently at. However, as they could perceive nothing in that particular spot, after a moment, they all turned back, shrugging their shoulders in puzzlement.

Hattie, shaking and straightening herself, said, "That's all very well, my dear, but what are we to do about Reginald? I mean, Mr. Tenbury?" she corrected herself, blushing.

"I might have something that works temporarily, but you'll need to find your orbs, and you'll need all the help you can get remembering as much as you can about your lives," she said, shakily standing on her already wobble-inducing Spanish heels.

Hattie followed her into the antechamber. It was in complete disarray from their recent fracas with Lydia. Vamelda began sifting through the rubble.

"Where is it? Where *is* that thing? It was one of the first you lobbed at me," Vamelda muttered.

"I most certainly did not 'lob' anything...at least, not at you. You know very well that I was merely trying to protect you from Lydia," Hattie contested sharply, annoyed with her companion's peevishness.

Vamelda pulled a face and said petulantly, "You could easily have injured me all the same."

Despite her exasperation, Hattie knew that this woman was Reginald's only hope and, as such, should be in possession of all of the events that had transpired here-tofore. Accordingly, Hattie commenced relating Reginald's tale to the medium. Hattie wasn't entirely sure the woman heard her as the medium tossed item after item over her shoulder. As she narrowly missed Hattie a few times (and in light of their recent conversation), she suspected that not every aim was as absentminded as the medium purported each of them to be.

Standing up with an "Aha!" on her lips, Vamelda pulled out an Egyptian curio. It was a statue of Isis, wings out-spread before and behind her.

Handing it to Hattie, Vamelda queried eagerly, "Well?"

Holding the weighty antique in her palm, Hattie stared blankly at the medium.

"Is it still inside?" Vamelda demanded in tones of frustration.

When Hattie did not respond, the medium, rolling her eyes almost into the back of her head, pressed firmly down on one of Isis's wings, and a little drawer popped out of the base. From it, Vamelda removed a diminutive container, carved out of ivory and filled with what looked like a bright green salve.

"Yeaaas, this will do nicely," she said with an air of great solemnity. "However, it will only be effective for a short time. You simply *must* find his crystal ball as soon as possible. I'm thrilled he's remembered so much, but it seems to be only enough to make him relive his last moments."

The two women returned to the kitchen, and Vamelda

generously and unabashedly applied the salve to Reginald's chest and abdomen. As though seeing time in reverse, Hattie watched in astonishment and joy as the wounds began to close – the flowing blood seeping back into the slashes of flesh.

"What *is* that foul-smelling stuff?" queried Harold.

"Oh, dahling, it's simply a concoction created by the Egyptian goddess Isis. I wasn't quite sure it would work because she *is* the protector of women and children, but she's also the goddess of healing, so I thought we might as well give it a try. It will not last, however. Her powers were only able to bring her own husband, Osiris, back to life for one night of glorious passion."

Vamelda's eyes flickered over to Bertram for a moment. His well-defined cheeks erupted into a rather magnificent smile, and she was temporarily lost in a fit of abstraction. Groaning, Hattie was forced to snap her fingers before Vamelda's face before the medium continued her account.

"When I communed with her on my last trip to Egypt, she made a gift of it and warned me to use it wisely. I've been saving it up for a special occasion, although I *was* rather tempted from time to time to use it on my own aging body."

Vamelda caught up a teaspoon and began looking at herself from varying angles, pulling back her skin here and there.

"*Vamelda!*" Hattie brought the medium's attention once again back to the matter at hand.

"Oh, yes, dear sweetums," she returned to her task. "There. That ought to do it. She won't see many people, you know. It was *quite* a task to get her to speak with me, but she *was* so interested in a particularly fascinating bracelet that I..."

"That's all very fascinating," interrupted Hattie, "But we must get on with devising our plan."

She looked down at Reginald's injuries, which were mere angry red marks now, rather than the gushing wounds they'd been a few moments before.

Pressing his arm in silent gratitude at the effectiveness of this painless remedy, their eyes met briefly and intensely before Hattie moved on: "Tell us more about these orbs, Vamelda."

"Oh! The orbs, yes. I've always known that they held a special power. Even as a girl, when I first became cognizant of my gifts, I knew they enhanced my skills, but I'd no idea until today how essential they are in your afterlives. Lydia seems to believe that if she's able to possess them, it will give her control over the dead to whom the orbs belong. I have noticed that some are dark, angry, and clouded, while others are light and peaceful, but this new theory..."

The medium looked strangely mystified. Hattie well knew that it was Vamelda's habit to brazenly bluff her way through any puzzle she couldn't quite work out, so this breakdown of her usual countenance of confidence troubled her.

"Before you arrived," the occultist continued, "Lydia

made claims about even using a death mask for purposes I've never dreamed of. Ambitions that could change the very fabric of the afterlife. I'm not certain, but that would mean..."

Vamelda ended haltingly, slipping back into her usual vague manner of speaking.

The room fell silent, and Hattie observed each of her friends as they absorbed these revelations. Bertram looked strong and manly – a pillar and such a comfort at a time as this. Harold, at last sitting down to his own tea, stared into the depths of his cup as though the answers lay therein. Although his color was returning, Reginald was looking absent-mindedly at Hattie's lap, his features expressive of much turmoil within his soul.

Hattie began running her thumb along her fingertips in a distracted frame of mind, thinking of what to do next.

A loud screech of chair legs being shoved back gratingly on the tile floor made them all affix their attention on Reginald. His eyes were staring, and sweat began to bead upon his brow.

"Oh, my dear one! Is it your wounds again?" cried Hattie, astounded by his wild looks.

"You...your fingers," he stammered.

"My what?!" asked Hattie, slightly affronted.

"The way you rub your fingers on your thumb," he took a step toward her.

"I...what?" Hattie was utterly lost.

She'd no idea of her habit.

"Oh, yes," said Vamelda, absently. "I've noticed it. It's a funny little thing you do when you're nervous."

"I am *never* nervous," Hattie lashed out, disliking all of this attention directed to her person.

"Uncomfortable, then," chimed in Harold. "I've noticed it occasionally, as well."

Hattie straightened up to her full seated height, back straight, neck taut. She turned to Bertram, a silent plea in her eyes.

Bertram shrugged, "I'm sorry, Hattie. It *is* a bit of a habit with you. *Some* men might, however, find it endearing."

He finished with a sly smile in Reginald's direction.

"Oh, you are a *card*," interpolated Vamelda, with both eyebrows lifted so high in jealousy that they practically retreated into her scalp.

Hattie promptly and a bit childishly sat upon both of her hands.

"I can't see how this is relevant to…"

She broke off as Reginald cut her short: "But *she* did that. The woman I loved. The one who kept me safe from Lydia's charms."

Feeling every bit as envious as Vamelda, she countered, "*What* woman?"

"I recall now that I was…*engaged*. To a young woman. It cannot be…is it…*you*?"

Vamelda interrupted, "Do you have it still, Hattie?!"

"Have what?" her eyes did not remove from Reginald's intensely questioning gaze, but she nonetheless answered the medium, unable to leave the woman's addled question alone.

"*That thing!* Oh, you know – that bit of a green thing that your nephew brought to us?"

Hattie's mind traveled vaguely to the new curtains in her room.

Exasperated, Hattie threw her hands up in the air. "What *are* you talking about, Vamelda?"

"Well, it's so obvious now, but these things can help – these *objects*. Oh, please tell me you still have it, Hattie. You would not have thrown it away?"

By now, Reginald's hands were enveloping her left one, stopping her from the finger rubbing that had unconsciously begun afresh. Embarrassed, she drew her hand away. Undeterred, he caught it up again and kissed each one of her fingertips, stopping at her fourth.

The volume of Vamelda's voice was visceral: "*THE RING!*"

Chapter Thirty-Four

Hattie rushed up to her room. They had all driven back in the Daimler – pressed up a bit too tightly against one another for a comfortable ride. Hattie wasn't quite certain where her legs ended and Vamelda's began.

Before they left, Vamelda had packed a few things, unwilling to stay in her shop alone for fear of Lydia's return. The medium's curative salve had banished any prejudice on the part of Reginald, and he, after a very obvious hint from Vamelda, had invited her to stay at the mansion.

"It *is* best that we all stay together," Bertram had confirmed.

Reginald agreed, "Now that we know Lydia is in England, we must set up some sort of defense against her, and remaining together is by far the best plan."

So it was decided, and Hattie helped the clairvoyant pack a few things before returning to the mansion.

When they arrived, Hattie offered to take Vamelda's belongings up to her room for the time being. They would determine a place of rest for her later.

Reaching her apartment, Hattie placed the bags just inside the doorway. She was arrested by the sight that greeted her in the dim light. Her bedchamber was in complete disarray. It was not merely the previous chaos of changing out the bedclothes and window coverings.

The mattress was upturned. The chair where Reginald had sat just hours earlier was upended and slashed as though a furious cat had had a fit upon it. Feather stuffings from pillows littered the room. One of the doors to her wardrobe hung askew.

Tredpidatiously, Hattie moved forward into the room, concerned that the agent of these violent deeds could still be within the confines of the space. Her imagination ran rather wild at the prospect of such an encounter, but she was determined to discover the ring that had grown, in her estimation, so essential and precious.

She had previously stowed it in a small, oval-shaped, velvet-lined jewelry box on a table near the window. That particular table had been knocked over in the wake of the interloper. Hattie walked around the bed to see what had become of the ring box. She crouched down and began to cautiously feel around in the shadows where she imagined the box might have been flung.

Several sharp creaks in the flooring erupted, making Hattie nearly lose her breath. Someone had entered the room. At first, she thought it could have been Vamelda coming to see what had become of her luggage, but

Hattie knew the medium would have made her presence known, whether intentionally or not. No, this individual seemed to have no clue as to her presence, as all below knew whither and for what purpose she had gone.

The hinges of the now-solitary door of her wardrobe groaned and scraped as someone opened it, as though it was resistant to the endeavor. Hattie could hear the trespasser begin to sift through her clothes, and she flinched as she heard material rip forcibly. A grunt of disappointment from the mysterious person came shortly after.

Hattie crouched perfectly still, keeping her shaking body in check as she waited for the person to finish their despicable task. She could hear item after item being tossed hither and thither, as though the intruder was a giant scavenger bird, picking through the remains of an animal's corpse. Soon, a dress was flung toward her, and she nearly cried out as the delicate lace brushed the edge of her jaw. Instead, she gritted her teeth and gathered the courage to try to discover the identity of this pillager.

As she lifted her head above the top of the bed, an unfortunately-placed post obscured the person from her view. Hattie dared not move more than that for fear of being discovered. However, her primary purpose remained: She must find the ring, and she must do it quickly before this vandal discovered and made off with it first.

The dawn was beginning to kiss the edges of her windowsill. Casting her eyes about in search of the jewelry box, Hattie's vision strained through the blushing aurora. Just when she was about to give up hope of discovering anything worthwhile in her current position, the plunderer tossed a coat in her general direction, sending a small box flying when it landed on the floor. The receptacle overturned in its flight and splayed open. There lay her quarry – just out of her reach – the emerald sparkling tauntingly in the ever-growing morning light.

The entrails of a favorite hatbox were landing in various states of disrepair and a snowfall of millinery was descending upon and around her. A muted groan of frustration reached Hattie's ears, and the footsteps of the ransacker receded, and then...silence.

After a few hushed moments spent in abject dread, Hattie ventured to stretch a trembling hand out slowly to the shimmering jewel. The muscles in her arms became taut and pained as they reached the limit of their capacity – in her fear, she was loath to move her entire person in case the interloper heard her and returned. Her fingertips touched the velvet edge, and the box tumbled upon its side as the circlet of precious gems flew, unbidden, through the air and struck the wall.

It made only the smallest of tinkling sounds as it clattered to the floor, but the delicate percussion must have reached the ear of the plunderer, for they returned in full force to the room.

A lamp was lit – the shadow of a person stretched across the floor toward Hattie, her outstretched arm, and the dazzling jewel. Taking a chance, Hattie's hand darted out to clasp the ring, which was now thankfully within reach. Recoiling into the shadows near the upturned mattress, Hattie willed herself to somehow become Lilliputian in size. Her view was such that she could only perceive the corner of the room wherein the table lay on its side, along with the now-empty jewelry box. The person huffed as they ostensibly bent over. Hattie closed her eyes tightly, as a child playing hide-and-seek, hoping against all logic that lack of sight of the intruder would equal their inability to perceive her.

Detecting a vocalization of disgust, Hattie's eyes fluttered open, half-blind with tears of terror. She saw the box that had so lately held her precious possession fall to the floor. Mumblings followed the obtruder out the door and along the passageway. Hattie listened, straining, far long after the retreating footsteps fell silent.

Attempting to raise herself up, she failed the first time, her arms and legs too weak with fright. She'd never felt so wretched as when her limbs gave out in that moment. All of the circumstances – equally painful and mysterious – along with the disagreeable particulars related by Reginald, had finally taken their toll on her. Drawing a deep breath, her fingers closed more tightly around the little trinket. The action had, simultaneously, a quietive and restorative effect.

As though a shock of brilliantly pure energy ran through her veins, she stood quickly and without pain. A warmth rushed into her being, inciting her to action. However, the zeal did not extend to foolish abandon. Caution was still uppermost in her mind. Hugging the shadows of the hallway, her footsteps as light as a dancer's, she made it to the top of the stairs undetected.

The ring felt cool and smooth in the palm of her hand, and she resisted the temptation to slip it onto her finger as she descended the staircase to return to the safety of her friends.

Chapter Thirty-Five

"Daaaahling – there you are! You've been simply *ages*!" Vamelda greeted Hattie as she swiftly glided through the door of the library.

"There's someone in the house! Upstairs," Hattie gasped breathlessly.

Bertram and Harold pushed past her before she had a chance to direct them any further.

"It *is* such a comfort to have a stalwart, devoted man at your beck and call, isn't it, dearest?" Vamelda said dreamily.

"You mean *two* men, don't you, Vamelda?" Hattie couldn't help teasing her, even at such a tense moment.

Hattie was about to disclose her adventures upstairs, but she was cut short as she observed the room. It was in even worse disarray than her own, despite its recent clearing out. Although it looked as though it, too, had been thoroughly searched, there was more viciousness to this wreckage in the library. Covers had been torn from precious editions. Pages had been scattered about, as though the perpetrator had some particular vengeance against their contents.

Reginald was bent over in a corner near the mantlepiece, collecting the leaves of a disemboweled volume. Hattie went to help him and as she collected a few pages, she noted that the sheets were from the book of Shakespeare poems they had read together so tenderly and so recently.

Looking into Reginald's face to see if he, too, felt their significance, she observed that his expression was full of anguish and dismay.

"Here," said Hattie, taking the scattered pages from his arms. "You shouldn't be doing such things in your condition."

Drawing him up to his feet, she unintentionally pressed the ring into his palm. He looked down at the glimmering, little trinket for a moment, and...it was as though time stopped for them both.

Vamelda gasped audibly, but neither of them were aware of it.

Not taking his eyes off of the deep green emerald, he took her hand in his and placed the circlet upon the fourth finger of her left hand. A tingling sensation radiated throughout her body, beginning at her fingertip and flooding through her entire person. Haltingly, Reginald looked up into her face. It was as if glowing embers had replaced his eyes as they searched her own.

The burning passion that had engulfed her during their first kiss seemed but the flickering light of a match in comparison to the feeling that poured through her now. A swirling wind that was no wind encircled them both, lifting them from the ground upon which they stood until the tips of their feet barely brushed the floor. Their arms enveloped one another as their lips met in a sacred heat that knew no equal.

Hattie's ebony hair was caught in the flurry and swirled about them in reckless abandon. So encompassed was she in their blaze of emotion that she did not note the changes coming upon them both. Each of their forms was undergoing a rapid and astounding transformation, witnessed only by Vamelda, who, shading her eyes, could observe but dimly in the brilliant light that emanated from the couple.

Memories flooded Hattie's mind. An accidental meeting by a lake. Reginald, a dashing, young soldier, rushing to rescue her sunbonnet that the wind had caught up and away from her. Their many returns to that same lake, rowing together in secret, unbeknownst to her aunt and uncle. Stolen kisses...a secret engagement of which her family would never approve. Him, kissing her hand in parting as he left for America to make his fortune.

And the staggering articles from the newspapers. The full story of the torn clipping came back to her – where she had read that he was nothing more than a murderer – a man obsessed with another woman. Hattie recalled the eviscerating pain that ripped through her soul when she read of how Lydia Campbell had implicated Reginald – convinced the authorities that he was a jealous former lover who had slaughtered her husband.

She knew that all to be falsehood now...the years of pain and self-doubt that she had suffered under for so very long came back to her, then disappeared as dewy rain-drops evaporating under the glow of the sun's resplendent rays.

Now, she tasted nothing but bliss and happiness and contentment and memory. She savored it deeply. The utter joy was almost painful – nearly too much for her soul to sustain.

This man before her was Reginald. *Her* Reginald. And nothing could part them now. Not Lydia with her strange powers. Nor even Reginald himself, with his stubbornness and bitterness. She could sense that those feelings were leaving him – being burned away from his very being with every passing moment as they communed with their past lives and forgotten love.

When the kiss ended, they were both gently placed upon their feet by some unknown – but still keenly felt – force. Drawing apart, Hattie knew that every remembrance that had rushed in a deluge upon her mind had entered his, as well. Smiling radiantly and serenely, she looked up into his youthful face.

For he was indeed young again. Just as she remembered him when they had first encountered one another. Before the agony of war had descended upon him to line his features or the pain of death had crossed his path.

His back was straight; his form lean. As she caressed the arms that still surrounded her waist, she felt his smooth, firm skin. And the most glorious thing of all –

at least in her estimation – was the disappearance of the heavy crease between his brows. No longer weighted down by the absence of memory. Clear of the loneliness and humiliation that he had carried upon his countenance for decades.

"My Hattie," he said with a wealth of tenderness in his deep voice, all gruffness and aged tones removed.

He pressed his lips and body against hers again, and, even though it did not have quite the same dramatic effect as before, it was somehow more whole, more satisfactory than their previous embrace.

"How touching," interrupted a sarcastic voice from the doorway.

A set of glittering teeth smiled menacingly out at them from a florid face. Hattie and Reginald turned, clinging to each other in surprise. The man stepped into the light to reveal a yellow-checked suit.

Chapter Thirty-Six

"Mr. Carrington!" gasped Hattie.

"Yes, my dear lady, it is indeed Mr. Carrington. I do wish you would call me Carri. It's so much cozier between such intimate friends."

He was carrying a glass of what looked like port wine. Stepping over to Vamelda, he placed a hand on that lady's slim shoulder. She winced under the pressure.

"You seem to have had quite the adventure this evening," he said, stooping over the medium and offering her the glass. "I do hope this will help."

"Don't!" cried Hattie, but it was too late.

Vamelda had tipped back the glass and drained its entire contents in a single gulp.

"Yes, that's it. Precisely what is good for you at this juncture, I think," he said comfortably.

Hattie was not fooled by him for a moment.

"What did you give her?" she demanded, stamping her foot.

"Ah, now that is very clever of you, Ms. Vavasuer. Just a little port wine and..." he paused, pulling out a small vial of some bright purple liquid. "And, of course, a little of my special tincture. Very good for taking care of these nasty, little problems we all encounter from time to time."

He bent over Vamelda, smiling warmly. Hattie rushed over to the medium's side and threw her own body as a barrier between them. Carefully studying Vamelda's face, Hattie saw it slip from its usual semi-vacant expression into one of complete mental absence.

"Oh, yes," he said. "I never did quite tell you how I came into my fortune, did I? I made the most wonderful tonic in the world. The ladies were simply gasping for it. Our little concoction made the skin youthful. Rich, old biddies would invest very heartily in my business for the simple favor of a lifetime's supply in return. More often than not, they would even will their estates to me as a token of gratitude for their newfound youth and beauty. It took *years* off until...there were no years left...and I became the sole recipient of their estates."

Hattie listened in horror – her disgust plainly written upon her face as she looked up at him.

"Don't worry – it was very pleasant for them," he continued, the tones of his voice sickly sweet in his complete absence of remorse. "No pain. Just a drop of my extra *special* tincture."

He shook the little bottle between his thumb and forefinger. "They couldn't feel a thing!"

Hattie, meanwhile, was jostling Vamelda by both shoulders, trying to compel her out of her stupor.

"Oh, fair lady, you overexert yourself. There's nothing to be done but to give her the antidote...and I'm certain you know that I won't hand *that* over easily."

Reginald was across the room and had Mr. Carrington by the collar in an instant.

"Oh, no, we cannot have that," Mr. Carrington said. "I'm not a gentleman of violence. Nor do I pretend that I could overpower you, my good fellow."

Mr. Carrington, despite his awkward position, looked him over calculatingly.

"Even before your youth was regained, you were still a force to be reckoned with. Yet I would thank you to unhand me. You couldn't think I would be so stupid as to carry the antidote upon my person? "

Reginald released him, shoving him back a little as he did so.

Mr. Carrington carefully straightened his lapels nonchalantly, although he did still keep a vigilant eye on Reginald.

"I thought that the dead could do no harm to the living?" said Hattie wretchedly.

"Well, now, that would be a little trick from my wife. For all intents and purposes, I should be unable to move about quite so freely as I do, considering all of those old ladies whose lives I cut short. You recall that Teddy's father is unable to move much from the ditch in which he died so unfortunately?"

From Vamelda came a suppressed gurgling that erupted as a foam upon her blue lips. Hattie looked up at Mr. Carrington with seething disgust.

"It seems the lady is suffering, so I shall be quick in my explanation. My wife happens to have a knack for all things mystic. When we met, I was merely pulling the wool over a few eyes here and there and making the odd dollar. But Lydia, now! There's a talent and no mistake. The tonic was all her idea. I was selling something alright, but she has this power – it really is delightful how she does it, but every life Lydia takes, she's able to regain some of her youth. It's quite a sight to see her murmuring over her mystical objects like an enchantress of old. That's why the tonic worked so well on those ladies, you see. She mixed in a little of her draft with mine, and, well, it was a match made in...hell?" he said, snickering at his own joke.

Vamelda had completely slumped over and was sliding to the floor. Reginald hurried over to the medium and gathered her in his arms to place her gently on a nearby chaise.

Over his shoulder, he roared, "What do you want, then? You have the antidote. You must want something in exchange. You couldn't find it on your own, I imagine?"

Reginald's hand swept the room. "This is your work, isn't it?"

"Oh, quite, quite," Mr. Carrington returned pleasantly.

The little salesman stepped forward eagerly and greedily.

"I believe you already know what I want. Otherwise, you wouldn't have hidden it so well. You, see, it's simply this: Ms. Vavaseur's orb."

"*Hattie's* orb?" Reginald returned, every ounce of his frame quivering with bridled rage.

"Why, yes. I thought you must have guessed. I suspected it was hers that we needed quite early on, but my wife was more difficult to convince. It's your fiancé's orb we've been looking for. I found yours, my dear sir, several weeks ago in a sewing box beneath her bed," he gave an amicable nod in Hattie's direction. "But I'm afraid we need *both* to complete my wife's transcendence."

Vamelda had begun to shake violently. Joining Reginald by the medium's side, Hattie was desperate to help calm her but did not know how.

"Ah, yes. Here is the last of it coming on. First blue about the lips, then the spasms. You haven't much time if you want to save your friend."

Hattie looked up pleadingly into Reginald's eyes.

"Very well," he said, and, striding over to the bookcase, he touched a hidden spring that revealed a small safe.

Quickly twisting the knob to the relevant numbers, he opened it to expose the orb – spiraling with lavender lights that seemed to kindle and darken while he held it in his hand.

In a moment, Mr. Carrington had darted forward and had it in his grasp. He flew out the door before Hattie could blink.

"The antidote!" wailed she, as Reginald hurtled after

him.

It seemed ages of agony before her own love returned with a little bottle of green liquid. The cork was popped, and he had it down Vamelda's throat before Hattie could draw her hands away from the clairvoyant's shoulders, which she had been ineffectually trying to steady.

"Where did you find it?" she asked as Vamelda stirred, and her lips began to shift from a slightly-tinged blue to their usual pink.

"I had him by the throat, and he said something about 'Ms. Vavaseur always enjoying her sausages,' so I ran to the breakfast room. He had hidden it in a warming tray."

"He got away?" Hattie's voice was rich with reprimand.

"Well, I couldn't very well save this woman's life *and* somehow convince him to follow me about while doing it, could I?"

"No...I suppose...I suppose not," she replied thoughtfully, a little embarrassed at her ill humor so soon after their sweet, romantic reunion.

"I did call to Bertram and Harold. They came tearing down the stairs after him once they saw me let him go, but I expect he got away in that flashy car of his," he grumbled.

Then, looking down into Hattie's wan and fearful face, he softened, "We have each other now, my love. There is nothing we have to fear if we face it together."

Their hands found one another, and hers gripped his tightly as she said, grimly, "I just hope they can catch up with Mr. Carrington."

"A most charming man, by all accounts," rasped Vamelda, who had begun, rather hazily, to come around at last.

Chapter Thirty-Seven

The next day was supremely gloomy. Gathered around the breakfast table, each countenance was downcast with the incomprehensible exception of Vamelda's. Considering what she'd endured the past few days, her lighthearted humming and hearty appetite defied all reason. She gaily gulped down her food with indulgent delight.

"Goodness, my dearies! I haven't had such lovely fried mushrooms in quite some time. Bertram, you really are a wonder...I'm curious how you'd fare with a nice, plummy sponge?" she said dreamily, stirring a finger in what must have been very hot coffee.

Vamelda didn't seem to notice as it sizzled, and steam wafted from its contents. Bertram, who had just poured her a bit more before her appendage entered the cup, tenderly lifted her hand away from the scalding beverage and wiped it gingerly with a towel that had been thrown unceremoniously over his shoulder.

Aside from Vamelda's often incoherent remarks, no-body seemed inclined to conversation that morning.

"I have it!" Vamelda jumped out of her seat, upsetting her cup of coffee all over the white linen. Reginald lunged out of the way just in time, knocking over his chair and cursing vehemently as he did so.

They all waited – breathless with anticipation for Vamelda's thought to cross her lips. Staring straight out of the window, she leaned across the table to Reginald's coffee-soaked mushrooms and speared one with a fork.

"You're finished, then? Sublime, my darling!"

As she noisily relished each bite, Reginald grew impatient with every movement of her jaw that did not produce an intelligible sound.

"Well, woman? What is it?"

"Wouldn't it be lovely if we had a picnic out on the lawn? Just there – under that *diviiiiine*-looking tree?"

Exasperated, Reginald looked as though he was about to unleash upon her a stormy rant. Hattie, every bit as infuriated, chose to calm herself with a deep breath.

She laid a hand on Reginald, throwing him a glance of commiseration before she said, "That sounds lovely, Vamelda, but it is quite stormy outside at present."

"Oh, that's very simple. All you have to do is kiss it away, don't you? I thought you knew that by now?"

Her bright eyes blinked innocently at the couple before her.

Hattie, the vexation growing again within her, moved to the serving table to placate her bubbling emotions with a nice, fat sausage.

"Oh, my dear sugarplum! Don't be shy! We can all look away or cover our eyes if you'd like, but you really shouldn't be embarrassed by it."

"Embarrassed by what, exactly?" Hattie said, her fork faltering as she came to the realization that she'd consumed five sausages already.

"Why, by the kissing! It's the only way to dispel this terrible gloom. Isn't it rather obvious that Reginald – Mr. Tenbury – is in complete control of the weather? It's entirely dependent on his mood. In general, the dead only affects the weather slightly, but Mr. Tenbury has quite an effect on it for miles around. Why do you think I've been so very keen to visit this house?" she said, looking around luxuriantly.

Hattie, putting down her fork, licked her lips and attempted to surreptitiously rub a quick finger across her teeth to detect any spare bits of sausage that might have established themselves between those pearly utensils. Shyly, she turned to Reginald.

He was staring out the window, and Hattie was a bit embarrassed by his inattention to her. Just as she was about to turn away from him, he crossed the room and had her in his arms. Time, place, and present company melted away into the outer voids of the universe.

Breathlessly, they drew apart. The sun was pouring in from the windows as gaily as a soft summer's day.

"There," said Vamelda matter-of-factly. "What did I tell you? Fascinating. I'd like to study more of its effects, so I can..."

Hattie cut her off: "Why don't you and Bertram plan our luncheon outing and in the meantime, we'll all have a good think?"

Vamelda, always delighted to be thrown together with Bertram, took up the idea immediately.

"Shall we try our hand at that plum pudding, then, *dear* Bertram?" her voice was thick with cloying flirtation.

The pair left arm in arm. Hattie and Reginald were lost again in their own world by the time the medium and her amorous chauffeur exited the room.

"I suppose that leaves me to play gooseberry with one or the other of you," said Harold. "Or perhaps I'll go polish some silver?"

The man was speaking entirely to himself at this point.

"As a matter of fact, however, I suppose I needn't complete my duties any longer, as good old Reginald has come to himself."

When he received no response, the faithful former servant shrugged his shoulders and sighed. Just then, Teddy strolled nonchalantly outside of the window. He began making faces at the intertwined couple before him.

They paid the boy no mind, but Harold took himself off directly, with, "I suppose I shall be able to find *something* to do with myself."

A few moments later, he could be seen sneaking around the corner of the house. Soon after, the young boy began racing away from the astute butler, and the two, it is to be hoped, had a very nice game of cat and mouse – all fun on the one side and all frustration on the other.

Hattie and Reginald, oblivious to any of this, were completely enraptured. Hattie's hair was getting a bit tousled as she nuzzled into Reginald's chest, but neither of them seemed to mind. She began fiddling with one of the buttons on his waistcoat, reveling in the simplicity of the mere act of touching a bit of his clothing.

However, the fastening began to feel a bit odd in her hand. Instead of the smooth, rounded finish that she had felt beneath her thumb, it became concave, as though a piece of it had been knocked away. Drawing her head back, she looked at it more closely. The entire button was gone, although it had been there moments before. She blinked her eyes heavily, unable to comprehend what she was witnessing.

Reginald's waistcoat had begun to disappear as powder dissipates when mixed with water. His entire being was evaporating before her into thin air.

An outcry came to Hattie's lips, and she began to scream as she had never imagined she could.

Her fingertips clawed after him, desperately trying to hold onto the particles that were dissolving before her. As she lengthened their reach, her own hands came into her sight. They, too, began to vanish. Quickly, she folded them into her, hoping against everything that she could, by this action, in some way prevent their crumbling disappearance. But as she did so, the cry in her throat turned mute.

Vamelda rushed into the room in just enough time for Hattie to deliver a single, pleading, wretched look as her consciousness fell into a gray mist.

Chapter Thirty-Eight

A bright light shone over Hattie's eyes. It must have awakened her, but she somehow could not open them to see her surroundings. Her body was sore – she felt as though every bone within it had been broken. A moan escaped her lips when a foreign hand passed over her face, evidently feeling for something. The cry escaped her more out of fear, although the pain was a close second. Unable to move, she could not tell if bonds kept her body restricted or if, with the agony that pressed upon her, she had lost the use of her limbs through some accident.

Searching her mind to recall...had she fallen from a horse? No...slowly, the thoughts came back to her. She was already dead. No accident could befall her that would cause such agony, unless...unless...

Reaching deep within her soul to muster all of the strength of will she had, Hattie forced one of her eyes open a sliver. A lantern was suspended before her face. She could distinctly see a shadowed figure behind it – a portly shape. She knew it almost instantly to be that of Mr. Carrington.

The sickening feeling in her stomach was amplified tenfold upon this realization. Unwilling to let her consciousness be known, she attempted to take in her surroundings as much as she could with her limited vision.

In the corner of the room lay a moldy-looking mattress, stuffed haphazardly with hay. A tattered, old blanket was strewn askew on this dismal sleeping arrangement. Mr. Carrington's familiar, yellow-checked suit coat and boater hat had been flung atop a nearby barrel. A mouse was scrambling to eat the remains of a small pastry before its presence was discovered. Hattie recognized the pastry as one that she had pressed upon Mr. Carrington during his last visit. All of these clues led Hattie to surmise that the man must have been using this as a makeshift dwelling place.

Funny – she had never inquired as to his living conditions. Not once had he invited her to his abode, and it had not occurred to her that he had need of accommodation, her own having been taken care of from the moment of her death.

These thoughts were arrested by several sharp splinters that were inserting themselves rather uncomfortably into her right side as she lay upon the floor. As the aching, terrible discomfort that she originally felt upon returning to consciousness fled, more pressing and immediate little miseries manifested themselves.

She moaned again, involuntarily, and in response, Mr. Carrington shoved the lantern closer to her face. Her opened eye watered, and she could not help but blink rapidly to cope with the searing irritation from the unwelcome light.

"Aha! You've wakened at last," he said in his usual, jovial voice.

It was as if the man were paying her a kindly visit in the hospital, rather than hovering over her menacingly in a darkened room.

Attempting to press herself up from the floor, she discovered that her hands were indeed bound behind her, clasped together with cold metal.

As Mr. Carrington drew the lantern back, another face emerged from the shadows. Horror crept upon Hattie. The flickering lantern did the face no favors.

The eyes were pure white, convex, and sightless. The mouth was a gaping hole that opened into a grotesque scream. The tongue lolled out as if lusting for her blood. The lips were pulled back in a snarl, revealing teeth that were upturned in impossible contortions that seemed as though the monster was consuming itself as well as reaching out to tear Hattie's flesh. Deep purple feathers surrounded the face, while a single jewel of the duskiest rose shone out from the forehead.

Its head jerked side to side like some twisted, inquisitive bird as its sightless eyes somehow peered at her. The body began twisting and contorting in a demonic dance as it moved closer and closer.

A scream was building up in Hattie's throat, and just as she was about to give it life, warm hands grasped hers.

The tenderest of fingers gave her engagement ring a little twist, and a sigh of relief replaced the cry. She was not alone – Reginald was with her. Feeling blindly behind her, Hattie found that his wrists were also clasped in irons.

He moved his body closer to hers. The mere heat of his form helped her steel herself against the garish ritual that was taking place before her. The creature leaped about, holding a crystal ball in each hand. By turns, flames and ice seemed to emit from the orbs as they twisted in the frenetic steps that accompanied the low chants that erupted from this bizarre being.

Hattie could determine no definite form. At first, she thought she could make out the feet of a lion, then a goat, now the tail of a snake. The apparition transitioned from one to the next so quickly that it was a blur of claws and scales and cloven hooves. Three things only remained the same: two hands clasping the crystal orbs – and the death mask.

Mr. Carrington watched the spectacle with a strange combination of reverence and glee. Bending over Hattie, he helped her sit up. She unwillingly relinquished Reginald's grasp. Mr. Carrington must have believed him to still be unconscious as he paid the man no attention.

"My wife is quite marvelous, isn't she?" he said admiringly.

Hattie's lips were dry and cracked, her voice hoarse as she responded, "You don't mean to tell me...*that* is Mrs. Carrington?"

"Oh, yes. She has used death masks before, you know. She can see into the afterlife so much better when she's wearing one. They've even allowed her to communicate with me, although we were oceans apart. That's how I warned her about your Miss Syd coming over to ruin our plans."

Faintly, Hattie queried, "A...a...and what plans might those be?"

"It's coming to pass at last. You see, with these orbs, she will be able to...to control all fates in the afterlife."

A wicked smile navigated over his features, giving him the look of a goblin in the shadowy half-light.

"All fates?" Hattie asked, almost choking as she said the words...bewildered from the all-encompassing physical agony and mental horror.

"Oh, yes. All will bow before Lydia to do her bidding. She will have the power to command the elements, to punish those who displease her, and to reward those who have proven faithful to her."

The man was waxing passionate, unmasking the facade of a devoted husband and revealing the raving worship of a fanatic. Despite her fear, Hattie was unimpressed by his fervor.

She interrupted, "Are you certain *you* will be amongst those she rewards?"

"Quite, quite. Once the ritual is complete, I will be there by her side, ruling with my goddess of the dead."

His eyes gleamed in the lantern light with histrionic

intensity.

"Oh, I'm afraid you are quite mistaken on that point," returned Hattie, mustering all her courage and strength to sound pragmatic.

Her calm, tranquil tones arrested him, and he gave her a sidelong glance as he returned somewhat to his conventional, offhand manner.

"Just what do you mean by that comment, Ms. Vavaseur? You cannot suppose that I have done all this just to be cast aside at the penultimate moment?"

"Well, to start, did *she* not poison *you*?"

"Oh, no, dear lady. You are quite mistaken. You see, the lovely Lydia's powers are extended when in the presence of a dying individual. Many times, we used the victims of my little tincture for this purpose – to see beyond the grave.

"However, there was only so far we could go with strangers. Lydia can always see further when she has close ties to the individual who is passing over. You saw something of that with Miss Syd and Vamelda."

Hattie recalled Syd's flitting and Vamelda's sudden calm that all was well with her. Although there had been no confirmation that her friend's predictions were correct, Mr. Carrington seemed convinced that the situations were of the same tenor.

The salesman continued: "I began to enjoy experimenting with various tinctures – seeing how far I could take myself to the brink. My darling Lydia could always bring me back. You have, perhaps, noted that she still looks very young? A special elixir and certain rituals have allowed her to keep her youth and beauty. I was never in any real danger with her powers at my disposal."

The man did not take his eyes from his wife as he continued warmly, "Eventually, she..." he shook his head, "...*we* came to desire something more than the riches we had amassed. More even than curiosity about the life beyond. Although we had gained some influence over death, it was clear to us that we were meant to rule it...to bend to our will every soul who has ever walked the earth."

He paused, his tongue rolling around in his mouth as though savoring the words he would expulse next.

"In her wanderings through the shadows, she gained much knowledge regarding how to bring this about. However, there has always been part of the ritual that could not be revealed – that she could not foresee: the location of these two orbs. They were the two objects missing that we desperately needed to complete the ceremony, yet we could not discover their whereabouts.

"Lydia knew that they were connected to this Reginald Tenbury and his fiancé," he bowed to her as though delivering a great compliment. "I was sent on to find them...to find *you*. When we read of your death in the newspapers, Lydia knew the time had come."

Hattie, still straining every bit of her powers to remain composed, gave a dry, little cough. It had the desired effect, as Mr. Carrington peeled his eyes away from the woman – the creature – before him.

Turning the lantern full upon Hattie, he looked deep

into her face, searching for confirmation of a doubt that lingered in his own countenance. Unflinching, she met his eyes fully and raised a brow to complete her air of disbelief.

"Has she not told you, then?" Hattie inquired, an impertinent tone in her voice.

"You think you have some information that she has not shared with me? Pah! Impossible!"

However, his tone had just a hint of ambiguity, which lent Hattie the temerity she needed to advance the knowledge that was within her power to topple his towering and terrible utopia.

"Everyone was there when she told us. Vamelda, Bertram, Harold. Have you never questioned why those *particular* orbs are so essential to her plan? Why Reginald's? Why mine?"

"I – well," the man spluttered, his brows creased in discomfiture.

"Did you never think that there was some special significance for Lydia in these orbs? It must have crossed your mind. Otherwise, any orbs for any souls would have worked just as well."

"She must have a reason, there must be...otherwise..." he faltered, looking pleadingly at the figure whose dance was becoming more unnatural with every movement.

"Oh, yes. Lydia certainly does have a reason. It is because she loves Reginald, not you," she calmly articulated.

Mr. Carrington struck her with so much force that her fettered wrists wrenched severely as she toppled backward upon them. A muffled outcry sounded behind her, and she could feel that Reginald was straining against his bonds, restless in his attempt to defend her and frustrated at his powerlessness. Eager for her beloved's safety, Hattie covered his cry with her own. Pushing herself up from the floor, she squared her shoulders with a haughty look in her eye, the red mark on her cheek florid and hot.

She was about to say more, but Mr. Carrington's manner arrested her verbal assault. The seed of uncertainty she hoped to plant must have taken root long before her lips expressed the idea. The man was pacing back and forth, eyeing his wife distrustfully.

"Never. No. She wouldn't. It's been too long. Too many years. Too many lives we took together. It is our destiny."

The man worried his collar nervously.

As though she was some strange, otherworldly water creature sensing the changing of the tides, Lydia stopped and turned to Mr. Carrington. Taking human form, she was suddenly resplendent in folds of pink muslin that clung to her body provocatively.

"My love. It is time."

Her tones were deep and heavy with seduction. The man melted visibly before her as he knelt at her feet. Kissing them, he simultaneously drew a long, silver knife from a belt at her waist.

Approaching Hattie, a wicked glint in his eye left her gasping for breath as he caressed her face with the blade. Closing her eyes, she held her breath. With a tug and a slice, she realized that he took, not her lifeblood, but a lock of her hair. The knife was so sharp that his recoil from the cutting grazed her cheek and left a thin, bright gash in the center of the bruise that was forming where he had hit her before.

Hattie could hear Mr. Carrington as he moved on to Reginald. He soon returned with another fistful of hair. Sensing her will, Reginald must have relapsed into his continued farce of unconsciousness.

Their backs to the two prisoners, Mr. Carrington and Lydia hunched over strange engravings in the floor. A small fire was lit, and a few hushed words were spoken in some unintelligible language. The smell of burnt hair reached Hattie's nostrils.

Quietly, Reginald began to move behind her. Twisting around as far as she could, he, at last, rose into her line of vision. His wounds were weeping again – Vamelda had mentioned the salve had limited effects.

Hattie could see that every muscle in Reginald's body was tense, preparing to spring into action at any moment. What he would do, she could not fathom, but she desired above all to be there beside him, helping to terminate whatever nefarious ritual was about to be completed.

She, too, arose without sound. He nodded encouragingly and gave her a sort of grim, half-smile as she drew herself up.

They had no chance to complete their mission. Two dark figures burst upon them through the door of the shack.

Chapter Thirty-Nine

Everything devolved into madness. The lantern was tipped over and extinguished. Cries rang out in the deep, thick night. Scuffling noises added to the confusion and all Hattie could see was the occasional luminosity of the orbs.

One seemed to float along the wall and to the door, and Hattie had a glimmer of hope as it illuminated the face and figure of Harold, the butler. The other orb escaped out the window, and Hattie's heart warmed even more as the bright purple light gave a glow to the features of little Teddy, whose countenance was as gleeful as though he was making away with a jelly trifle.

Lydia gave a murderous shriek as the orbs disappeared from her view.

"After them, you fool!" she screeched at Mr. Carrington.

He disappeared into the night, the lantern swinging dangerously as he did so. In the darkness, Hattie felt behind for Reginald but merely grasped at the cold night air that poured in from the window and door.

A flicker of flame illuminated the death mask moment-arily as Lydia lit a match. Reginald was standing face to face with the woman. The sightless eyes stared at him until the match singed her fingertips. She lit another, and Reginald had stepped closer. Then another and an-other. With each match that burned, Hattie could see him maneuver his way toward their common enemy.

Standing at last before Lydia, Reginald removed her mask gently, tossing it onto the nearby bed. He stared down into the woman's beautiful features. Leaning in close to her, he whispered something in her ear. As though mesmerized, Lydia wrapped her arms about him and pulled him to her. In her eagerness, she dropped the match, which set the makeshift bed alight.

For a single, terrifying moment, Hattie believed that the enchantment had worked – that Reginald was under Lydia's spell and was compelled to do her bidding. In a moment, Reginald's hands were freed from the iron clasps that bound him. When Lydia reached up for a kiss, he retreated. Both women knew in that moment that he had not succumbed. One countenance was full of relief – the other full of disbelief and ire.

Apparently in shock that her allure had not accom-plished her desires, Lydia tripped backward, falling onto the mattress. What had begun as a small flame had now burst into a full-fledged fire. It swallowed up the woman until all Hattie could see was a pair of pale, star-ing eyes.

Before she could comprehend what was happening to

her, Hattie was pulled from the shack that was quickly going up in a blaze. Reginald had her firmly by the arm as he steered her out into the inky night. Rushing into the nearby trees, their only light was the moon.

Hattie had never run so desperately fast in her entire life. Her lungs ached with the sharpness of the night air. She stumbled once or twice, but Reginald kept a firm hold on her arm, righting her each time she nearly fell to the earth. Behind them, they could hear the petrifying screams of Lydia.

When the blood-curdling sounds began to die behind them, Reginald and Hattie at last slowed. Leaning against a tree for support, Hattie attempted to catch her breath. Just as she was about to speak, she spotted a figure at the edge of the wood. It couldn't be...it was...Lydia.

She again had donned the evil mask and was making her way through the trees toward them. Reginald, who was facing the opposite direction, began to speak, but Hattie shook her head violently and jerked her chin toward their pursuer.

They both looked on with bated breath as the huntress wove her way between the trees, searching for some clue of their presence. Softly, Reginald put a tender hand upon Hattie's head, and she felt a lock of her hair slip out of its pin. Next, she detected pressure upon her wrists as Reginald attempted to free her with his makeshift lockpick. Biting her lip in an agony of anticipation, she watched Lydia, prepared to forfeit the freedom of her hands in favor of their liberty from this diabolical woman.

Just as the lock clicked and her fetters dropped softly on the turf at her feet, a fiendish cry rang out amongst the trees. Hattie was certain they'd been discovered, but she saw Lydia's silhouette running to the right of them. In horror, she watched as the woman viciously attacked a figure in the darkness.

Lydia's knife lustrous in the moonlight, she sank it deep into flesh over and over again, her frenzy seeming to overpower her reason.

"You. Will. Not. Have. Him!" Lydia screeched with each plunge into the innocent deer.

Upon hearing those words, Hattie realized in horror that Lydia meant each plunge for her own person. Beside her, Reginald crouched down amongst the ferns and pulled Hattie down close to him, wrapping his arms around her. Holding perfectly still, they watched in terror as the scene unfolded before them.

Seeming to realize her mistake, Lydia pulled herself from the carcass and tore through the woods toward them, her maniacal performance having heightened her hysteria, as though the wetting of her knife with blood made her lust the more for it.

Although she did not know whether the knife would have any power over their souls, Hattie had no wish to find out and so kept silent beside her Reginald. Lydia passed close by them in her pursuit, her dress bespattered with the animal's blood. Hattie shut her eyes tight, willing herself to unsee the gory sight.

After what seemed like hours, Hattie's legs began to

ache with their cramped posture. With a warm squeeze to Reginald's hand, she stretched up to her full height against the tree that had sheltered them from Lydia's seemingly sightless gaze. Reginald stood beside her, and together, they made their way through the wood and toward the manor house.

Just at the edge of the trees, before the sloping green that led up to the French doors of the breakfast room, they stopped to take in their surroundings. All was stillness – no movement could be detected. Reginald began to move forward, but Hattie paused and drew him back out of the moonlight.

Taking his face in both of her hands, she drew him to her, and they shared a long, tender kiss. There was a depth of meaning in this kiss that even Hattie did not quite understand, but there was a sense of finality for both of them...as though such a kiss might never happen again.

They drew apart, and, hand in hand, crossed the unsheltered lawn, through the doors, and into the silent house.

Chapter Forty

As they entered the house, a cry sounded, but it was not the howl of a murderous witch. Instead, they were greeted by the hysterical wailing of Vamelda, who stood in the doorway of the breakfast room, as breathless as Hattie and Reginald themselves.

"Oh, my *deaaars*! We've been *so* worried about you! I guessed what had happened. I've heard of such spells but have never seen one put into practice, not having a taste for such dark deeds. I never imagined that we'd ever be able to find you, but then little Teddy was *so clever*, you know. He knew all along right where Mr. Carrington has been staying."

Vamelda gathered them into her and, slipping both heavily bangled and bescarved arms into each of theirs, led them proudly into the library. Hattie had never held Vamelda's adornments in high esteem, but they felt comforting and familiar to her as she acknowledged the presence of such stout-hearted friends.

All were gathered in the library. Harold was there, somewhat the worse for wear, but gave half a smile and a nod as he handed over one of the orbs. Little Teddy puffed his chest out to its full breadth as he delivered the other into their keeping.

A dishevelled Bertram stood up from a chair, but the lipstick on his collar belied the reason for his untidiness. It was not from heroic deeds, as Harold and Teddy's were, but rather the effect of an amorous interaction with Vamelda, Hattie was sure. As she looked him over with a critical eye, the man at least had the decency to blush at the mute assault.

With her usual, strange acumen, Vamelda said to Hattie, "Well, what *could* we do, my dear, but comfort each other as we anticipated your return? Teddy and Harold had things in hand."

It was Hattie's turn to redden slightly at her friend's keen sagacity.

"You're safe now, and that's all that matters. Without the orbs, Lydia cannot call you to her as she did before," Vamelda said, nodding knowingly in accompaniment of this statement.

"She may come at any moment, however," stated Reginald. "We must do something to ensure the safety of the orbs."

"Indeed," agreed Hattie. "Give the other to me. I believe I know just the place."

"My love..." Reginald remonstrated, but Hattie had his orb in hand and was out the door before he could say another word.

Hattie left the library and walked quickly down the ill-lit hallway. Half of the lamps were extinguished, as no one had had the time or the inclination to keep up with the banal niceties of housekeeping. Reaching her destination, she closed her eyes tightly as she opened the door to the mirrored room. One after the other, she gently rolled the spheres in, hoping – nay – *willing* them to reach the back of the closet without damage.

However, Hattie's mission was twofold. There was something she needed from that closet desperately. Feeling around blindly, she caught upon the object she was searching for, then placed it delicately in her bosom for safekeeping.

When she returned to the others, Reginald greeted her with a tight embrace and a slight remonstrance, whispered in her ear: "Don't leave me like that again, will you?"

Hattie shook her head to reassure him, but with an arch lift of her brow, intimating that she could do as she pleased. He punished her truancy with a kiss. Just as their lips were about to meet, Hattie gave a little, strangled cry.

Lydia and Mr. Carrington stood in the doorway. The mask hanging limply at her side, Lydia's clear and breathtaking features stood out starkly from the smattering of dried blood that had stiffened upon her dress.

Stepping forward, she began chanting an intoxicating string of mellifluous words in a strange tongue. Slowly, Reginald turned toward her, disbelief and determination carved upon every feature.

Leaving her husband in the doorway, Lydia moved toward her prey as softly and exquisitely as a panther.

"Come to me, my love," she sang out, in English. "We are destined to be together. You feel it as I do, I know...this pull between us. Do not deny it."

"Never," growled Reginald. "You did not have me then. You shall not have me now. You have no power here, Lydia."

Locking eyes with him, she began the chant again. This time, even Hattie felt the compelling pull of her enchantments.

"What are you doing, Lydia? That's not the chant that we..." questioned Mr. Carrington, his voice angry and confused.

Twisting her head around to her husband, Lydia revealed a blackened and burned scalp at the back of her head, devoid of the lustrous hair that had once adorned it.

Looking more closely, Hattie realized that the woman's hands and legs were bloodied, not only with the fluids of the stag, but also with the crimson of blistered, weeping, and scorched flesh.

"You idiot!" Lydia turned her venom upon Mr. Carrington, at last revealing her true design to this, her most faithful of servants. "You are *nothing* to me! *Nothing*! Simply a pawn in my brilliant game. I have no further need of you! Reginald is my only muse – the only one who could ever inspire in me feelings of adoration and affection! How could you possibly believe that I could ever love *you*? You, with your balding head and your grotesque suits!"

Mr. Carrington seemed dazed for a moment – but only a moment, as he calmly returned, "Well, my dear, you're not such a lovely specimen yourself any longer."

"Oh, this?" she cackled bemusedly. "You know I can solve this with one, simple death. A little potion, a little spell, and I'll be as good as new. You've seen the wrinkles and sagging skin disappear easily enough before! Do not be so foolish as to think that I cannot remedy *this*!"

She passed a hand over the back of her head, hardly wincing in her demented zeal.

"Perhaps a nice, juicy, fellow medium would do the trick!" she said, turning her eyes on Vamelda. "But beauty can wait, can it not, my love?"

Her attention had fixated once again on Reginald.

"Beautiful or not, you repel me, you evil...*thing*. Woman is too good a name for you. You're a possessed, vile creature, and I will not – hear me – I *will never* relinquish my love for Hattie! You were unable to overpower me then, and our love is only stronger now, for we know what it is worth. It has stood against time and death and, yes, even hell! It *will* withstand you!"

Reginald drew Hattie near to him, and their fingers entwined behind Hattie's back, squeezing each other so hard, the tips of them began to lose all feeling.

"I'll never stop, Reggie," Lydia's eyes were somehow colder and more threatening as her cheeks reddened with a strangely becoming blush of vexation. "As long as I draw breath, and even after, there is nothing you can do to stop me. You *will* give in. I have bent far stronger men than you to my will. I can bring you back to *life*, Reggie! We can be as one – as we always longed for. Just think of it – our bodies entwined? Alive, flesh upon flesh!"

Reginald, disgust lining every feature, looked to Hattie for comfort. His countenance cleared the moment their eyes met.

Enraged at her lack of effect upon her desired one, Lydia turned her malevolence upon Hattie: "As for this...*fiancé*...of yours. She is nothing compared with me! Just look between us and see, even with this scarred body, that there is no comparison."

"I do see," said Reginald, still looking upon his beloved, his eyes tearfully filled with all the softness of love a true man's heart can possess.

"I see a woman rich in kindness and love who has been through so much, yet still strives to do what is right. I see a woman whose loveliness surpasses all because of her keen intellect and her faithful heart. I look down into the eyes of a true woman who loves me back with a tenderness so full and deep and rich that I can hardly begin to comprehend it. I examine her closely, and I here behold the most beautiful woman in the world because she is stubborn and outspoken and challenging in ways that are intricate and meaningful and creative and...*human.*

"You are correct, Lydia. There *is* no comparison. There

was always something unnatural and licentious about you, even with all of your charm and your fine clothes and your flawless form. There was nothing ever real, warm, or divine about you. You never could have tempted me, you vile succubus, because you've given up the most beautiful thing about any person: your soul."

With every word out of Reginald's mouth, Lydia began to tremble and seethe.

Volcanic rage overtook her until she ruptured with: "Bah! This is but nonsense, my love. You'll soon see it my way. I can sense the orbs are near. They do not need to be fully in my possession to complete the ritual..."

Donning the monstrous mask once again, she recommenced her mystical chant, but just as she began to contort her voluptuous body in the otherworldly dance, a shot rang out.

Chapter Forty-One

For a moment, Hattie didn't comprehend what had happened. Lydia's form had paused momentarily in her demonic movements, but then she seemed to writhe in even more frenzied maneuvers before her body dropped with a soft thud to the floor.

At first, it was difficult to see the blood as it seeped through her dress, the deer's reddened fluids having soaked the front of her garment during the attack. Soon, however, Hattie was able to distinguish the more lustrous crimson from the dried russet as it seeped out from the little hole in Lydia's chest. As her lifesblood drained from her heart, Lydia looked shocked and vulnerable. For a moment, a softened innocence, as that of an injured child, played upon her features, revealing what her nature could have been as a very young girl.

The unblemished expression was short-lived, however, as anger, hatred, and unbridled passion overtook the exquisite countenance. Scarcely had this momentary transformation taken place when the eyes went blank, and Hattie knew she was gone.

Every soul in the room drew a collective breath of relief as they watched their common enemy expire before their eyes. Hattie looked around to discover their savior.

The barrel of a familiar, little revolver was peeking into the half-open window opposite her, glinting in the lamplight. It moved toward her, followed by a trouser-clad Syd. Placing the gun neatly away in her vest, the adventuress helped a trembling Gerald through the window after her.

No one said a word as the shock of what had just played out before them seemed to settle into their minds.

"Serves the old hag right after trying to kill me!" Syd's voice resonated loud and strong in the soundless room.

"You're alive after all – I knew it!" cried Vamelda, the first to attune her senses to the circumstances.

"Of course I'm alive!" Syd interrupted herself with a fit of coughing. "She may have pushed me onto the subway and set my hotel room afire – I'll grant you, she nearly had me there – but you didn't think a woman like *that* would be the end of me?"

Syd hobbled to lean against a nearby wall; her broken, casted leg obviously causing some discomfort.

Gerald crossed the room and stood over Lydia's remains, looking stunned.

"I...I can't believe she's actually kicked it," he nudged the body with his toe as if in disbelief that revenge could be taken so quickly and coolly.

Half limping, half shuffling, Syd joined him and looked down at the grisly corpse. Gerald directed his gaze from the macabre sight to the woman standing next to him. Abruptly kneeling before her, he seized her hand in his.

"Oh, you magnificent Sheba! You've done it! You've bumped her off for me with that bean-shooter of yours. Marry me! You're simply the eel's ankle, my sweet. Will you be mine?"

"What?" Syd withdrew her hand from Gerald's very sweaty looking grasp. "You sweet idiot. Of course, I won't marry you! I'm not the least in love with you. Just because I saved you doesn't mean I *want* you. Get up from that ridiculous position this instant."

Vamelda came close to the both of them.

"Oh, but my darling Syd! What will happen to you?" Vamelda placed her hand on her friend's shoulder comfortingly.

"First, would somebody in this house *please* get me a chair?" Syd demanded. "For being the hero of the hour, I'm certainly not being treated as one!"

Ever the faithful servant, Harold rushed forth and produced a comfortable seat for the audacious maiden.

After settling sufficiently, Syd at last replied to Vamelda's inquiry, "Well, I think it's off to the gallows with me, I'm afraid, old chum...unless I can plead insanity. My record should help my case. Hopefully, they'll simply throw me back into the looney bin, and perhaps, someday I'll be 'cured.' I've been missing how the nurses fuss over me a bit, anyhow. Or if I do end up paying the price for my sins, I shall make a nuisance of myself at your notable establishment, Vamelda. Perhaps I'll even find it in my heart to haunt a few ill-beloved relatives here and there. I expect I shall be quite alright in the end, whichever fate awaits me."

Backing away from the body, the two other mortals each found a nearby seat. Everyone seemed to discover their voice at once. Reginald was shaking hands with Bertram. Teddy and Harold were sitting together in a corner, most likely swapping tales of their daring, mutual adventure.

Hattie once again looked down at the body before her, studying the physiognomy of this woman who had caused so much trouble to her in life and in death. It seemed strange that a person could at one moment be full of life and emotion, and then next...nothing...nothing...

Was it nothing? Hattie rubbed her eyes. It couldn't be...but had there been a slight twitch at the mouth? No – it was impossible. Hattie knew she was exhausted from the events that had transpired. Perhaps only a trick of the light?

There it was again.

Panic set upon Hattie's soul. Eyes, glazed in death, snapped back to life and focus once again.

As though a puppeteer's strings were pulling at her wrists, Lydia's full form elevated from the ground to an upright position. Hattie tore at her own throat, as though in a nightmare and unable to vociferate a warning to her loved ones.

Standing before her was indeed Lydia, yet her body was still laid down upon the ground. This new form was perfect. No dark void caved at her bosom. No burned and blistered flesh. No blood drenched the pink taffeta of this resplendent gown. A wicked smile played around the spectre's plump lips.

"Lydia!"

It was a strangled cry from Mr. Carrington in the doorway.

A full, arch smile crossed the ghostly features as it ever so slightly inclined its head to her husband's call. Nonetheless, in death as in life, Lydia's obsession remained unequivocal as she laid a hand upon Reginald's chest.

Apparently deaf to Mr. Carrington's exclamation, Reginald covered the hand with his, most likely believing it to be that of his beloved. Never could a man look more aghast to discover his grave mistake. Dropping the hand as though it was a hot iron, he stepped back, his entire visage contorted with terror and loathing.

"You fools! You've only made my position the stronger in this afterlife! Here, I have the freedom to call all dead to my aid. Perhaps I can no longer *force* you to bend to my will, but now I have the power to make everything you love a misery until you bow to my every whim! *You will still worship me, Reginald Tenbury!*"

At this moment, Hattie's full memory returned to her. The pain and anguish of what happened in America. Believing that her betrothed had not only been unfaithful but also a murderer. A billowing, desolate fabric made up of years of pain, loneliness, and self-doubt stretched out behind her.

Every passing heartache. Every tender kiss she observed that was shared between two young lovers. Every longing look at a child who dandled upon its mother's knee.

More anguish than could be contained in a single soul swelled up within her, as a rushing stream flooding the banks of a river after winter's thaw.

Yet, chasing after the excruciating deluge of bitterness came a strange sort of peace. The knowledge that each little sting in life could be replaced by such unutterable happiness and wholeness...this...*this* gave her courage.

"Oh, I think not," Hattie had found her voice at last.

Her tone was calm, collected...confident, even. The splendidly serene statement was met with a cackle of deranged laughter.

Facing Hattie, Lydia screeched, "*You*? I will torture your very being until you cry for my mercy! You will gladly deliver his soul – his love – to me once I'm through with you! You miserable, ugly, old woman!"

"Fascinating that of all the flaws in my character to choose from, you alight upon my looks. It's unfortunate that your disquieted, trivial mind can never see past the physical...or is it metaphysical now?...appearance," Hattie shrugged her shoulders nonchalantly.

Confused by this placid and intelligent rejoinder, Lydia pushed out an alluringly pouty lip in frustration and confusion.

"I can see you are easily flummoxed by simple moral logic. I could recommend a few books, but, you see, *you don't have the time*," said Hattie.

Puzzled further, Lydia, rather than attempting to combat Hattie in this phrenic repartee, looked upon her desired lover pleadingly, instead. Her eyebrows crossed petulantly when she elicited no response from him.

At this opportune moment, Hattie withdrew the small object that she'd stowed away in her bosom.

Opening it carefully, she said, "Since I cannot seem to elucidate you on these matters, perhaps you'd like to take a look at this?"

Hattie opened the little compact in her hand and pointed it toward Lydia. What next ensued took place so gradually, the woman did not seem to notice.

"You *are* very beautiful, Lydia. Even I cannot deny that. Particularly your hands, I've noticed," Hattie said.

Looking down at them, vanity dripping from every pore, Lydia turned them over, admiring them. Only...something was amiss. They were more translucent than they should be. Lydia realized too late what Hattie had done.

"No," she said slowly. "No. It cannot be. *How?*"

The woman's face contorted in fury as she realized that her entire visage was being sucked away. The resplendent body of which she was so proud gradually began to lose form. Her transparency increased little by little until there was not much left of her but what could truly be considered a ghost.

Just as the last bit of her form was fading, she turned to see Hattie, who was tranquilly holding a little mirrored compact open in the palm of her hand as the full essence of the woman disappeared into it. Hattie snapped it shut as she heard the cry of Lydia's tortured soul erupt from within the little trinket.

Dropping it on the ground before her, it smashed into a million tiny pieces. As though ridding herself of a pesky troop of ants at a picnic, Hattie serenely ground each little sliver of glass to powder as the most chilling shriek resounded in all of their ears. It died out as the last tiny crystal dissolved into nothingness beneath her heel.

Chapter Forty-Two

Slack-jawed, each person in the room watched the scene play out before them. Not one of them had stirred from the moment that Hattie revealed the compact. Reginald, recovering himself the fastest, gathered her into a worshipful embrace.

"My darling. How did you know?" he whispered into her ear, his voice full to the brim with wonder and admiration.

"Bertram told me some time ago that mirrors can be dangerous to those freshly dead, but I wasn't quite certain that I wouldn't disappear along with her....and I'd no idea how we were going to kill her in the first place. I...I didn't want any of us to become...a *murderer*."

Her eyes swept a rather shy, sideways glance at Syd, but the lady seemed preoccupied with adjusting her injured leg on a cushion with the help of an obsequious Gerald.

"You have indeed been very brave, madam...er...Hattie. Your soul could have been sucked straight into the glass, as well. You risked everything – for him," Bertram nodded toward Reginald. "You're a fortunate man, Reggie."

"*Don't* call me that," Reginald reacted, his shoulders nearly touching his ears as he shivered in disgust. "Only *she* ever called me that, and I have no wish to hear the nickname ever again. Reginald will do very nicely. I always loved that you called me that, Hattie. Never tried to shorten it. Say it now to me, my darling. Let me hear you speak it as a countercurse to all that has passed."

Obedient to his request, Hattie was rewarded with a loving kiss, although she blushed at the attention given them during that particularly interesting moment.

Syd, sounding slightly petulant that her part in all this wasn't met with any sort of adulation, interrupted, "I don't see what all the fuss is about. One of these other fellows – even Vamelda – could have gone and fetched it. Hattie didn't *need* to risk her existence."

Gerald, looking around to discover to whom his newly beloved was speaking about, delivered a puzzled, "Ah, oh?" to the room at large.

"I had thought of that, as well, my darling. That was very silly of you, Hattie, you dear sugarplum. *Any* of us could have fetched it for you if only you'd said," interpolated Vamelda.

"Hattie? My *Aunt* Hattie? She isn't *here*, is she, Vamelda? I always assumed her visits were restricted to your shop! Then again...that floating compact being smashed to bits nearly had me running for the hills."

Gerald gathered his suit jacket tightly around him,

tucking one front flap over the other. His stint in jail seemed to have had an anemic effect on him, as he was thinner than ever, so the jacket served more as a comforting blanket than it would have mere weeks earlier.

"I hadn't thought of that in the moment, I'm afraid," Hattie's dignity was a little wounded, but she also knew deep inside that somehow, *she* needed to be the one to put Lydia's evil soul to rest in the end.

After all, it was her own love that had been targeted – her life that had been destroyed by this woman. When she seized the mirror from the little closet in the hallway, she realized that she was endangering her own soul, but she did not care. Merely desiring to give Reginald a chance for a peaceful, unfettered existence, she knew that if things had not gone just so, she could be sharing Lydia's fate.

A little shiver ran through her as these thoughts did the same. Reginald only held her all the more tightly.

Another ghastly thought came to her mind, and she pulled away from her beloved, looking behind her toward the doorway.

"Wherever has Mr. Carrington gone?" she exclaimed.

"Do you mean the fellow in the checked suit?" queried Syd.

Hattie nodded while her nephew scratched his head in utter confusion.

"What fellow?" he asked in a dazed sort of way.

"I saw him slip out some time ago. I didn't register that

he was Mr. Carrington! I should have guessed. I did try to warn you about him, you know. It's unfortunate that Hattie didn't think to turn her little mirror on him, as well!"

"Turn the mirror?" Gerald was looking very much like a little lost lamb.

"I'm not sure it would have worked," Hattie said thoughtfully. "Lydia performed all sorts of spells on him when they mutually agreed to his murder...or would it be suicide?"

She shook her head, trying to work it out, before she continued, "I don't believe he has the same vulnerability the rest of us do after death."

"I doubt we've heard the last of him," Reginald agreed. "He may not have Lydia's gifts, but he's certainly a greedy little man, and he doesn't seem the type that would casually write off being made a fool of. For now, he seems to have cut his losses and made a run for it."

"We may want to check on the orbs, just in case," said Hattie.

Harold volunteered himself, and she told him of their hiding place.

"A most clever locale, if you don't mind my saying so, madam...ahem...Hattie," he responded.

As he returned with the precious objects, both glowing and resplendent in the palms of his hands, he placed each in the care of its owner.

Reginald studied his own orb closely. His forehead

wrinkled in puzzlement. He scratched his bearded chin, then pulled a bit at the skin of his cheek.

"It can't be!" he exclaimed in disbelief.

"What is it, my love?" asked Hattie, concerned.

"Why, I'm *young* again!"

"Of course you are, my darlings. You *both* are," interjected Vamelda, as though this was the most casual, natural thing that could have possibly taken place.

Hattie looked into her own orb and admired the twinkling young eyes that blinked back at her. She had felt the full transformation take place and somehow guessed it from Reginald's appearance but had had little time to give it thought.

As she smiled winningly at herself, behind her orb, she could see Reginald look down at his chest.

"And I'm healed!" he proclaimed in delight. "Look, Hattie! Not a scratch on me!"

Blushing, Hattie walked lightly over to her beloved.

"Yes, *yes*, my own love. You are safe at last," was her sweet, reassuring reply.

"Here I was, thinking that I was a disgusting old man compared to the likes of you, feeling guilty that you'd strapped your fate to a miserable cuss, but see?" he stretched his arms out wide, laughing joyfully.

"I'm not certain that an auburn beard is as appealing as a snow white one, but I'll make do," teased Hattie, giving the aforementioned plumage an affectionate tug.

"Oh, my own Hattie," he said, folding her into his arms.

Vamelda and Bertram followed suit, although their embrace was rather louder and included a lot of wet-sounding kisses.

Repelled, Gerald looked on at the medium's seemingly erratic behavior.

Teddy had somehow got ahold of a washbasin and was about to pour it over the unsuspecting mortal's head.

Syd was watching Teddy in delight and anticipation.

Harold was looking politely away into a corner.

Hattie surveyed the room contentedly. At last, she had discovered the true meaning of her existence. It was not protecting herself in bitterness and isolation. Nor was it merely enduring the fate that society and circumstances had thrust upon her.

She had always had the power within her to do something more – to love and be loved. Hattie merely had to reach out, grasp it by the lapels, and give herself wholly over to it. Looking into Reginald's deep amber eyes, that's precisely what she did.

LA FIN

Afterword

Thank you so much for taking this journey with Hattie! If you've enjoyed uncovering the mystery alongside her, please share your experience by leaving a review. I can't wait to hear from you!

M. Rebecca Wildsmith

Made in the USA
Monee, IL
30 September 2021